KING OF THE MISSISSIPPI

A NOVEL

HOGARTH
London New York

Published in the United States by Hogarth, an imprint of the Crown Publishing Group, a division of Penguin Random House LLC, New York.
crownpublishing.com

HOGARTH is a trademark of the Random House Group Limited, and the H colophon is a trademark of Penguin Random House LLC.

Library of Congress Cataloging-in-Publication Data is available.

ISBN 978-0-525-57378-4
Ebook ISBN 978-0-525-57380-7

Printed in the United States of America

Jacket design by Matt Dorfman
Jacket photographs by (knives) © Don Troiani/Bridgeman Images;
Two businessmen shaking hands/Bridgeman Images

10 9 8 7 6 5 4 3 2 1

First Edition

For all the good people of Houston and the other hurricane-ravaged Gulf Coast towns, and to the long journey of change ahead

IT IS THE EASIEST THING IN THE WORLD FOR A MAN TO LOOK AS IF HE HAD A GREAT SECRET IN HIM.

—Herman Melville, *Moby-Dick*

WHO DARES WINS

—Motto of the British Special Air Service (SAS)

PART ONE

1.
THE KING DECLARES

"Not everyone is meant to be a CCGer," Brock Wharton said to himself as much as to the staffer who fumbled with the applicant folders.

Great consultants mastered the management of time. The muggy fall day that would usher the war home to the future managing director of Cambridge Consulting Group had commenced, like any other for change agent Brock Wharton, on the fast track.

"Next up in the holding pen," Carissa Barnett said, pulling a manila folder from the stack.

Holding pen. She had not been on the job five weeks and already acted as if she were a veteran consultant with a short attention span. Confidence was contagious at CCG, even for the support. Wharton conceded to himself that the new twenty-five-year-old recruiting coordinator did carry a disproportionally generous bosom on her slender frame, which was managed expertly—the old conceal and reveal—in her pairing of formal business suits with blouses his colleague Piazza labeled "plunging." Wharton waited for her to set down the folder she held out for him, as she exaggerated multitasking with God-knows-what application on her new smartphone that had transferred none of its claimed intelligence to its owner. That Carissa ran the task force to recruit a wider collection of out-of-the-box thinkers troubled Wharton, who as a principal at CCG had pushed the initiative over the summer after feedback from a client critical of CCG's junior-level consultants.

Seven of them sat erect in chairs in the four-walled glass room. From outside the fishbowl, their conversation buzzed like a horde of caught flies against glass. All faked pleasantries with the other applicants while nervously hoping their newfound friends fell flat on their faces during the case interview. Although these seven applicants had done their first-round interviews at the smaller Dallas office, Wharton recognized a couple of the applicants from networking events the Houston office had sponsored. Five guys and two girls. Or was that six male applicants and one female applicant? Wharton studied the cropped hair and suit style of the suspect candidate. CCG was really leading the charge to beat McKinsey and Bain in their recruitment of the best and brightest from the LGBT community—though if pressed Wharton would be forced to admit that although he knew what the first two letters stood for, he wasn't sure those belonging to the third letter should have their own category, and was still confused as to what the fourth letter represented in this "community."

"Topper." Wharton read the first name at the top of the résumé aloud and waited to gauge the manner in which he rose. The tall candidate was an easy read for the ex-quarterback. The burgundy tasseled Ferragamo loafers with yacht-stitch detail, though not on the level of Wharton's bespoke shoes, were a touch of class by Topper Musgrave IV. He wore a practiced smile (to match the sheen of light mousse he put in his hair) as easily as he wore a tight-fitting, European-cut suit favoring his athletic build. On the older side of applicants, he was close to Wharton's age of thirty-three. Wharton predicted that within a year of starting, Musgrave would be on the website and in company recruiting literature under the caption *For me, CCG is not only about developing the strengths you have but also about growing intellectually in a field where the learning never stops*. His was an image cut from the Brock Wharton Catalog for out-of-the-box thinkers.

Wharton led Musgrave down the all-white hallway to put him through the obligatory case interview. "How was the flight from New York?"

"Nothing quite like coming back home to Houston from the city." Wharton understood this code-speak: I can play with the big boys on Wall Street, but I have chosen to return home and be a big fish in a small pond. Wharton liked the play. Wharton had benefited from comprehending the big-picture value of leveraging his fading status as a hometown hero. In New York, he would have joined the mile-long list of ex-athletes turned traders and bankers. But in the good-ole-boy network of Houston, Wharton was the marlin hung on the office wall.

Inside his office, Wharton allowed Musgrave to take in the football given to Wharton by the Houston Texans on draft day that was mounted on its own wall. On the other wall hung his framed University of Texas jersey from the Holiday Bowl. Next to it was his Harvard Business School degree encircled by a bright, crimson-colored frame to achieve a layered effect juxtaposed with the majestic Longhorn dehydrated orange. Never one who was much for the aesthetics of interior design, Wharton adhered to a guiding principle of honoring achievement.

After sufficient time had passed for Musgrave to be intimidated but composed, Wharton put the résumé down and examined the applicant's features for signs of awe or reverence. No wrinkles on the field under the perfectly stationary, coifed brown hair or above the thin eyebrow trails; big hazel eyes dialed in on the prize; the symmetrical nose and ears showing no genetic slight. Only born assurance. A familiar face stared back at Wharton in the award-winning pedigree of Musgrave: here was a CCG man.

Wharton began, "I usually begin a decision-round interview by providing the candidate with a face to put with our international reputation of excellence and seventy worldwide offices. Then I will ask you a few questions about your background to get to know your story, allowing you to walk me through your résumé. After which time we will proceed to the case portion of the interview, and then wrap up with any questions you might have. Sound good?"

"Sounds great."

Wharton motioned to his football jersey upon concluding a brief internal debate to lend his own face as the best example. "When my football career ended in injury before my first NFL preseason, I asked myself, 'What other challenges are out there for a game-changer in life, Brock?' At first glance, it was investment banking. Which I did here in town at arguably the best bulge-bracket investment bank for four years—logged a lot of hours and got up to speed on everything I thought there was to know about business. But it was while learning the case-study method at Harvard Business School that I realized a well-trained monkey can perform the functions in banking." Since Musgrave, a native Houstonian, had opted for Wall Street, Wharton decided to forgo his polemic on oil and gas as unnecessary; he calculated he was not alone in his derision of the industry as not meeting the ambitions of someone of their talent level. "It was that epiphany—which came to me during the twenty-fifth mile of the Boston Marathon—that made me realize consulting was the only place in the business world that provided a daily intellectual challenge for the extreme competitor in life. If you're a competitor, you will never be bored and your future is limitless at CCG." Wharton stopped to point at Musgrave and asked with a turn of the palm up to show the oyster that could be held there, "In what other job in the world can a recent MBA graduate stand in front of a Fortune 500 CEO and tell him how to fix his company? So, Topper, why do you wish to be a part of CCG?"

"Because it's the best. And it can grow further."

"*Further*," Wharton said, wrapping his tongue around the length of the word approvingly, in the manner of a python encountering a small mammal.

"Houston was the number one city in job creation at three hundred and nine percent this past year. It's about to overtake Chicago as the third-largest city in the country. *This* is the downtown where I wish to log my future late nights."

Directed by this exhortation to his lectern, the future mayor asserted, "It's not just an oil town."

"My grandfather used to say, 'Oil is a commodity you own, not something that defines you.'" Musgrave did not have to spell out for Wharton that his grandfather had uttered the platitude as a cabinet member in President George H. W. Bush's one-term administration.

"You can't be inimitable if you float on the same rising tide as all boats," Wharton crowed, now rehearsing his speech as the first Mr. Houston recipient who would reject the celebration of oil—in his case, as not celebratory enough of his own distinguished talents, any industry that ultimately derived its success from the luck of drilling into the earth's right spots. Where was the sport in that?

"At every stage in my life I've been the best, gone further. Whether it was graduating at the top of my class and still finding the intestinal fortitude to captain the basketball team at a little school in Boston, or serving as a leader after that by besting my peers on the trading desk."

Little school in Boston. The competitor speech had sunk the hook deep in this billfish. "Captained at Harvard, eh?" Was it even necessary to insult this captain by asking him for a solution to a case study? The rest of the interview would be better spent shooting clays. What a joy it would be to open the gate for such a competitor. To hit him with a tight spiral in the end zone during the Consulting Bowl. Even the future king of a city needed his lieutenants.

"All-Conference in the Ivy League can't match being drafted in the seventh round," Musgrave said with a fellow-club-member-sized grin.

Wharton marveled at the young pro's subtle dropping of draft placement. Musgrave had clearly scouted CCG in Houston and researched some national who's-who list of upcoming talent to watch. Wharton scanned to the bottom of the interview report and found the box labeled *Fit for CCG?* Wharton checked it and wrote beside it in his best mock Shakespearean: HIRE HE OR EXPIRE WE. Next to it he sketched a small hourglass with an arrow pointing to the small amount of sand left in the top half and printed GRANULARITY UNNECESSARY.

Each applicant was scored by the assigned interviewer in three categories: behavioral assessment, case performance, and fit for CCG. It was nothing if not subjective—something Wharton favored, though the case interview portion was supposed to be an objective measuring stick to compare the competing applicants' analytical abilities. Wharton always tested one of two case problems. Both problems were based on actual consulting assignments he had worked on at CCG for six and eleven months respectively. The Dr Pepper branding case was his preferred test to sit in judgment of. In an interview, he allowed twenty to twenty-five minutes to present the case portion. He looked at his watch; they had plenty of time. Wharton shuffled the charts on his desk and called an audible, "Change of plans. You already did three cases in the first round, right?"

"Two cases."

"*Two* cases, *three* cases," Wharton began, rolling his eyes to telegraph his would-be future protégé to play along with one of his favorite pastimes, "are we accountants? Well, you have at least three more to work through today anyway. I think at this point, with your credentials, it might be more interesting to stick with the behavioral part of the interview. Have you scan some charts and graphs and discuss what qualitative data you can pull from them." Pull qualitative data to make more money, that inalienable American commandment from J. P. Morgan that Wharton had taken an oath to uphold while in the womb. "Every top consulting firm can walk into any elite business school and come out with enough number-crunchers to boil the ocean, Topper. Between you and me, what we really look for are people who are not afraid to make a decision when faced with an impossibly large amount of data. We want the alpha male in the pack who sails across the ocean. I will ask you a favorite question here at CCG: What is your biggest failure and your biggest success in life?"

Musgrave suddenly lowered his imperious forehead and pantomimed a hesitant neurotic, only to shoot up to the surface and lock eyes with an awaiting Wharton to complete the variety act. "Is it wrong to confess that I can't think of a failure?"

"*No*," Wharton said, rising from his chair, unable to stay seated in his excitement that the recruit had hit his line, "that's the right answer at CCG!"

• • •

Gatekeeper that he was, even Wharton had to admit recruiting had brought in a great class. It was the first time he could remember checking the box to hire all the candidates he had interviewed on a decision-round interview day. Though none of the three other candidates he interviewed reached the exalted heights of the poised Topper Musgrave IV, Wharton thought that, under his leadership, the remaining three could be valuable assets to him one day when he was managing director. Obviously, he would still have to run them through his own version of consulting boot camp first. But if they could survive his finishing school, then yes, they—including the girl with the butch haircut who had cracked a new trial case in an innovative fashion by suggesting the client further outsource all but one of the divisions to Eastern Europe—could be potential CCG all-stars. Wharton would have loved for it to have been a game. Much more so than football, a sport he had excelled in and never liked, but loved telling people how much he had never liked it more than he had in fact not liked it. The real adversary was the river of time, which must be dredged, channeled, dammed, and prioritized. He would have lost—*was* losing—head to head against time of course, everyone did, but it would be close, yes, Wharton outdistancing his peers in the race.

The shine and swagger of a new day. Great Recession? Not Houston. And yet, and yet there had been a speed bump in September 2008, sure, but that had been assessed and corrected; and now the city of Brock Wharton seceded further from the rest of the flatlined country in the first week of September 2014. As Wharton was considering whether to rearrange his weekend schedule to pencil in sex with his wife, one of the strangest men he had ever laid eyes on breached the space of his open doorway. Of average height, the boyish, sun-cooked man appeared taller than he was as his askew brown hair lashed out in every direction. His rangy build (accentuated by the too-small, off-the-rack, navy double-breasted suit he wore as if he were a redneck admiral at a regatta that Wharton would never enter) seemed pulled at the sinews' seams. It was the sort of flawed build that none of the South Texas ranching families would ever breed. If not for the intensity of the blue eyes—divided by a comic eagle nose that dived toward raggedly chapped lips—so nakedly sizing him up in return, Wharton would have dismissed the figure as an apparition too absurd to be real.

Unnerved by the fixed eyes that looked through him to some burning skyscraper or falling zeppelin outside the window, Wharton twisted around, anticipating to be hit by a tornado. But the downtown skyline was undisturbed. Annoyed by this intrusion and humiliated that he had been tricked into a search beyond his window, Wharton spun around in his chair to regain the initiative. "Who—"

"You're the man to beat?" A smile the size of the intruder's face tore through the puffy lips and exposed a series of swollen red gums congregated around two monstrous white tusks for front teeth, which, if not fake, the hospital-white fangs had avoided the yellow staining of the other teeth and clearly swam in their own current in the man's mouth. A muddy five-o'clock shadow surrounded the giant mouth, which surely, upon closer inspection of this dark facial sandpaper, would be attributed to not shaving than to some celebrated regeneration of stubble.

His piney, log-cutting aftershave sprayed Wharton's office with his scent. A hand slithered in the air above his desk toward Wharton. He stood and asked in a harsh tone that betrayed the mask of imperturbability he wished to project, "Who are you and what is the nature of your business in my office?"

"I'm Mike Fink," the man said in a mysterious dialect, a dialect hailing from a region that Wharton could only place as from the land of the lower class while his limp hand was grabbed by Fink. His flagrant confidence-man grin expressed an expectation that Wharton knew the name, if not the reputation. "I'm here for the leadership position."

I, Wharton declared to himself, will personally see to it that that never happens. This was a case that needed no analysis. Wharton pulled his hand from Fink's clasp and came around from his desk. "Be that as it may, I have never heard of you. I am sure we can resolve this misunderstanding in no time if you would please . . ." But Wharton trailed off, watching in horror as Fink plopped down unasked in the chair across from Wharton's desk and wriggled his lanky body to find an incorrect posture. This creature's cheekiness apparently knew no bounds. Wharton found himself slightly behind Fink and facing his back; Fink tapped his right foot, waiting on the start of an interview

Wharton was not about to give such an entitled lout. *Leadership* position? Papers rustled behind where Wharton stood, but he could not take his eyes off the hunched back of Fink.

"I see that you used your Special Forces navigational skills to find Brock's office, Mike," a squeaky voice said behind Wharton.

"Too easy, Carissa. Didn't even have to *consult* the compass."

"Consult," Carissa repeated in a higher pitch that no doubt carried a waving of a finger at clever schoolboy Fink for his introduction of an unimaginative punning attempt to their colloquial exchange. "A good consultant never consults a compass."

"Miss Barnett, what is going on?" Wharton asked, as he swung around to see the top-heavy recruiter giggling and swaying her head to the savage's tapping beat. Was she blushing? Her lips certainly now bore the mark of lipstick, adorned in a Valentine's Day red to match a pair of six-inch stiletto heels that had magically sprouted up from her earlier flats like weeds in a trailer park. She was without her jacket, and it appeared that—was it possible, even amid the other illusions?—she had lost three or four buttons, too, judging by the excessively gratuitous amount of breast on exhibit. All at once, Wharton felt the butt of a joke, a weary traveler who had stumbled into some rustic country inn for shelter only to be mocked by the randy bar maiden and the regular patrons.

"Oh, Brock, I'm so sorry. I guess you hadn't been notified that Mike would be interviewing this afternoon. He was traveling from New Orleans and wasn't able to make it for the morning block of interviews." She ruffled through the stack of papers in her hand and pulled a badly mauled page out and passed it to Wharton. "Here's a copy of his résumé. Like I told Mike, you are the only one left to interview him before the meeting in the conference room in half an hour to decide on who the new hires are."

Wharton waved her on before she disclosed any more details of the hiring process. Oblivious to the intent of his wave, she leaned over to Wharton with the bright eyes of a much younger child, a mercurial silver sparkle that screamed antidepressants, and whispered audibly for Fink to hear, "He's a Green Beret."

"I don't care if he's the pope, Carissa, as I have only a half hour to give an intensive interview," Wharton said truthfully, for despite his conservative Christian upbringing, he now cared little for religious figures. Indeed, besides possibly salvation, little reward stemmed from religious fervor beyond the required Christian affiliation among his strategic-friends crowd. Wharton thought even less of people in the military, despite the nauseating resurgence of post-9/11 glorification of a segment who'd been the frequent subject of derision prior to that day. In Wharton's youth, the military was the last stop for the talentless who could not do anything else in life. It usually wasn't even much of a choice: *You can go to prison, or be all you can be in the Army.* Now everyone was expected to shake their hands, pick up their checks in restaurants, turn over first-class seats to them on airplanes, and worst yet, stand up and clap for them at sporting events while nodding that the only reason the sport is even being played is because of heroes like them fighting in some country with cities no one can pronounce. An inane rah-rah yellow-ribbon patriotism, a shared ritual offering peace between the jingoes, Middle America, and pinkos where everyone emerged feeling good about their participation. Doubtless this explained how this Fink character was granted a CCG interview.

"Well," Wharton said to Fink, shutting the door on Carissa, "it appears I am to interview you. I'm going to take a minute to scan through your résumé."

"Take your time," the applicant advised the interviewer. "There's a lot there."

There, Wharton quickly realized, was not a lot there: current employment listed as *none*, no work experience (unless ten years in the military counted), a 2.9 GPA, and a bachelor of arts in English literature (was that not the easy major?) from Tulane University (a bottom first-tier university that CCG did not even review applications from) the same year Wharton graduated. Lo and behold, Fink's résumé was actually a mirror out of a fable, in that if you held it up, your exact opposite looked back at you.

"An English literature major?" Wharton murmured, bringing the CV closer to his eyes.

"With a minor in theater. I read somewhere that English majors make the best consultants. Stands to reason."

Had recruiting seriously thought the SPECIAL FORCES bullet in bold letters at the top alone merited an interview? Special Forces could not be that special if Fink lacked the cognition to apprehend that he did not belong at CCG. That his presence, an interloper squandering his time, was offensive to a Brock Wharton, who had conducted a life cultivating a résumé. Fink was a great example of a candidate not having researched CCG; how had he passed the first-round interview? In fact, Wharton assessed it to be the most heinous résumé ever submitted for his review: not even the oversized font or alignment from section to section was consistent in what amounted to only a stretched half page of largely questionable achievements (high school senior class president?). Wharton looked up at Fink in time to see him fondling his Texans football!

"Put that down!" Wharton pointed at the ball holder on the wall next to Fink, who on his orders positioned the ball upside down on its seam.

"I apologize. I had forgotten that you were drafted in the last round after playing for UT."

Wharton searched the blue eyes sunk back in the triangular face for an intended slight in the usage of "last" to describe the still-prestigious seventh round. What it seemed Fink hadn't forgotten was the chatter of sports columnists, recruiters, superfans, and boosters who had once ranked Wharton the top high school quarterback in the South and proclaimed him the next UT football savior. He in turn ranked this same mindless mob number one in cowardice after four years of enduring their catcalls every time he was injured and being denounced by them for betrayal when their impossible expectations for their fair-haired boy were not met on the field. "Were you drafted as well after graduating college?"

"Drafted by our country," Fink said, startling Wharton with a belly laugh loud enough to be heard down the hall.

Wharton avoided Fink's face to conceal the anger he was sure must be reddening his own cheeks. He found refuge in Fink's résumé. A review of it demonstrated that the undereducated Fink knew absolutely nothing beyond the art of exploiting some tax credit for businesses that interviewed veterans. Another bending of the laws, no less egregious than allowing veterans a pass in public with their PTSD service dogs while their pit bulls created anxiety for everyone else. Wharton pushed aside the flash of resentment that made him want to physically kick Fink from his office. He settled on an approach he was convinced would inflict far more damage to this impertinent CCG impostor's candidacy: cede the stage to an unwitting Fink and allow the veteran to shoot himself, hailing as he did from a demographic statistically known for its high suicide rates.

"Thank you for your service. Now why don't you walk me through your academic accomplishments?" Wharton began anew, chumming the waters for that pesky foe of Delusion: Fact. "I see here that you had a two-point-nine grade point average at Tulane."

"Two point nine four five to be exact, but if you round that up it is a two point nine five, and if you're really telling a tale, you could round that to a three point zero."

"CCG, almost as a rule, requires its applicants to have a GPA of three point six or above from a top-ranked college. You are applying for the position of consultant with an undergraduate GPA of two point nine against a field of applicants that all have MBAs, and, in some cases, two advanced graduate degrees. Have you done any graduate-level course work at all?"

"The Special Forces Qualification Course."

Fink was making this easy for Wharton. "I don't think I follow," Wharton said, baiting him to continue his charm offensive and rambling lack of reflection, which conformed ideally to Wharton's plan of wrestling back control of the interview. "Can you elaborate specifically on how this course qualifies as graduate school and how it relates to a career in consulting?"

Fink straightened up in his chair. His arrowhead chip of a face leaned in over the desk. Was he applying for a job or auditioning for a small part in a play?

"*De Oppresso Liber*," Fink said, enunciating each Latin word for Wharton's appreciation.

Wharton stared dramatically at the now confirmed lunatic and awaited a further terse three-or-four-word inadequate explanation that was not forthcoming. It was not as if Wharton lacked experience playing a part; he knew full well what was expected of him in life's starring role. Finally, Wharton asked, "Excuse me?"

"Motto of the Green Berets." Fink thumped his chest with his fist (in the spot where the handkerchief, which could have been the only item to make his costume more ridiculous to Wharton, was missing). "It means 'To Liberate the Oppressed.'"

"What does this have to do with consulting?"

"For a decade I trained not only on how to operationally liberate the oppressed, but also how to free my mind from the oppression of conventional thinking. A consultant referencing unconventional thinking in a plush CCG office and actually being unconventional when the stakes are high are as different as a yellowbelly catfish is from a bullhead catfish," Fink exclaimed. He had also managed to concurrently use his hands to grotesquely elucidate the contrasting courage of each subspecies by forming what Wharton interpreted as human female and male genitalia. "Like consulting, it's about being adaptable. Who is the most adaptable? Ain't that America? Now, I'm not a big war story guy, but you asked me to describe a situation where I had to lead a group of people and convince them that an unconventional solution was the right way, and to that I say: how about *every* day in Iraq! If that—"

"I didn't ask you anything of the sort. You are barking up the wrong tree."

"I once stared the bark off a tree I was so riled up," Fink offered as further qualification. He laughed and winked at Wharton. "Too much time overseas in the sandbox dodging death this past decade will do that to you. The relevance of my graduate work in the Special Forces Qualification Course is that I have unique professional training and a record of success in solving and analyzing complex problems. As I explained to the senior partners, and this perhaps fails to come across in a limited reading of a CV, there is a value in being able to establish networks of influence—"

"Influence," Wharton repeated. "You are claiming to have acquired this from the military?" Here was a hick who could not influence the next banjo number at a hoedown—could Wharton get a witness among the kinfolk (because they're all related) messing around on the hay bales?—and yet Fink thought himself up to CCG snuff. The true tragedy of these small-town military applicants not being that bright was that they were unaware of it. Seeing how everyone else was afraid of the possibility of veterans returning to the office and shooting up the place, Wharton saw it as his duty not to coddle military candidates, but rather to use the interview as a teaching moment to direct them to their intellectual rung below dieticians. He did not doubt that they probably thought his posture that of a cheese dick. But comporting yourself as such was part of the game, be it assimilation of the fittest douches. In Wharton's CCG class, there had been an ex–Naval Academy nuclear submariner who had lasted a year out of the Houston office with his conventional mind-set, his pervasive logical staleness onsite incapable of turning the client ship around. He'd even had a gut.

"May I please just be allowed an opportunity—" But a knock at the door cut Fink off before Wharton could cut him off again.

Nathan Ellison, a senior partner in his midforties with the body and energy of a younger man able to both network around town at all the right social gatherings and find time to teach Sunday school, stepped inside. "Didn't realize you were still doing an interview." He apologized to Wharton, then noticing Fink, asked, "Is Brock giving you a real pressure cooker?"

"Can't complain, no one's shooting at me," Fink said, bounding up from the chair to straighten his corkscrew backbone into an erect figure of authority for a handshake, with a nod to Wharton. "Yet." Their hands met and held, arm wrestling blue veins popping out in the kind of kingmaker handshake set aside for finalizing backroom palace coup plots. They smiled at each other and continued to ignore Wharton as if he were a naked man changing in *their* locker room row. "Only jesting. He's great, Nate." Wharton brooded over the liberty taken with Nathan's name, paraded as it was by Fink, who no longer sniffed the air but deeply inhaled the noxious fumes that he had introduced to the office.

It dismayed Wharton that the late-afternoon autumn light from his window slightly softened the crags of Fink's bird-of-prey profile, the challenging mannerisms and hillbilly hostility of the hawk-nosed dive bomber jettisoned for the litheness of the assassin, high on hash and his mission, who moves limberly along the corridor wall in wait on the balls of his feet. "Unlike our intellectual discussion, Brock and I were sparring about the value in establishing networks of influence onsite with clients. I suppose we represent differing schools of thought"—Fink motioned with his hands to group him and Nathan on one side against Wharton on the other—"regarding the best method of how to mine pertinent data to achieve effective results. Just waiting on him to give me the case, but if you two are in a rush to get to your meeting, I am happy to skip over the bio part."

"Can't talk about it," Nathan said, and turning to Wharton, added, "or he'd have to kill us." Was the newly christened infantile persona Nate, once a sober CCG senior partner by the honest Christian name of Nathan, as high as Fink?

"Influence." Fink flicked his wrist in the air to snap an imaginary towel at Nathan, who laughed and closed the door. Fink's reciprocal laughter, forced to begin with, stopped the moment the door shut.

Wharton hypothesized that Fink's true intellectual capacity could be brought to the surface quite easily with the right application. Deployed not to the Middle East but to the far more unsympathetic region of high finance, how would Fink operate in the world of big money?

"Let's play with some numbers. We have to know that you are comfortable with numbers and speak the language of the business world while coming up with unconventional solutions to complex problems, as I recall you endeavoring to frame it earlier. The best way for us to discern whether you have the skill set required for the intellectually rigorous environment of consulting is by walking you through a case and seeing how . . . you . . . compete."

"I like to win . . . in . . . life."

Win? Was Fink attempting to commandeer *winning*, the very ethos Wharton lived by? Wharton handed him four clean sheets of paper and a clipboard with a pen attached. "How many in-flight meals were prepared on an average day last year for flights from George Bush Intercontinental Airport?"

"Forty thousand."

"Come again?"

"Forty thousand."

Wharton could not have been felled harder had Fink launched his entire gangly frame at his knees. *In point of fact,* Wharton would have normally explained if Fink had not rendered him speechless, the correct answer to the market-sizing question was forty-three thousand after factoring in the four thousand meals for the international flights. Wharton attempted to salvage some dignity from this unfathomable opening checkmate that had always stumped even the smartest business school students by an incorrect margin of at least ten thousand. "Would you care to illustrate how you arrived at that number?"

"For the reason that around forty thousand is the right answer," Fink charitably clarified.

"I am interested not in Hail Mary guesstimates but your thought process. That you were on the runway for ten minutes and watched two other planes touch down that you then multiplied by six to calculate how many per hour. You then extrapolated out that there were three runways total and each plane on average carried one hundred forty-five passengers. Which you multiplied by twenty instead of twenty-four, as the time from midnight to four in the morning is essentially a dead zone for departures. And that, of those domestic flights, only twenty-five percent of them provided a meal service."

"Which is how I arrived at around forty thousand meals. Just do the math like you just did. I solved it like I had one shot, one kill. Some of us applicants have been vetted—and I don't mean at an investment banking desk job playing with myself and numbers."

Fink released a cackle of a laugh aimed to pierce what patience Wharton had left. The Prohibition gangster–suited Brer Rabbit across from him had duped Wharton into illustrating a method aloud that backed Fink's wild-ass guess, now claiming ownership of Wharton's mathematical reasoning. What next: squatter's rights to Wharton's office? After Fink's barrage of assaults on football, his manhood, and the nonvetted like himself who had played with themselves while investment banking, Wharton suspected that his colleague Piazza was behind all of this. The explicit attack on investment banking by Fink was an overplaying of the inside information he had been fed, revealing the puppet strings. It was time to cut them, as Fink was still an applicant applying for a job at Wharton's firm. Why hadn't he stuck with the Dr Pepper case, a straightforward branding case? Fink could not even articulate his own identity. "You will need to write down your calculations and structure an outline for the remaining part of the interview. And I will be collecting your notes when we finish for confidentiality purposes."

"I understand. You're talking to a holder of a Top Secret security clearance."

It occurred to Wharton that such a fact, if true, did not bode well for national security. Wharton got up and walked to the window. "For the sake of simplicity, let us use the number forty thousand meals a day." He faced Fink and began the mad minute of firing. "Our client, a company called Swanberry Foods, is responsible for fifteen percent of the daily in-flight meals at George Bush Intercontinental Airport with a profit margin of one dollar per meal—but the meals only stay edible for eight hours. Recently, management at Swanberry Foods has been considering an overhaul, moving to frozen meals that stay edible up to twenty-four hours, enabling our client to increase its profit margin twenty-five percent per meal. The technology and new equipment to switch to the frozen meals costs fifteen million dollars over five years." Fink's pen lay untouched atop the paper. "What would you advise our client to do under the circumstances? You may take a minute to structure your—"

"I'd pull the trigger and double down on this new technology if our client's only objective is to maximize profit over the long run. You've got to roll the dice to make money."

"Please demonstrate beyond the usage of military and gambling metaphors how our client should strategically approach this decision. This time, be so kind as to walk me through your calculations that support your hypothesis after taking a moment."

Fink held up his index finger to Wharton and began to scribble manically. The same index finger reappeared two more times separated by three-minute intervals between flashes. It took all the reserve in Wharton not to snatch the finger on its third appearance and break it.

"What do your numbers say?" Wharton asked, putting an end to the longest ten-minute silence of his life.

"Profits of almost six million dollars a year if Swanberry switches to the proposed plan. That's before I shave their fixed costs to trim them down."

"I think you mean variable costs," Wharton said, allowing a laugh to escape at such amateur histrionics. He leaned over to try and read the chicken scratch on the top piece of paper. He was enjoying this and shook his head slowly at the illegible writing, indubitably representative of the mind that had dictated it. "God only knows where, but I'm afraid you have an extra zero or two in there somewhere. I don't know where to begin helping you because I can't make out a single number on your paper. This is why a *successful* applicant will use this as a dialogue and voice aloud each major step in his or her explanation; that way we can help guide you a little should you stumble in one of your calculations. Had you done the math correctly, you would see that at their projected rate of sales Swanberry would lose almost a quarter of a million dollars per year over the next five years, and that it would take almost six years just to break even after the investment if they could withstand the initial losses."

"I was shooting for long term, the big picture."

Like the trajectory of a clay pigeon, Wharton had anticipated this rationalization before he fired. "If you were thinking 'long term' and the 'big picture,' you would have noted they needed to increase their market share by marketing to airlines that their newly designed meals would last longer and save the airlines money compared to the other products being offered by competitors. Even acquire a competitor and streamline costs. And that's only after analyzing whether the industry is growing. You would have recommended that they diversify with other products or at least expand their current market into supermarkets, hospitals, retirement centers, prisons, and even your military-base chow halls. And that is exactly what we did, because I worked on this for eleven months—though the real company was not called Swanberry."

"Not bad, though, for ten minutes versus what took you a year, right?"

Wharton did not bite on this tease designed to distract him from closing in for the scalp. "Where's your outline or structured strategy? I need to collect your scratch paper as well."

Fink first handed Wharton a sheet from the bottom, the outline. "There might be a gem or two buried in there y'all could use," he thought he heard Fink say as Wharton gazed transfixed on the only two things written on the paper: PROFITS = REVENUE – COSTS, and circled below it, ALWAYS LOOK AT THE REVENUE.

"'Always look at the revenue.' I don't even know what this means," Wharton muttered in shock, letting the outline float down to his desk. "This is your foundation?"

"Winning," Fink instructed, standing up and tapping with the familiar index finger on the written equation at the top of the outline. "Or in the more narrow terms of this particular world, maximizing profits. In a wildcatting oil town like Houston, a thin line—"

"I must conclude this interview, for I have to attend our office meeting," Wharton said, rising from his chair and sparing himself from Fink's clichéd interpretation of the essence of Wharton's hometown. "Do you have any questions for me?"

Fink held up his hands as if about to make a confession. "I've got nothing for you."

Wharton thought it was the first valid point Fink had made.

• • •

"I'll never get that wasted half hour of my life back!" Wharton pronounced as he walked into Cambridge Consulting Group's conference room.

Wharton waited on Mitch Piazza to announce to the room his

usual refrain upon a late Wharton entrance, *Nice of the crown prince to grace us with his presence.* Oh, the relief to be greeted by the jaunty Piazza with his engraved cleft chin only overshadowed by his long nose, his self-important triathlons and life-altering training regimen, the obnoxious habit he had of jogging around the neighborhood with the ever-present headband but no shirt on! Somehow, this same Piazza, whose résumé listed Princeton football without clarifying that he played on the under-one-hundred-sixty-pound-man Princeton sprint football team, was Wharton's closest friend at CCG. But his friend's utter disinterest brought Wharton up short. Stopped him cold.

Piazza sat at the far end of the egg-shaped conference table, his attention to the right of where Wharton stood to address the managing director at the head of the table, flanked on each side by the two senior partners. "I met him briefly between his interviews with each one of you. I must say I thought as well that he possesses not only a colorful way of distilling a situation but also a raw intelligence in conversation. And as you said, he passes the airport test with flying colors." Musgrave was praiseworthy all right, but this much praise from the ass-kissing Piazza was reserved normally for cornholing the assenting senior management. Even then Piazza usually had the tact to do it in relative privacy when it was just his long nose and a partner delayed in the airport lounge. "He also has that rarest of qualities: all-American charisma." Wharton checked his hands for hives. "With his distinct bio and fiery personality, he has the ability to connect on a basic level with a lot of our newer clients."

Wharton attempted to cut off the office sycophant. "I presume you can't be talking about—"

"I even thought Fink was an MBA, as in our encounter he humbly made no references to Special Forces. Because this guy has the kind of military background that would have a great deal of traction to influence our growing number of nontraditional clients."

The characteristics describing another side of anyone other than the interviewee Fink ricocheted around inside Wharton's head: Intelligent. Charismatic. Talented. All-American. The only all-American (third team selection in one paper long since put out of business by the Internet) was Brock Wharton. There were two Americas, all right, but

CCG only consulted for one. And Wharton led that reasoned charge in the opposite direction of Fink, who drove his wagon train toward the endless horizon of psychosis. Wharton had been delayed not five hours but twenty-five minutes with Fink, an airport test that Fink had failed abysmally with his inability to talk about anything other than the military. "Okay, my friends, who orchestrated that prank?"

"Would you mind ending your own prank, Brock, so we can resume this meeting and settle on the candidates to whom we should extend offers?" Ernest Seymour asked. The managing director motioned for Wharton to sit in the chair next to Piazza. "So we're all in agreement that we should extend an offer to both of the women? That includes you as well, Brock?"

Wharton nodded his head in favor.

"Which leaves Topper Musgrave, but only Brock wrote a strong evaluation of his unoriginal why-I've-been-the-best shtick. A Green Beret and two female MBA students it is."

"I give up!" Wharton yelled, actually hoping the meeting would adjourn with this vote and a pie of whipped cream thrown in his face. There was no way to equate Fink with the standards of CCG unless it was part of a sick Friday joke. "I know I never lose, but you all win. I'm buying drinks for whichever one of you concocted the idea to hire that actor to play Fink. Pure genius. Platinum, I tell you. I thought he was a real applicant. And everyone pretending that we're not going to hire Musgrave—the best candidate in at least a few years to interview here. You can't beat a CCG Friday when we're all in the office and at the top of our game!"

"We are not going to hire Musgrave," Stanley Weinberg said, extinguishing Wharton's hope once and for all of a CCG hoax. Weinberg was a thin, bespectacled man in his early fifties with salt-and-pepper hair combed straight back from his forehead. The Snail. More an intellectual consultant than a business generator, the Snail had started as an analyst and inched his way up to senior partner engagement by engagement. His Hollywood-silent-film-star hair aside, there was nothing slick about him. Not even his horn-rimmed glasses, which he had worn so long that the style had recently been poached by a small cohort of hipsters. "Too much baggage. He's too assured and supercilious, and I for one wouldn't want to work with him in a small-team setting. There is such a thing as too much confidence."

"We are talking about the same Topper Musgrave who captained the Harvard basketball team and whose grandfather was commerce secretary, right? That's as all-American as it gets."

"Yes, the same greatness that helped bankrupt his employer Lehman Brothers and the economy by making a nice personal profit trading credit default swaps. Good for Musgrave's savings account while the run lasted, but not so good for America's savings account. I would venture that his politician grandfather would approve of his seamless transition. He even boasted he was given a salary raise by Barclays when it picked up his whole trading desk."

"Fink would bring diversity of talent to our portfolio," Nathan Ellison interjected. "His military background is a perfect fit with the male-dominated oil field services segment of the industry, and his out-of-the-box thought process is nicely suited for the unconventional drilling era." It always mystified Wharton how much Nathan's attractive brunette wife could pass for his sister, and yet here he was arguing for diversity.

"He has an out-of-the-box thought process," Wharton said, "because he's not even aware of the box."

"I remember someone pushing to net more wild cards," Piazza croaked.

"Let's be the first-movers of the consulting firms to really attach ourselves to the new generation in energy," Nathan said. "An operator like Fink who has the ability to turn on his English literature background with the C-suite, but who is also capable of speaking in the native vernacular to gather intelligence with the roughnecks in the field, is invaluable to business. He could also tap straight into the current pro-military business landscape with our other patriotic clients. His heavy soft-skills style would be perfect for Dr Pepper."

"Dr Pepper would eat him alive. Name one category in which Musgrave loses to Fink," Wharton said, daring the group.

"Captaining a sports team and captaining a small team of the nation's most elite operators behind enemy lines are not even in the same universe, and I say that having captained an Ivy League squad," Piazza said, snatching a Piazza-like opportunity to elevate himself, snipe at a vulnerable Wharton, and slip in a kiss to his boss's ass.

"Fink was the worst candidate I have ever interviewed. Even with what Nathan is saying, what would happen when the time came to put him in front of traditional clients? Consulting is presentation. Fink can barely speak coherently."

"What are you talking about, buddy? We all heard the two of you laughing in your office when you were interviewing him. It sounded like a party."

"That was all him. He is like the madman at the opera."

"I wouldn't have thought a 1-performer like you would have needed Nathan to spell out the strategic significance of a hire like Fink with the recent percentage jump of our business from both shale and expanded deep-water drilling," Seymour said. "Unconventional Drilling, Digital, Big Data, other national brands like Dr Pepper, let's capture all of this new business. How should we bucket Fink? By leveraging the cachet a combat veteran possesses from having done something distinctive with real stakes involved, where part of the sublime feat had an element of risk to it. Is he a hiring risk? Maybe, but in our post-9/11 world these heroes are a lot more real to clients than another fresh-faced MBA."

Heroes! Wharton swallowed, CCG's newly formed House Committee of American Activities waterboarding the good-for-business patriotism down his throat. To Wharton's mystification, society had begun to abuse the hero designation in its post-9/11 dementia, handing it out willy-nilly to anyone who could not obtain a decent-paying job but was given an American flag to sew on their uniform sleeve as a consolation prize. As he waited on the anaphylaxis to seize his esophagus, he wondered how Fink had brainwashed the heads of the office in a few thirty-minute interviews. Was this not an age-old variation on the case of the handyman *leveraging* his inferior social standing over the soft-handed upper class? That same working-class hero who overcharged for a shoddy job all the while ogling the wife of the same client he openly disparages? His airway still open, Wharton wanted to bemoan an age where it was considered blasphemy to say what all knew—that full-time salaried firemen barely even break a sweat for just two workdays a week—but the only siren he sounded was "Fink knows nothing about the art of consulting. He couldn't even work through a case, and he offered solutions that were completely incorrect."

"No one knows anything about the art of consulting—that's why it's consulting!" Nathan belted out exultantly. Wharton felt the bullying spotlight of a comedy club single out his place at the table. "If people knew what we actually did, do you think we would have jobs, Brock? We'll train him up. There is no right or wrong answer to a case anyway. He answered the case I gave him in an unorthodox manner, too, yet basically arrived at the same solution. At hundred-dollar-a-barrel oil, we need bodies for expanding the pie."

"We can't just mass-produce CCG consultants to meet the demand."

"Ninety-nine dollars a barrel," Piazza cut in, reminding everyone that the person behind his lifeless shark eyes had once traded oil at Morgan Stanley for all of eleven months. "Dropped to close just below the hundred mark today."

"He's never even had a *real* job!" Wharton pleaded.

"That's enough," Seymour said. "Everyone has weighed in. Fink is being extended an offer." Seymour stopped himself to look over at Wharton and wait for the silence in the room that would shortly follow a look. "You neglected an interesting data point when you were blinded by the bloodline of Musgrave, Brock. You missed that our new man from Louisiana comes from an even more illustrious family."

"What?" Wharton barely mustered.

"He's a descendant of American folk hero Mike Fink."

Again, Wharton continued his tailspin before his colleagues' stone faces. The stillness in the room churned the isolation all the more for the fighter pilot sealed in his cockpit and falling to Earth. "Folk hero? Like Paul Bunyan? How can you be descended from a fictional person? With his wavy hair and prominent nose, I thought Fink was Jewish."

This drew an audible gasp from several of the people at the table, who turned toward Stanley Weinberg, compelling him to defend his religion. "Yes," Weinberg began, "I see." The affectation of the Snail was such that, even when salted, it often called for an extra second or two to stir its mouthpiece. "There can't be a Jewish-American folk hero? Are all Jewish folk heroes supposed to be consigned to living on a roof in a Ukrainian ghetto and speaking Yiddish between sets on the fiddle?"

"That's not what I meant," Wharton said, protesting the latest of unwarranted charges: anti-Semitism. True, he felt no need for them to be welcomed into the Houston Country Club. But if anything, his detestation of swine like Fink surely granted Wharton some brotherhood with even the most orthodox of Jews. "I meant I don't understand. Who *is* Mike Fink?"

Seymour snapped his suspenders and roared, "King of the Mississippi!"

2.
FOREIGN INTERNAL DEFENSE

The strategic decision to strand his pregnant wife at the airport was the easiest of Wharton's consulting career. The standard risk-versus-reward matrix, pulled right out of any consultant's ass, made the calculation even easier. Normally picking up his wife during a workday was not even an option he would entertain, pregnant or otherwise, whatever the short-term benefit might be to their marriage. But normally a Monday did not see Wharton "on the beach," the consulting expression for those left idle in the office between assignments.

Wharton's wife, K.K., had flown to South Texas to surprise her family with the news that she was three months pregnant with their first child. It was a big announcement, made bigger by her family's preoccupation with breeding, and K.K. had waited until her family would all be herded at their flagship ranch between polo tournaments to share the news. That, Wharton dreaded, would force him to disclose the news to his parents: the disengagement strategy that included a phased withdrawal from parental interaction would not be allowed to run its course.

He presumed he had made the airport ride error after K.K. had put her parents on speakerphone, when he had been distracted by a rare display of praise from his in-laws (happily, a far cry in tone from the epithet they used for their oldest daughter's husband of "bum steer," which among the moneyed South Texas families was still grounds for defamation). Wharton believed he deserved points for his bull-like potency, in that he had succeeded in impregnating K.K. within a week of removing birth-control obstacles. He knew it was actually within five workdays of trying. Just as he knew he had given his reedy, brunette wife a son if she could uphold her end of the procreation handshake and close. None of which had been on his mind a minute before when his wife had called from the pickup terminal. The surprisingly chilly wind for early October added an electric-chair distortion to her anger that she ground out with her riding jackboots while he pissed a signature worthy of a founding father in the snow-white toilet of their guest bathroom.

Picking his wife up from the smaller airport south of downtown, driving first through the yellow and orange storefronts with barred windows that were always in the news for something called human trafficking, and the shift away from a game-day mentality that it would require were not in his priorities of work. Not on what would be Fink's first day at the office. Emotions were best kept out of management consulting, as evidenced by his wife's fury that clouded her from ever seeing how Fink pertained to her abandonment at the airport. With hate-fueled memories of Fink's interview with Wharton five weeks prior providing focus, Wharton had spent the entire weekend setting new milestones for himself. The first and last milestone: rid CCG of Fink.

Over the weekend, Wharton had read every yellowing book on Fink's supposed great-great-great-great-grandfather after a search through Houston's secondhand bookstores. The Mike Fink of legend illustrated: a flamboyantly long red feather erect in an Americana boatman hat atop greased hair, a scruff of a beard covering a woodcut of a face, usually dressed in modish striped pants paired with loud shirts, his trunk and arms enormous, standing over the rudder of a keelboat. And of course outfitted with the perfect accessories: knives of all sizes and serrations, an armory of chic cross-body-strap gunpowder horns that did not constrict, and modified Kentucky rifles long enough in barrel length to befit a man who liked to tickle tourists out for a stroll on the far levee. If Marlboro were sponsoring a postapocalyptic survivalist table at an NRA convention, cock of the roost Mike Fink would be blowing squall smoke rings and taking down libertarians' email addresses behind it. And in all the tales, Fink's violent insults and boasts were delivered in a parlance priding itself on spitting on the King's English. Without fail cheered on by his fellow unenlightened outcasts, who could not get enough of the fights and challenges of the variety in which third-degree burns equaled laughs.

As far as Wharton was concerned, the "Last of the Keelboatmen" or "King of the Mississippi and Ohio Rivers" was nothing more than a nineteenth-century tall tale passed by drunken frontiersmen from one boat to the next to mismanage the long hours in an unsettled country. Alone in his media room, he had taken much comfort in his first-time viewing of the old Walt Disney movie, in which the blowhard Mike Fink is upstaged by his rival Davy Crockett and has to eat his hat after losing a keelboat race down the Mississippi as a result of a blusterous wager. Wharton would see to it that there would be some hat-eating in the near future at CCG.

Wharton understood that he did not mix well with the folksy working class. His fallback conversation when having his shoes shined was always his own football career. Invariably this led to a reference of a former teammate or opponent who went on to far greater playing glory. His bona fides and street credibility established, Wharton would disengage mentally from the shoe shiner, who would be predicting the home team was going to come out like gangbusters.

Thankfully Wharton had risen fast enough in the elite world of strategic management consulting that he was largely able to avoid such interaction and mainly informed executives with an already great degree of wealth how they could make even more money. Lasting were the memories of the first consulting project he was assigned after business school in dreary Manhattan, Kansas (the "Little Apple," as its residents lovingly referred to the forgotten pit on the prairie). By day, he ingeniously streamlined a utility company's maintenance system; by night, he endured a zombie milieu in which the only recourses for dinner were garishly colorful chain restaurants off the dead main street, dining establishments in which the waitress inevitably sat down in the booth with Wharton in a futile gesture of conviviality to solicit the largest tip possible for bad service. Some served; some achieved.

So were Wharton's thoughts as his brisk cold shower spiked a return of feeling to forgotten zones, where increased circulation increased life expectancy. The same processes tugged at the life-shortening clingy bacteria unearthed by minted smart floss. Wharton weaved the engineered thread through a procession of sticky teeth, the transient whiff of death decay bleached and sanded away with gritty toothpaste suds. He did not rush the heated-cream-and-straight-razor shave that would even have cut the ego of a British House of Lords member. Or completion of the pharaoh's pyramid of tightening push-ups that deposited him aloft.

Swollen from the push-ups and secured in an armor of starch against the swamp humidity his azalea landscapers were already crouched in, Wharton descended the stairs of his Southampton Place home in the center of Houston with all the urgency of an emperor entering a room full of subjects. He opened his laptop at the kitchen table and clicked through the news links. Protein shake in one hand, he used the other hand to wave off his new Central American housekeeper, who approached with a presentation of steaming poached eggs and peppered bacon. His second time seeing her (Inés, maybe?) on his wife's rotation of three housekeepers, Wharton was sure her name had an *ñ* in there that he would never pronounce. Her long hair was the lighter-color brown of those corn husks they ate their meat out of. He speculated not many smiles had flashed under her thick mestizo brow that, like her squat shoulders, slumped toward the earth, bogged down by carrying the fall of her ancient civilization or whatever revolution she had lived through. Refusing to be served guilt with breakfast, Wharton took refuge in the front-page *Houston Chronicle* article on immigration reform. He found none. Instead there was a picture of his new maid's people tanning atop slow trains in migrating packs for days. All some sort of fiesta by way of an illogical Great Depression mode of transportation that spoke more about their poor time management skills and choo-chooing mañana attitude toward life. You didn't have to be a strategic management consultant to see why the conquistadors had restructured the organization. After a search of ten minutes, Wharton located his car keys under his spread copy of *Leading Change*.

Wharton turned down the air conditioner as his BMW kicked up the chalky concrete dust that coated downtown. Since childhood, Wharton's sensitive skin had been a source of inconvenience. It was a struggle, especially in a city at the mercy of air conditioning, to find a temperature in which his skin could just be. The itch. It often forced artificial temperatures to be recalibrated several times an hour. Sometimes, too, it wasn't the temperature. Hives had a way of appearing after he ate a dish he had consumed a hundred times hitherto without the risk of anaphylactic shock. In this way, these bizarre red welts on his body first engendered a concern by his father of a latent weakness in the genetic line. Allergists (one who had even treated the Bubble Boy) were brought in to test for food allergies, but they, too, were at a loss as to which substance Wharton's body rejected. He stopped carrying the emergency injection pen of epinephrine after a presentation to his eighth-grade speech class, the mortifying bulge in his front pants pocket even more humiliating than the earlier fear of accidental needle injection to his penis and the consequent amputation of the tumid organ. By high school, he had given himself over to the proverb passed to him by his father in a rare fit of compassion: pricks don't get prickly heat.

Under the semiromantic atmospheric layer of pinkish smog, familiar and new orange construction barriers were dropped about to reroute the whole city through the haze of the energy boom. Like Islamists, Houstonians shared a fanaticism for knocking down landmark buildings, but Houston developers differed in that they replaced the blown-up sites with gaudier concrete complexes and usually refrained from massacres. Enclosed within the vanilla leather padding of his sports car, Wharton dodged across lanes and cut back left onto San Jacinto Street at the red light; he eluded the rush-hour traffic blocking the entrance into the primary garage used by Cambridge Consulting Group and the truly enormous front grille of a bus by about eight inches. Rigidity: leading cause of death in sharks and management consultants. Not by accident had he been the University of Texas starting quarterback, thought Wharton at the sight of the newly minted traffic jam in his rearview mirror, ignoring the car horns, acknowledging the dips by the multiplying cranes above. After all, Wharton believed, talent was talent. He imagined the hapless nonconsultants bedeviled by the same laws of traffic when it came time to execute their exit strategies. It was as though they did not wish to compete with the Whartons in life.

Agent of change Brock Wharton had his disgust with the herd's inability to think outside the box tempered by the air, cool and directional, along the Houston One Center lobby wall. He floated up a floor on the vast escalator once used in an awful eighties movie he had seen as a child to depict the long ride up to heaven—the only element of the movie he identified with. In the incomprehensible plot, the bumbling protagonist kept receiving second chances from a most benevolent God (miraculously, thought a young Wharton), yet was still unable to develop and implement a successful plan.

Wharton held the elevator for an attractive redhead. In a gray pencil skirt and a cream button-up, she scrambled in heels over the polished white marble floor like a knock-kneed fawn. Her spicy perfume rode up forty-four floors with Wharton, though she, an almost-certified architect, with a large bag flashing a glossy exam book, departed the elevator with what Wharton felt was a strut reserved for him on the twenty-third floor. Two floors above the nation's largest independent oil and gas exploration company, and one floor above the largest investment bank, Wharton alone exited the elevator into the Houston office of Cambridge Consulting Group. On the top floor, the consulting office fittingly topped the totem pole of intellectual hierarchy in the Houston business world.

Wharton had not been at his desk for five minutes when there was a knock on his door. He stopped spinning his gold wedding ring between his left thumb and index finger as Ernest Seymour strode in and sat down in the chair across from Wharton's desk. Seymour's white shirt was almost translucent around his damp armpits, his crimson Harvard necktie serving as a bull's-eye between his royal blue suspenders. Trademark suspenders. Never trust anyone who sported a trademark, Wharton would train his sons one day, for it was a lesson he had learned the hard way from his childhood. Like a beard, they hide behind it.

"I don't suppose you would have any interest in a social impact engagement?" Wharton's pro bono offer of disgust must have been transparent, as Seymour answered for him, "High-impact results for a public education or an international nonprofit, not my cup of tea either. No margin, no mission. Headquarters is pushing it out to offices as a component of our new brand image. I told them we were too busy printing money in Houston."

Seymour had been with Cambridge Consulting Group twenty-nine years, seven as managing director. Wharton planned on achieving the same position in half that time. Not too long ago, Seymour had been the reigning cutthroat of strategic management consulting in Houston, the image of him with his jacket off and striding around in his suspenders at the downtown businessmen's clubs and eating establishments well etched. That was before McKinsey and Bain appointed managing directors younger and hungrier than Seymour and he became a drag on the CCG ticket. Dead weight, as any CCG-trained consultant counseled, should be cut loose. Wives number one and two had shucked the suspenders. And his new marriage, if thoroughly assessed, was probably tenuous given the fifteen-year difference in their ages and Seymour's long office hours that left his wife idle. Thirty years in consulting and suspenders turned into lifelines. But to count out the ex-Iowa-state-high-school-wrestling champion was as foolish as attempting a hasty takedown, for the nimble Seymour had a history of pinning challengers, his undersized ears flat against the freckled skin of his head with one ear always to the ground.

"In regards to actual branding, I'm back onsite at Dr Pepper corporate headquarters for three weeks next Monday."

"Impacting a client's and our company's bottom line, always socially impactful. Big account for this office's portfolio, Dr Pepper, especially because of the status its brand carries regionally in helping us attract new clients. Might there be an additional enablement this time around if packaged creatively?"

Wharton hardly needed to be goaded, having done more than anyone else at the firm to nurture the relationship. He'd brought Dr Pepper aboard as a client two years ago as a mere project leader. A repeat customer of CCG, Dr Pepper had become a client after Wharton's wife invited her third cousin, the Dr Pepper chief operating officer, to a University of Texas football game. By the time they left the stadium box suite during the third quarter in a blowout against some Division I-AA team that had more players than fans, Wharton had made CCG millions with a Fortune 500 company. The signature a few days later on the contract requesting a half-year consulting engagement to assess a possible merger merely made official what had already been agreed to over beers at the game. It was the first of three major clients he brought into the CCG fold in his first five years with the firm. Not even yet eligible to be a partner, he was the stuff of legends, a folk hero of consulting.

"Seeing how you are on the beach for the next week," Seymour continued, "I am assigning you and Phillips-Goydan to train up Fink before we attach him to an engagement. His orientation week went well, according to one of the boot camp instructors I talked with this morning by phone. She said, 'He is a take-charge kind of guy.'"

"Why not just assign Phillips-Goydan?"

"Phillips-Goydan is only an analyst. You're our star principal, so show Fink what will be expected at the consultant level. Even you began at the same humble level after business school."

"After business school, *after* being the keyword." Repetition was in order for Seymour's baby ears. The ears, so reduced in presence to the rest of Seymour's sizable body that they must be the inheritance of generations of Iowa farmers not putting much stock in the value of listening to their crops. To Wharton they were the ears of a sociopathic mercenary's shrunken-ear necklace, not the auditory organs of a CCG MD.

Seymour fooled with his phone, stood up, and approached the door. He seemed to hesitate. Wharton decided Seymour was one of those people who were always uneasy with any situation needing a paternal hand, something Wharton well understood because of his own only-child upbringing with a demanding tyrant. One of the saving graces of a consultant's busy life was that there was less direct interface with the boss than in most other business jobs. "I would have agreed with you before, but the talent pool has shrunk. We're not just competing with I-banking and McKinsey for the best MBA graduates anymore, now that start-ups, private equity, and attractive industry jobs are circling the waters. I'm under the gun as it is to satisfy an increasing client demand for experts in industry, or consultants with actual job experience in solving unconventional problems. A lack of authenticity is hurting our accounts. If nothing else, a Fink is someone who is *real* to clients like Dr Pepper—which is part of the reason I thought his conversational approach and EQ might fit well in our portfolio. A red, white, and blue hire like him lets us show clients that the three letters of CCG are a stand-in for *USA* among consulting firms and that we understand the very American issues these businesses are dealing with."

"My intuition tells me that he will demonstrate incompetence to be universal."

"Develop him on a steep learning curve—I'm sure a scrappy guy like him can handle it. He's seen a lot of stuff overseas."

Not the ambiguously designed seen-a-lot-of-shit-overseas card again. Otherwise known as the unqualified veteran's oldest trick in the book. "That qualifies him as a consultant how?"

"If he's anything like his ancestor, he has the potential to make quite a name for CCG."

Wharton was still putting hexes on his boss's suspenders when he found Pat Phillips-Goydan in the silvery state-of-the-art office kitchen constructing an elaborate coffee drink. Who knew how long he had been at it, shifting between the four machines he simultaneously worked. One for foam, yes. One for milk. One, presumably, for the coffee beans. And that crucial fourth machine to stir up Wharton's hate. No sociologist could convince Wharton that he and Phillips-Goydan were technically of the same generation: the beady-eyed and bald Phillips-Goydan and his mandatory quality coffee drink every day no matter the consulting location or whining ensued at escalating volumes. Wharton wished an Internet virus on all of these *millennials*. Even Phillips-Goydan's mother, a prominent local socialite, had called once during his first year to complain to Seymour that her son was not being allotted enough time for sleep while on assignment.

And there was always the affected pose struck by the slippery Phillips-Goydan, dressed in the hyper Hipster Nerd style of the new analyst breed CCG hired straight out of undergraduate from the Ivy League schools. Today's ensemble—no doubt thought about by Phillips-Goydan for the eight hours that he should have allotted to sleep—was a pair of tight, gray, flat-front slacks that were tailored to suffocate his tiny penis and narrow until they became as tight-fitting as leggings around his ankles and his multicolored Italian ankle boots. If only Phillips-Goydan had been burdened with carrying around an epinephrine injection pen in those pants, thought Wharton, he would surely have had an accidental discharge hit its target and learned his lesson. Phillips-Goydan's gray color scheme was balanced by a shrunken red V-neck sweater and a purple-and-white polka-dotted oxford shirt that showed at the neck and wrists. All worn with irony for having a corporate job like the ones Wharton had only known his adult life and, strangely, in line with the trend among a growing number of black rappers and athletes that the Caucasian boarding school–educated Phillips-Goydan felt akin to. Have your cake and eat it too; these hip-hop heroes of Phillips-Goydan's both were allowed to mock the square, white Whartons of the world and yet wanted—and apparently were, by the likes of Phillips-Goydan and the legions of his wired peers—to be taken seriously at the same time. Wharton pined for the flannel and grunge of the nineties counterculture; with them, at least, you knew where they stood.

"You want a cup of *qahawa*?" Phillips-Goydan asked Wharton, who assumed the last word meant coffee in some language Phillips-Goydan wanted Wharton to know he knew. Wharton could not with a hundred percent certainty say what Phillips-Goydan's opinion of him was. But Wharton believed he had a pretty good idea of the nitwit's view of him beneath that wraparound pate of foreskin that occasionally became distinguishable as a face when the wisp grew out his judgmental goatee.

Easy there, killer, Wharton breathed to himself. Phillips-Goydan was a clever weasel whose slimy tail needed to be stroked. "No thanks. You know the two of us got assigned to bring an off-cycle hire up to speed. New guy named Mike Fink. By the by, Stanley and Seymour were in my office earlier asking me again about how well you did at the closing presentation at Gulf."

"I thought the Snail wasn't coming in today because of a prostate appointment."

"I think he just stopped by briefly beforehand," Wharton said, looking to recover. How he hated Phillips-Goydan's inquisitiveness. Phillips-Goydan had a talent for knowing; the smarmy know-it-all in class who knew everything but knew nothing. Wharton did not trust this kid with a handshake. Yet some female, a consultant at Deloitte, had married this homosexual. He had even taken her last name, adding a hyphen, in some deranged "show of respect" that Wharton rightfully took as an homage to the eunuchs of a more castrated bygone era that spoke (squealed, really) to Phillips-Goydan. "You could tell Stanley's fasting all right."

"You don't have to fast to meet with your surgeons to discuss the procedure." He loved to display his seemingly vast knowledge of medical protocol that Wharton assumed stemmed from the hairless Phillips-Goydan being a sickly child, yet another irritating aspect of his personality. Wharton, despite never having played on the defensive side in life, fought the overwhelming urge to deliver a bone-jarring hit to the frail spine of Phillips-Goydan.

"I told them how you wowed the CEO and COO during your part of the presentation with your suggestion to buy a wastewater management company that would save their company millions a year long term over continuing to contract it out." He left out the part about how furious he was at Phillips-Goydan for wearing a cream-colored three-piece suit to the closing presentation and reminding all of the Gulf Oil & Gas executives how much they detested the newer generation of consultants. Everything about the Finkgate fiasco could be traced to the pushback from clients concerning Phillips-Goydan and his cohorts at CCG; redefine the consultant image to offset them, okay, Wharton was all for it, had spearheaded it, but employing Fink to trick companies with some sort of all-American con was not the solution when CCG already had the all-American market cornered with Wharton.

"Who's Fink? Was that the guy in the ridiculous suit during decision round?"

Wharton passed on the opportunity to point out contemptuously the irony of this coming from the punk kid who showed up to the closing presentation for a client dressed as a British cotton broker inspecting the wharves of the Nile. Wharton still wished to con the too-cool-for-consulting Phillips-Goydan into handling this "support the troops" charity operation of training the hapless Fink. "Sounds like someone wasn't impressed, huh? It might be better to have you run him through some exercises and you could write up one of your trademark no-nonsense evaluations for Seymour afterward."

"Would that I could, but I just had my jersey number called about fifteen minutes ago to help with a full court press on a pro bono engagement for a refugee nonprofit this week. Finding solutions to this Middle East refugee crisis is going to be tricky," Phillips-Goydan said, carefully layering some whipped cream on top of his coffee. The absurdity of sports references coming from Phillips-Goydan, who had never worn a jockstrap in his life, struck Wharton as fitting, given the equal absurdity of the task of grooming the feral Fink. "Good luck with the mentoring. I think I remember hearing someone say last week that the new off-cycle hire coming in has a lot of sand. Guts of a man's man. We can always use guts on the CCG team." Following this lecture on guts from the most gutless little jellyfish in the CCG Houston office, Wharton awaited a berating on taste from the foppish metrosexual as a further punch to his taut abdomen. But Phillips-Goydan decided, for a change of pace, to attend to work.

His failed plan to manipulate Phillips-Goydan to his own ends left Wharton alone in the swanky kitchen cursing fate. Now Wharton would have to train up Fink. Even if it were possible to get Fink up to the level that he needed to perform his job at, Wharton did not wish to be the one responsible for the river stray finding a home at CCG. To achieve his milestone, Wharton would have to pivot.

Before he could pivot, Fink stomped into the kitchen and bellowed, "I should have known I would find you in here hiding out from work!" He swung open the massive metal refrigerator still thrumming from his entrance and fished out a box of pastries, biting violently into a large éclair. Wharton watched in horror as Fink's lips rolled away like a shark to display the bottom and top teeth needlessly ripping back and forth in a struggle to break away half of the soft, pudding-filled pastry. His mouth still full from the carnage, Fink garbled, "That's my favorite part about consulting, free food."

The milky pudding of the éclair, now relocated to the corners of Fink's mouth and on the sleeve of his navy blazer, allowed Wharton to regard him at face value: Wharton's prized CCG had lowered the standards for Fink. Why were there standards if they weren't to be upheld? Wharton did not buy the value-add of veterans. Not that Wharton had anything in particular against veterans (as he suspected Fink thought he did), though he acknowledged his opinion might be less disdainful if not for the fact that he had zero friends who had served. For all the lip service about the supposed intangibles a veteran can bring to a business environment, the meritocratic Wharton had not seen it in his encounters with military personnel once they were out of uniform and looking for a civilian handout. If anything, it seemed to Wharton, they had a sense of entitlement to be repaid for what he had thought was service. "The soft drinks and chips are free. You are eating someone's dessert." Fink let the remaining third of the éclair fall from his hand into the box and attempted to hide it in the back of the refrigerator.

"I guess we have commenced with the mentoring," Fink said, after shutting the refrigerator door. His focus was now on Wharton's tailored shirt. "Are those your initials monogrammed on your sleeve cuff?"

It was too early in the day for class warfare. That was not the battle Wharton wanted to engage Fink in, a contest predetermined by birth where the victory always went to the one from less means. What Wharton sought was a competition, man to man, in a controlled environment. The victor emerging as king. Any verdict Wharton desired regarding who was tougher would be inconclusive if set against the backdrop of their origins. Wharton was sure to receive an unfair ruling by an arbiter who would be influenced by whatever wild yarn the imaginative Fink would spin about sucking from the teat of the she-wolf that raised him. Or the drunken trapper father who would skin and then douse a flayed Fink in bootleg hooch to make him dance for nickels down on the corner. All of this would be contrasted against the immense affluence of Wharton's childhood in River Oaks and Sunday brunch with the family at the restricted country club. "Yes, now follow me to the back room, as your comment regarding dress reminds me why we should have you watch *Backpack to Briefcase*. The video should help illuminate a lot of these questions you have. I need to run you through a few drills beforehand. It's important that you sit back and observe this week since you will be shadowing me for some on-the-job training."

In the back room, Wharton found himself full of envy as Fink struggled with the consulting exercises. Life must be considerably different—and a lot more fun—when the expectations were so low. It struck Wharton that nowadays he was often the sole driver putting pressure on himself. Even Katie Kidder had removed herself from the partner track. He tried to remember when the last time was that he had been freed from promise. When time had slowed down. Like it was currently with Fink's constant use of the computer mouse. Wharton whipped the air with his fingers and said, "Let me drive." He motioned for an uncomprehending Fink to stand up and relinquish control of the computer. "You have to know the Excel shortcuts, how to fly a computer without a mouse." Wharton used the keys to navigate to the shared network and selected *Backpack to Briefcase*. "Last Friday I held a competition with the analysts where no one could use the F2 key. Watch this video until the conference call."

Wharton went in search of Katie Kidder. A striking six-foot-tall blonde, Katie had walked down catwalk runways and taught linguistics at Middlebury before becoming the top consultant in the year group above Wharton at CCG. Only to walk away from it all. She had shocked everyone, most of all Wharton, who had spent years undercutting the achievements of the person he felt was his biggest competitor, by recently abandoning the rat race for partner and seeking out the staffing manager position. She had eliminated the brokered deals in the black-market netherworld of staffing engagements, replacing it with a fairer and more efficient black box system of assigning a balance of new hires and proven talent in certain specialties to projects.

Wharton found her in her office at her new standing desk. "I guess I owe you for not assigning Phillips-Goydan to Dr Pepper as the fourth person."

"Thank the black box," Katie said from behind her giant computer screen, "for a more just staffing system. It took me accepting a pay cut to change CCG culture."

"Your desk looks cool. Does it feel healthier?"

"Sitting is the new smoking. Most dangerous thing you can do is work in an office. Scientific research suggests that a standing desk reduces the risk of obesity, diabetes, cardiovascular disease, and cancer and even lowers long-term mortality risk in consultants. Allow CCG to sponsor *you*!" Katie jumped out from behind her desk and pointed at him but hit her hand on the top of her computer screen.

"Someone must have had a good weekend to be so refreshed and energetic for CCG."

"Gosh, I'm retarded."

"Mentally handicapped," Wharton corrected. For as long as he could remember, he had hated when people used that crass term. His dad had certainly been fond of labeling anyone with it, especially Wharton. Inexplicable as it was to even him, Wharton's one soft spot had always been for the mentally handicapped, who often were denied a shot when everyone else was busy squandering theirs. A young Wharton had never joined in during the teasing of these kids when all his classmates were mocking them. Too easy a target, perhaps. As if the mentally handicapped did not have enough challenges, they had to endure these taunts that they were expected not to feel. Although it would have driven his father mad to have had a mentally disabled child, Wharton would have been fine with having the company of such a sibling. No kid would have said anything either about his brother, not when Wharton was the star quarterback. On this matter he had never cared what others thought.

"Mentally handicapped. I apologize. I clearly did not get enough sleep."

It was hard to take the new Katie Kidder, who seemed almost happy. Looser. So loose she bordered on goofy, like your college roommate's kid sister from the Midwest who was of legal age but seemed younger. Wharton still viewed Katie's new position and attitude as a ruse to lure Wharton into complacency as she leapfrogged past him on the CCG fast track. This was still Katie Kidder, who had more talent and balls than any of Wharton's male colleagues and whose only marriage had been to her work. He had tried many times on assignments late at night to imagine what it would be like to be married to her. Or more appropriately what it would be like to have sex with her, until the thought of being mounted by a smarter and more ballsy version of himself stopped him from playing out the fantasy to its end. It never helped Wharton's imagination that she preferred earth tones and non-form-fitting outfits, which had to make her the worst representative of an ex–fashion model ever. Yet her high cheekbones and fitness routine had always kept the former model looking a decade younger than the two years she had on Wharton, who had started noticing gray hairs on his own balls. If there was one woman who tested the lingering hold that his faux youthful conservative Christian persona still had on his moralism, it was Katie Kidder. Her big eyes positively beamed her intelligence to everyone who interacted with her.

Katie twisted a curl of her hair below her ear with her finger. Wharton pushed away any thought of sex, or the newfangled notion of snuggling with Katie, so he could influence the engagement. "What the project could use is another marketing guru like Ursula. Maybe Amber?"

"There's hope for you yet. Begin by accepting the possibility of the black box."

• • •

You would be fucking lost without us! he all but spewed at the black boomerang speakerphone in the middle of CCG's conference room table. But Wharton responded outwardly to the final inquiry by the Dr Pepper brand manager with the decorum of a principal at CCG, for all he said was "Ultimately it is client impact that sustains a competitive marketing advantage for Dr Pepper that we're committed to with this problem-solving study." Sometimes Wharton compared the consultant-client interplay to one of the platonic relationships at Bigger Brother Little Brother, the professional providing his costly time to guide the needy orphan whose lack of parents was off-limits to criticism.

"Okay, branding team, you guys can jump off now and I will finish up," the chief operating officer of Dr Pepper, Kenneth Klay, said, addressing the conference call. There was a pause for the brand managers to hang up. The sane voice of Klay had come back on not a minute too soon for Wharton, who believed Dr Pepper would be lost if Klay had not had the genius to bring aboard Wharton and CCG. "A better integration of branding strategies needs to be a deliverable from this project, Brock."

To the right of Wharton sat Ursula and Connor, who compared airline frequent flier benefits on their laptops. They were both junior to Wharton at CCG; he had worked on several projects with the stocky, Switzerland-born Ursula, who had even become something of a specialist in the consumer beverage market during her time at CCG. This was the first engagement in which he had been assigned the milquetoast Connor, an ex–systems engineer, who still seemed dazed by Wharton's Ritz-Carlton Platinum Elite member card that he had passed over to him earlier at the start of the conference call (he had to give the kids something to aspire to). To the left of Wharton, Fink plowed forward with a pencil in a small moleskin notebook that had a water stain across the top, its pages swollen with the pattern of a geological cross section. The moleskin cover looked like a hide still tanning. When Fink flipped the crackling pages of his notebook, pencil depressions on the backside hung there for those tracking in lunatic Braille. If the actual prospect of being a consultant besieged observing consultant trainees with anxiety, as Wharton had seen twice before in his five years at CCG, they left on their own volition within the first few months. Quit. In disgrace. With a tall tale needed to explain the inevitable gap on their résumé. It was usually more professionally damaging than a firing.

"What's the burning platform?" Wharton asked, ignoring his buzzing phone inching up his thigh to the lip of his pants pocket. "Dr Pepper needs to start making a profit. Often branding is more a matter of assessing that the market has shifted. Either way, after a rigorous analysis of the situation, we will develop a customized solution for marketing. Tell us if you envision anything else for this quick win." The marching orders ran through his head as Klay recapped the deliverables. Wharton mentally dispatched workstreams to himself, Ursula, and Connor before he caught his vibrating phone as it poked out. Three missed calls from K.K. Okay, okay.

Wharton pointed at his phone for Ursula to cover him for a minute. He stepped out of the conference room back door into the hallway. "K.K.?" He heard only the sound of car horns on the other end of the line. "Is something wrong?"

"I'm calling you at work so you won't be able to claim again that you forgot," a recognizable voice on ice answered, confirming everything was okay with his K.K. He guessed that she was at the Galleria, probably waiting on the valet. "We're now hosting the committee dinner on Wednesday at our house since the Fords are sick. And my parents are staying with us this weekend. Polo tournament. So I'm going to need some help from you to prepare."

What was the point of paying housekeepers if K.K. still needed him to help prepare for a dinner he would gladly pay to get out of? And what was the name of the new housekeeper, the peasant-looking one? Though what he really burned to ask was: how many goddamn polo tournaments could her bum-of-a-billionaire father have in Houston this fall? Her parents had already stayed with them last month. Trying to impress his in-laws was already a full-time job on top of his demanding daytime job, much like if the court's greatest knight had married the princess but still continued to hold down his position for the sake of his own self-worth. Though K.K.'s parents were far less of a torment than his parents, Wharton thought he was within his rights to want to selfishly enjoy this memorable phase of a first pregnancy alone with his wife. Her growing porcelain hump had started to fascinate him as if it were a science project, which it kind of was, with the distinguishing feature that this one allowed rubbing without any threat of being reported to the principal for perversion. On the subject of true perversion, Wharton had always thought there was something sexual between female equestrians like K.K. and their horses. But K.K.'s polo-playing father had made the case that there were also at least a few perverse men beyond the perimeter of border-town donkey shows. To see the heir of the fabled ranching fortune (his great-great-great-great-grandfather might as well have been the King of Texas) take out a whinnying horse at his thoroughbred stables and stroke it with his dainty hands was enough to spur nightmares. The second time Wharton witnessed the act, he had whinnied louder in horror than the horse being touched. It all had the unlikely effect of making even Wharton long for more family time to be allocated to visiting his parents. A glimpse of Seymour's familiar blue suspenders through the sliver of glass next to the conference room door bucked Wharton out of his contemplation of family vis-à-vis horses to end his call with his wife.

"That was precisely the reason for merging operations eighteen months ago," Klay's voice boomed on speaker as Wharton reentered and regained his seat. Seymour fixed on the speakerphone in the middle of the table as if Klay were sitting there. Ursula was covering her laptop screens with notes next to the copyboy Connor, who followed her lead. Fink's pencil was a seismograph needle recording tremors in his notebook. Though tough to conjecture midconversation, Wharton surmised Klay was referring to the silo effect, that corporate bastard of decentralized management gone overboard.

If he knew Dr Pepper, more silos had probably shot up since Wharton had last stepped in a year ago. His job would be to find and fix eighty percent of this problem in twenty percent of the time, enabling value creation. He leaned forward in his chair to address the matter but was overtaken by Fink. "This is Fink again." Again? "Well, I would have advised against it." Against what? "That said, I wasn't with CCG a year ago for that engagement, Klay." Klay & Fink, just a couple of old military buddies out on a shore-leave lark. Not a COO of one of the major soft drink companies in America and a consulting trainee under orders to observe a conference call. "I know you have to attend a meeting, though I will say this: sounds like a case of conflicting brand management. Cooperation on a unified strategy for a company as diverse as Dr Pepper is but the first step in encouraging best practices. One of the first workshops conducted onsite by us should be to assemble the brand managers." *Us?* More alarming, Seymour nodded across the table. That Fink had tripped by chance upon one possible reason for Dr Pepper's dip in sales in conflicting brand management, Wharton could not argue with. Though unlikely to be the root cause, at the very least it would have to be disproved by Wharton's team. Wharton did not linger on where and how Fink could have learned to identify such a problem as the rogue puffed out his peeling lips again in a mating dance, his hunger to participate in and proceed toward a decisive outcome naked.

"I can set that up. See your team next week, Brock. Give my best to K.K. Later."

"Strong work! You just worked your way onto your first engagement, Fink."

"Katie already is slotting another person for the project," Wharton said, suddenly finding himself a champion of black box project staffing.

"Start filling him in on Dr Pepper over lunch, Brock."

"It's the training taking over. Always take the initiative and take command of a situation," Fink said to Seymour. Although he put nothing past these huckster veterans, Wharton doubted that *act unprofessional to make yourself look professional at the expense of your colleague* was in the Army training handbook. Wharton glared at Ursula and Connor, who both folded their laptops and followed Seymour out.

Wharton rotated in his chair to dress down the take-charge upstart. He stiffened at the idea of condemning zeal and assuredness. But Fink's act of ordainment could not be allowed to go unchallenged. "Kenneth Klay is the COO of a company, not some buddy of yours back on the block, Fink." Wharton detested addressing anyone in person with solely their last name, which always returned him to the sports field with his father as coach. He equally hated how some veterans acted like they had a monopoly on leadership. Was that their one big contribution? Did Fink, too, get drilled on it since he was old enough to hold a football? Did he require himself to read every business book on the subject of leadership? "You don't offer up hypotheses when you're shadowing for on-the-job training as an observer. Certainly not to a client–a COO. Though several years apart, Kenneth and I were both Baker Scholars when we were at HBS. Baker Scholars. That follows you around on your résumé for life. Precedes you. He's that much smarter than your average COO, that is, the person you were just impermissibly consulting."

Fink's concentration was on Wharton's right hand punctuating the end of each sentence, the mongoose-versus-cobra face-off only broken up by Piazza's entrance through the back door. Fink stood, adding, "Would a leader in a remote consulting outpost sit back and wait for permission to solve a problem when it arose?"

"Not at CCG they wouldn't," Piazza said, slapping Fink's back. Piazza had bounded into the room, his cowlick up and ready to tangle. Idea Man. Idea Man was the name given by others in the office to Piazza's manic persona, a persona that flashed about once a month for a day with a certain backlit gusto but fell short of an amount that could be adequately deemed infectious. Which was not to say that Wharton did not have ample wonderment for Idea Man on a high swing, when his enthusiasm for new ideas channeled into an ability to fixate on a task to exclude everything else in Piazza's life, most especially his high-strung wife. "Shall we take lunch at the Coronado Club? Have you ever eaten there, Mike? You have to be with a member like our boy Brock here. The gray hairs of Houston business and Brock Wharton."

"Jacket or suit only in there," Wharton said, educating the nonmembers. Not that Fink's Joseph A. Bank buy-one-get-six-free suit would pass club scrutiny. Such an outfit would not even be allowed to stink up the club's Churchill Lounge smoking room.

"Or we could show Fink the tunnels?"

Although relieved they would not be lunching at the Coronado Club, Wharton would have preferred to not be sinking down the Houston One Center's escalator with Fink toward the tunnels. Down twenty feet below Houston's skyscrapers and downtown flood-prone streets, another world existed in the tunnels. With no homeless people to trip on in the six miles of climate-controlled succor from the Houston heat wave that was about year-round, working professionals stepped it out in the city's largest underground mall five days a week.

The tunnels were a scene, though not exactly Wharton's scene. The winding underground maze had too much of the human element up too close. There were the same escaped stiffs at the shops and coffee stands each time Wharton passed by, ready to mainline the caffeine right out there in the open to make it through another workday, their craving laid bare under the glow of the hospital lighting, everything and everyone so sunken that the tunnels were hardly a humane shelter from the aboveground world.

"Did you have a beard and long hair?" Piazza asked as they waited for their order. His eyes, already too close to his big nose that had been hurriedly molded together, now had a cross-eyed expression that stared out past his mountain of nasal flesh at Fink. "I've seen pictures of Special Forces guys on horses dressed like Afghans calling in airstrikes against al-Qaeda."

"Unfortunately, I missed the boat by a few years. Our main job was the less sexy Foreign Internal Defense mission of training our allies. Kind of like military consultants. The objective being to prevent America's direct participation with boots on the ground in future wars."

"I saw a television documentary this past weekend about the Green Berets and Special Operations in Iraq and Syria," Piazza continued once they had all sat down at the small food court table and unwrapped their orders, "now battling ISIS."

Wharton's turkey sandwich was dry and tasteless, the sourdough crust he sucked down with his scorn stabbing the rings of his throat. But Wharton slowed to a chew when the redhead from the architectural firm came out of Rajun Cajun with a to-go bag. He himself had hungered for a catfish po'boy at Rajun Cajun, though he had not dared insert Fink into his more native element. Wharton had not noticed the bounce in her breasts before. The breasts, while in no danger of needing full jib sails for a bikini top, were still designed to be more than abundant for the beam of her body. Wharton recognized that the worst part about getting older after marrying too young was not all the girls he had missed out on. Far worse was the newer doubt that nagged wifelike at him regarding whether he even still had the talent to score such a babe if he were single. It did not help matters that K.K., the woman he had been faithful to, had recently adopted a delight in constantly pointing out his one or two gray hairs and wrinkles. There had certainly been many opportunities to cheat when out on the road on consulting engagements in earlier years for such a good-looking, in-shape former star quarterback from a major program turned wealthy alpha consultant. If it weren't for Wharton's personal code of honor. He knew it was silly that it ate at him that bachelor Fink had the freedom to court any redhead he wanted with his little skunk of a penis, but it did. Wharton's first blowjob had been from a redhead of similar physique when he was a junior in high school. And for a person with no affinity for music, he had oddly always related it to a great guitar solo (he had been standing during the act). In seven years of marriage, he had received a single blowjob from his wife. Coming on their African safari honeymoon while camping in a lavish campaign-style canvas suite, it had been tainted by Wharton's inability to remain erect as he associated K.K.'s soft conditioned hair with the mane of a restless lion gnawing his dick.

"Brock!"

When Wharton came to, he turned to find his best friend, Richard Muncher, and a group of identically dressed males off to his right. The archetypal insecure Houston energy investment banker: plainly striving harder in his Ferragamo-walnut-shoes-and-Hermès-pastel-tie wardrobe to feel as legitimate as his Wall Street peers. The only thing separating the pack was that half of them had discarded their suit jackets to put on gray fleece vests. Wharton normally approved of anything with Fifth Generation Old Money White Houston Male embroidered on it, but only if it had sleeves. Their own daydream was to be viewed as wolves, but Wharton now questioned how in his twenties he had ever thought dominating such a flock of lambs was a challenge.

"You guys go on. I have to solve where HCC's Mr. Texas in football has been hiding."

Wharton smiled and stood up for a bro hug. "I could use an HCC cigar bull session."

"That's Houston Country Club for the rest of us," Piazza explained to Fink. Prior to Piazza's explanation, Wharton would have wagered Fink's first guess to have been Houston Community College. Richard sat down across from Wharton and next to Fink.

"You still on the waiting list at HCC?" Richard asked Piazza, getting a reliable laugh from Wharton.

"I don't think K.K. and I are doing Aspen this Christmas, Richard."

"Because she's pregnant? Oh come on, Brock my boy, you are becoming a recluse on me. That's when you go to Aspen, so your unborn child can taste it. Before you summer there." From the sea of his northeast boarding school to the shining sea of his in-laws' vacation homes, Richard was a snake of the first order no matter the location. His appearance as a diminutive man whose unfortunate face and black hair bore a resemblance to the muskrat of his home state of Mississippi sold him short, claimed Wharton, who was all too happy to have an inferior-looking best friend for scale. "Hey, you better not be sneaking off again to that inbred place in Maine."

"Prouts Neck is not in the plans," Wharton said, grateful that even his wife had grown tired of drinking the cult Kool-Aid required there by the two hundred off-market families. The peninsula was far from being "remote"; the buzzing northeast WASPs descended on each other at their shitty pint-sized private beach, with sand and freezing water reducing your already small penis to a gumdrop should it have survived the unabashed sight of pasty and cellulite-riddled skin that was the hallmark of the unimpressive white tribe there. The problem was K.K.'s two unmarried best friends from boarding school were chained to the fading place and its hollow culture of New England prominence. Lily was an untalented but gregarious writer, always flitting about town and with a remarkable penchant in her dating life for intimately connecting only to coke-addicted cheaters, and whose only work as a scribe of nothingness were her cute monthly reminder emails to her father to write her Soho rent check. Usually a softie toward redheads, Wharton had little sympathy for the abrasive ginger Mimi, an exceptionally well-bred twit in her midthirties who was secretly in love with the flake Lily but was unable to come out of the closet because her liberal San Francisco family's net worth was so high, and thus in the rationality of Prouts (where air-conditioning was *beyond* flashy), a paragon at the country club for her deprivation. The only good thing about the old-moneyed sanctuary was that if God forbid a French Revolution ever came to America, Prouts Neck would buy Wharton's own highborn neck time before it kissed the guillotine blade. For worse than even the nightly themed cocktail parties in this enclave was the Cliff Walk, the Prouts Neck pride and joy, a public trail only accessible to the homeowners gated inside the oceanside loop path of privately held rocks that, for centuries, had brought a serenity to the clans, a sacredness to their special community, as they circled. Some surprise that resident Winslow Homer had focused on inanimate hostile rocks in his paintings of the place.

"How is the price of crude affecting deal flow, Tricky Dick?" Piazza asked, bringing Wharton back from the brink of mad Maine to the saneness of the market.

"Merge. Acquire. Restructure. We make more money when everyone else is losing money in this town." Richard either noticed or perhaps chose to acknowledge Fink's presence for the first time, asking, "What's your story?"

Piazza volunteered with an eagerness that made Wharton switch the ass cheek he balanced his dislike on. "This is Mike Fink. He just joined us from U.S. Army Special Forces."

Richard pulled his head back to examine Fink's hair, which was not shaved on the sides in the Army fashion. Which was a pity, as Wharton delighted in the buzzed Mohawk hairstyle that served as a form of birth control for this military class that would breed like rabbits if left to their own ways, for no woman would sleep with a man with such a haircut. Neither Richard nor Fink, whose fingers fiddled with the last bite of his food, offered a handshake. Amused by the conundrum of

Fink, Richard smiled when Fink nodded in a simultaneous confirmation and deflection of Piazza's statement. Richard asked with a tilt of his chin skyward, "You ever kill anyone?"

Piazza's rubbed-raw nose bobbed above his open mouth. For a passing moment, Wharton thought about doing his part as a mentor and doing anything other than slipping his wedding ring on and off his finger. But Fink answered without moving, "Only on workdays."

After Fink splattered on his own face a smile that the shell-shocked Richard might have worn earlier, Wharton said to Fink, "Come on, we need to put you through some tests."

3.

UNCONVENTIONAL WARFARE

"What *is* Dr Pepper?" Wharton asked the room of Dr Pepper brand managers as he paced in front of the whiteboard.

The men and women responsible for managing Dr Pepper's brand stared back at Wharton from their seats. Wharton decided to give them another minute, and so he occupied himself with the view overlooking the western part of the Dr Pepper corporate headquarters campus. Outside the floor-to-ceiling glass windows was a corporate park. The centerpiece was a health and wellness fountain too shallow for the employees to drown themselves in at lunchtime. Because of its uneven concrete foundation, unwanted pennies often corroded like half-submerged shipwrecks in parts, and Wharton believed that behind each lay a wish to be anywhere other than at the Dr Pepper headquarters in Plano. As he had not intended for his question to be rhetorical, Wharton returned his attention to concluding the workshop.

Wharton knew he better lead with the answer or it was going to be an even longer Day One onsite than usual. "Since we've already addressed which market research you've been using, why you made the branding recommendations you did, and how you communicated that to other departments, let's circle back to the primary goal of this workshop, which is the branding strategy of Dr Pepper. I think the branding strategy of the Dr Pepper Corporation is to be the number one market-leading beverage brand in the world. What do you think?"

"I believe our branding strategy, as much of our polling indicates, is to be the most sustainable beverage company in the world," answered a junior brand manager in her late twenties named Maggie. "To be synonymous with quality rather than quantity to achieve our mission."

"Right, so I think what you're saying, what we're both saying," Wharton said, dragging the branding managers toward buy-in and away from the black hole of sustainability, "is that the strategy is to be the best, the most *profitable* beverage company in the world."

And Dr Pepper wondered why it was perennially in the crosshairs as a company to be taken over. Not that Wharton cared if it maintained its proud independent tradition. He only cared insomuch as he might lose Dr Pepper as a client if it was acquired by a massive conglomerate. They were onsite for the next three weeks to lead a comeback in profits, not to warm the hearts of Dr Pepper employees, which was beyond the scope of their engagement.

"I might be picking up a different frequency, but is that what you are saying, Maggie?"

Maggie looked over to her interpreter, Fink. "I believe our branding strategy is built around integrating sustainability into every aspect of the business and customer experience."

This was why workshops onsite with a client's employees were a check-the-box, Wharton wanted to bewail. A mere formality for buy-in, the listing of pros and cons up on the board an unnecessary time-consuming debate for a principal like Wharton who knew his client's company better than the client did. Rather than white-board an all-American branding strategy concerned with a fiduciary duty to being the most profitable, these social media–era brand managers could spend all day on their favorite adjective, *sustainable*—that is, what those in second place worried about. No executives at Coke ever lost a second of sleep over draining sacred rivers in India to dilute the holy acid they poured down customers' throats on the way to financing the construction of additions to their second homes.

"You're getting at tying CSR to the brand to enhance the value," Fink pointed out.

Corporate social responsibility was the new gypsy switch that corporations used to assuage the guilt of employees that they did not in fact work for a diabolical behemoth raping the world to ensure earnings perpetually higher than the previous quarter. The patron saint of Little League jerseys for every bleeding heart stuck in middle management down to the common foot soldiers wheeling cases of Dr Pepper around who needed a reason to believe. Fundamentally, Wharton believed, it was an un-American business idea and an unnecessary pacification of the faceless workers at any large corporation. A perfectly suited concept for an out-of-touch Fink.

"I see CSR playing a positive role in brand development and fulfilling the company mission of increasing Dr Pepper's sales," Maggie said in an increasingly louder voice, correct in finally landing on the mission, but incorrect in that corporate social responsibility was almost impossible to monetize.

"There it is," Wharton said, "the branding strategy is to be the best beverage company in the business. Maybe another workshop on CSR and an exploration of its brand impact could be done in the future. I want to thank you all again for participating in this workshop."

Four minutes later, after hustling the brand managers out of the room, Wharton pointed a dry-erase marker at the remaining CCG team seated at the table. He grinned and said, "As I suspected, there are conflicting brand strategies because there is a conflicting overall strategic direction of Dr Pepper. Sometimes the problems present themselves within the first hour onsite." Wharton turned around and said while writing on the board, "What is Dr Pepper?"

"Nobody at Dr Pepper knows, that's for sure," Ursula said and chuckled.

"A company at a crossroads," Connor said.

Wharton spun around and said, "Right, but better yet, where could Dr Pepper be a year after we present the findings of our assessment in three weeks?"

"Enablement project! Enablement project!" Ursula hooted, chanting the CCG mantra for new business.

"No one ever said the Swiss didn't have an ear for the sound of money. Yes, I see an additional enablement project coming out of this engagement, Dr Pepper taking a leader mentality with a new playbook."

"*The art of the possible*," Ursula crooned.

"I will set up a meeting tomorrow morning with William Marles, the new head of product development. He's a new Klay hire and a Rice grad/Rhodes Scholar, so he should be receptive to our recommendations. Connor, I want you to take a deep dive into the soft drink market, the brands within Dr Pepper, and especially the emerging health drink brands as a point of comparison. Here, start listing." Wharton tossed him the marker. "Look at the margins, competitor benchmarking, and amass all the market research you can analyze. It's my hypothesis that the health drinks market offers the most potential for differentiation and the market in which we could better position Dr Pepper products for what should be its only short- and long-term goal: to be the most profitable. Ursula, you concentrate on retooling advertising expenses and a branding strategy beyond *sustainability*. And since you're the subject matter expert on the beverage industry, collate the marketing data they should've collated. Target whoever you project the most profitable beverage consumers will be in the next few years. The numbers never lie." Fink's pencil rested atop his moleskin notebook, the compass needle that would not point him out of the wilderness this time. Not when Wharton controlled onsite deportation to the desolate interior. "What do you think your workstream is?"

"My workstream?" Fink asked. He looked to Ursula for help, but presumably sensing what was in the air, she lowered her head closer to her laptop. "Uh, my task?"

It was all ripening for harvest. "Wouldn't a deliverable from you be exploring CSR in more workshops, as you seemed to take quite a fancy to its relationship to branding?" On the remote chance of any findings, Wharton would bury it in the report appendix. "Or pursuing possible restructuring of divisions at Dr Pepper as well, based on marketing statistics?"

"I would like to conduct more workshops and engage with employees across different levels. Find out what Dr Pepper wants to be and the reason it is Dr Pepper. As any Southerner will tell you, Dr Pepper has always been a different kind of soda. One way to adjust fire on the branding strategy would be to get more participation and personal investment from employees in building the brand and creating the strategy instead of broadcasting messages at them."

"You do that." Wharton would be the last person to hold up Fink's voluntary deployment to a Siberia of workshops, to not give him the rope he needed to hang himself with. At the end of the second week, Fink would be left riling up his own shadow. By the end of the third week, his lifeless rubber chicken carcass would twist below whatever makeshift gallows pole Wharton could jury-rig to stretch Fink's crane of a neck to the utmost. "Conduct as many workshops as you think time permits." *But leave time to make arrangements and have the champagne on ice for one last workshop titled How to Workshop Yourself Out of a Job on Your First Engagement.*

"I was thinking about that. Perhaps we could switch to a hotel out here to give us more time onsite? Or if there's no availability, maybe stay at a motel so we still minimize commute time?"

"Stay at a mooooo-tel," Wharton mooed. Ursula and Connor stopped working to join Wharton in his laughter at the suggestion of leaving civilization and their Dallas hotel. "Someone has yet to learn the first rule of consulting."

• • •

By the end of the second week at Dr Pepper, Wharton could report up to Seymour that it was a case of "hands" with Fink. Hands: *the interpersonal skills of a consultant in relation to a particular group of people.* Fink's lack of hands had completely exiled him from the CCG team gathered in their base camp room. It was more the exile of a registered sex offender and his or her hands. The beauty was that Fink had exiled himself voluntarily. At the end of each workday over the last two weeks he had asked Wharton for permission to continue conducting more workshops on the Dr Pepper campus, a wish that Fink was all too easily granted. Wharton smiled, returning his gaze from the fountain to his computer screen, which he had to tilt toward him to read as sunlight had cracked through the room. Next to him, the keyboards of Ursula and Connor chirped back and forth as they typed out their final pages for the presentation draft. In the corner of the room were their three roller Tumi suitcases and Fink's black sports bag.

"Just forwarded you the new deck from the Best Little Slide Sweatshop in India, Brock."

"God bless outsourcing. But try keeping a straight face, Ursula, when Kenneth goes on about how professionally done our slides are compared to ones produced by his in-house team."

"Are we still doing the progress review today? Because we are missing our great Village Stability Operations counterinsurgency strategist if we were planning on making our flight."

"Perhaps Fink would prefer to stay across the street this weekend rather than travel home," Connor said. "The way he raved about Holiday Inn's American breakfast almost made me believe that maybe the three of us had made a mistake in not relocating from the Joule."

"There is still time for me to sign off on more hotel relocation requests for next week for those on the team interested."

"Consulting is not for everybody," Ursula said.

"A consultant can't win the war if you commute to it. Let go of your thirty-thousand-foot view. We have to live among the villagers. Dress like them. Eat with them. Sleep with them."

"Crazy Americans. By the way, are we dressing for our client presentation in Halloween costume like Dr Pepper employees are doing on the thirty-first?"

"I will get us around that. The only tradition that Dr Pepper leadership should be focused on next Friday is how to make a profit. I should probably catch the end of one of Fink's workshops to see his work." He omitted that it would be wise to do so for the purpose of further documentation of why Fink was not qualified for the job.

Wharton walked through the colonnaded section that jutted out from the backside of the southern wing. If seen as a whole, the building's architecture was asymmetrical, as no colonnade spanned either the backside or any side of the northern wing. The narrow circular beige pillars that funneled to a choke point always sent Wharton into a spasm of wondering why he worked so many hours on location at sites he detested. Before the obvious set him straight: to uphold the world he had built, otherwise the sandstone colonnade of his own world would crumble. None of which he could explain to anyone besides K.K., who he pushed each stone for, his labor ending at her feet, as the others only saw the final creation of a world he had been provided regardless of his efforts. What he loved most about K.K. was that she understood the unrelenting pace he ran at in life to remain the best. But how could his wife not? Once she had been chosen by Wharton, her own life had been affirmed as the best, a portal into the most desirable world. He pulled out his cell phone and for a moment he stared at a picture of his K.K. Klay Wharton before it was erased to show an incoming call. He answered the phone. "Was just about to check in with you."

"Bring me up to speed with a fast and furious, as I've got a dinner in five minutes with the big guns of Phoenix Energy," Seymour said. "This tumbling oil price of the past ten days looks to be a harbinger of things to come, which is going to take a bite out of our core clientele."

"Had another great lunch earlier today with the head of product development, William Marles, the new star here who I think will push Kenneth and the CEO for big changes. I will send you the draft of implementation recommendations later. Since you're making the trek down, let's strike up the band to play a favorite number of yours called Enablement Project."

"Love it."

"There is the issue of Fink, and his lack of . . . hands."

"If his background can't help him connect well with the employees of Dr Pepper, he isn't going to play well in energy's culture either. And with this gathering storm hovering over energy, Brock, we need all of our clients."

"I know, I know," Wharton lamented into the phone, praying secretly for nothing less than a repeat of the 1986 oil bust that wrecked Houston. Only the old families had the means to weather that perfect storm.

"Keep me updated, as Stanley and I will definitely be there next Friday. Got to run."

Wharton found the room on the northern side of the campus. For a sign, a leaf of CCG letterhead with the barely legible handwritten words VETERANS WORKSHOP. Wharton peeled the sign off the door. He folded the sign with its unmistakable handwriting and slipped it into his pants' back pocket. He could hear Fink's raucous voice on the other side.

Wharton walked in and jerked back upon sight of William Marles, who was nodding in agreement with something Fink had said. They sat across from each other in a circle of twenty occupied chairs. The gung-ho Marles had earlier made no mention of plans to attend a CCG-led workshop while lunching with Klay and Wharton, a lunch conversation that had managed to cover the sad state of UT football, undergraduate life at Rice, mutual affluent Fort Worth acquaintances, and Oxford versus Harvard. Lord knows they had never discussed consulting the advice of veteran employees on anything. And here the Dr Pepper head of product development was sitting among them, seemingly, as any talking head on television would stress, being a part of the conversation. Wharton remained standing. He leaned against the wall and found to his mild surprise that he no longer viewed Marles as the smartest employee at Dr Pepper.

Fink acknowledged Wharton with a flash of his right hand in the air and said to Marles, "I can relate to what you're feeling, William. All of us here have known that feeling. Can be lonelier than a one-man patrol behind enemy lines. I think even the most squared-away soldier experiences difficulty and doubt when transitioning to civilian life. All that additional Special Operations training hadn't prepared me any better either. Which is why I want you to carry on with what you were saying before that about Dr Pepper, as this seems to be a common thread." Wharton sensed a confessional ring he was outside of, which Fink clarified with his knack for subtlety. "Pardon me for a moment. Is everyone okay with my nonveteran colleague Brock Wharton sitting in our veterans group workshop? You never served your country, Brock, in one of the armed forces branches, right? We don't count Coast Guard, do we?"

Marles spoke up over the howls of laughter from the scruffier-looking rabble in Dr Pepper factory uniforms, many of whom were wearing a ball cap with a branch of service on it (as if that were not ostentatious enough, they had made pin cushions out of the hats with shiny metal unit decals and medals). "Come on, guys, our whole discussion has demonstrated how it would be beneficial if he was allowed to sit in on our session. There's too great a disconnect as is between veterans and civilians." Marles bulldozed the air toward Wharton with the back of his left hand. "Not that I could even really begin to describe my three years in the Corps to you in one workshop, Brock." William Marles was in the Marine Corps? Were the rest of these grease gorillas once in his platoon?

"Yeah," Wharton said, not wishing for Marles to give it a try either. Wharton had come to document Fink's "contribution" to the engagement, of which he had already seen enough. "I'm sorry I can't stay. We have our CCG progress review in ten minutes."

This drew no reaction from the veterans in the circle or the CCG employee it was directed to, the latter of whom addressed Marles again. "But you're uncomfortable with any branding strategy distancing itself from the soul of Dr Pepper?"

"Yes, that's *not* an all-American campaign."

Wharton grunted as he caught his right leg from kicking the chair in front of him. An overweight fifty-year-old with a grizzled handlebar mustache and ball cap turned to assess Wharton. Printed above the screaming eagle on the bill of the black ball cap was HAITI VETERAN. *Haiti?* fumed Wharton. *Was that really a war?* he wanted to shout, but he checked himself to direct his anger toward Marles's contradiction of his earlier agreement with Wharton's branding strategy.

Marles continued on, accompanied now by a thousand-yard stare. "When a boy on a factory tour asks me, 'What is Dr Pepper?' I want to be able to hand him a can of the finest soda, as a Dr Pepper Museum tour guide once handed to me when I was a nine-year-old, so he will forever identify the brand with our unique flavor."

"Twenty-three unique flavors," the Haiti veteran said, his eyes still on Wharton.

"I hear you, Brother Marles," Fink said. The ring of veterans applauded the breakthrough. "It's why the U.S. Patent Office couldn't classify it as a cola. Who are we connecting with, if not the individuals out there who are each as original as the flavor itself?" Fink capped off the act by walking over and handing Marles a warm Dr Pepper can that Fink had removed from his briefcase. Taxed as he must have been by the cache of emotion that Wharton felt was required for the sham, Fink still found the energy to yell at him as he exited, "Be there in five minutes to bring it all home. Wrapping it up, Wharton!" *Wharton! Get back here, Wharton!* Fink *was* bringing it all back home, thought a fleeing Wharton. For Wharton's perpetual coach father, who had never served in the military, also used to military-like-command Wharton as a child on the pee-wee football field as he ran away, all after his father had berated him for some mistake and Wharton had ritually thrown his helmet in resistance, sprinting for home in escape. In high school, his father had served as an unwelcomed second coach, never missing a practice as he hung over the fence to form the critique that would be unsystematically delivered at dinner.

It was forty-five minutes later when Fink entered their base camp room to interrupt the CCG progress review meeting to proclaim, "Collected some great intel from these workshops," holding up a stack of completed questionnaires for Wharton, Ursula, and Connor to behold.

At the dry-erase board, Wharton resumed his drawing of an impotent bananagram that graphed the shrinking market share and its correlation to shrinking profits. "Thus, what we have all individually concluded these past two weeks is that the overall strategic direction of Dr Pepper isn't just off a few degrees and therefore has had its two worst quarters in a decade, but that the company's entire future is at stake if it doesn't drastically bend to the new beverage market with a more agile strategy for competing. Less a question of branding of the product Dr Pepper, and more a shift in the beverage market as a whole."

Wharton stood erect and observed his team members, who, except for one, all had their laptops open around the table. In front of Fink on the table was the stack of confessions he had extracted from employees. Half of whom rightfully feared that their jobs were at stake, jobs they had assumed would always be there when they signed up with Dr Pepper if they just showed up on time, stained their teeth yellow with pride for their product, and avoided risk until thirty years had passed and seen their youngest children graduate. From Wharton's experience, the simplest factory managers transformed into poets laureate about the impossibility of automating the complexity of their jobs as soon as CCG consultants arrived onsite for the assessment phase of how to best optimize processes. If Fink's sideshow with the veterans and the turncoat Marles were a bellwether, his findings interviewing these types of employees would range from a mishmash of contradictory statements to self-serving lies by voices irrelevant to the project's conclusions.

Wharton continued, "We have the next week to formulate and present a new strategy. We need to stress divestments in some of its traditional segments and further shift the emphasis to a continued investment—especially acquisitions—in the new wave of healthy drinks and prescribe a marketing strategy for carving out a niche in that market. The whole company is structured to be as inefficient as possible and is begging us to reorganize it appropriately. Costs and nonessential personnel need to be cut." Out of the corner of Wharton's eye, a mop of hair shook. With the belief that Fink scrutinized the board for a flaw at the crux of the argument, Wharton felt prompted to preemptively strike his inimical teammate. "You disagree with this summary?"

"I've got to be honest, I don't see how this floats. This ain't my first rodeo—"

"This is your first consulting rodeo. And you're the only one who hasn't turned in his section of the presentation to me yet." Wharton resumed his speech to the team. "We've gathered and analyzed the information. Complete your new tasks assigned earlier and we will edit our presentation together and incorporate any further data for next Friday. Go ahead and pack up here so we can catch our flights back for the weekend. Except for Fink. I wish to hear more about your objections from your fifty-thousand-foot view."

When the others had filed out, Wharton asked to see Fink's slides.

With a white background selected to optimally highlight the absence of any graphics or visual design, Fink's four slides only had one to two bullets per slide, consisting of either a sweeping-generalization blurb or a question in all capital letters crafted, Fink-like, to contradict the team plan.

"How do these slides fit in our deck?" Wharton asked, taking a picture with his phone.

"I can't say I agree with the conclusion on the board. I'm not sure we've analyzed all the factors of the decline. What's the so-what?" Fink's efforts to act out in accordance with his image of how a consultant might approach a multilayered problem were even more grating than his normal bumptious nature. Fink was actually more tolerable as Fink, Wharton thought sadly.

"What do you not agree with?"

"It's more of a lead I'm still tracking down." Fink stood up and put his hand to his chin professorially. "But I think our client needs to get back to the basics and marketing what makes Dr Pepper unique, rather than spreading itself too thin to attack everything or shrinking to concentrate on the latest trends." Fink walked over to the board and unveiled aloud his big contribution to the engagement. "The trend that is the important trend is never the trend."

Wharton was not fooled by Fink's new school of brawling by way of a nonsensical Zen style and syntax mixed with a buzzword. "The team has concluded differently."

"The *team* hasn't reached a conclusion. Let's slow down our gunslinging attitude right now of recommending that they cut jobs as a proper solution. What kind of square-deal strategy is that, to tell a bunch of people who have been working here for years for what they thought was the best beverage company in America that they are not part of the plan going forward? That's the native vision we're imposing? A lot of the employees I met this week are combat veterans. And veterans find a way to make it happen. Talent like that can't just be outsourced to China. That might be how Pepsi operates, but that sure as hell ain't what Dr Pepper is about. Ask yourself not what but *who* is Dr Pepper? Because we're here to execute, not be executioners."

"Consultants don't make the decision to cut people, they only recommend. Your populist rhetoric and folksy integrity aren't helping out any of the employees here if the company continues to adopt bad strategies and goes under. That would be a loss of American capital. And CCG is in the market of growing a company's capital. The rest of the team has agreed to a strategy already, and we're driving down the field toward the end zone. We aren't sure whether we can put you in the game. As consultants, we have to deploy every week. If you don't think you have what it takes to win, I suggest you confide in Seymour when he flies up here to attend our presentation that strategic management consulting is not for you."

Fink ran his hands through his wavy hair and tilted his head back to stare at the ceiling as if illustrating his burden to Wharton of having to actually employ an ounce of intellectual thought over the workweek. Fink seemed determined to frame his coming termination as a pageant of martyrdom. "I want to have a warm and fuzzy that our proposed solutions have been chewed on and are spot-on and not railroaded through by way of groupthink. So we can save this great brand and positively influence the lives of Dr Pepper employees. There are a lot of different tribes here, each with its own culture. We can't be afraid to mix it up out here and be unconventional." Not *unconventional* again! Did these brain-dead Special Operations commandos ever exhaust a word more to establish legitimacy? wondered Wharton. "Choose the hard right over the easy wrong on the way to victory. That's why I signed up for this profession. This calling." At his core, Fink did not lack passion for defending the little guy who cannot keep up with the change in his surroundings. Such humanity would be fine if Wharton's profession were not consulting—in which it was his responsibility and Fink's to usher in unwanted change! "A calling in which you help your client continuously improve and adapt its identity to create its own destiny!" Fink grabbed his briefcase and turned away to spin the locks. He pulled out a paperback copy of *Don Quixote* to hold up, a formidable righteousness fortifying his gangly frame. "'Draw on what you know,' they instructed us in consulting orientation. I've been doing just that with literature to help me better connect to the emotions of the workers and why the brand has drifted. To *see* the human condition in the modern business world."

Don Quixote. This was his north star? "They didn't mean literally. That advice is intended for consultants with professional backgrounds relative to a client engagement. Not English majors."

"We have to believe again if we want Dr Pepper to risk believing in our solution."

Fink's false sincerity about their profession (a new audacious gambit Wharton begrudgingly admired) did not lure Wharton into mussing up the advantage. He was one chess move ahead of the Mississippi Madman. "Fink," Wharton said, draping his arm around Fink's wiry shoulders and leading him out of the room, "you just reminded me why I fought to hire you in the meeting last month when others raised their objections to your lack of business experience and education."

"You fought for me, mentor?" Fink asked indulgently. A bit too indulgently, thought Wharton.

"Sure did, teammate," Wharton said in the same playful manner of a charade. "I told the nonbelievers that here was a man not afraid to deviate from the script and speak his own mind. And that, along with your unique way of analyzing cases, is special."

"Special Forces," Fink explained happily. "Diplomats with automatic weapons."

"*Right*," Wharton said quickly, refusing to be derailed in their brinksmanship of chicanery, "which I don't want you to be scared of doing next week during your part of the presentation. Never stay silent if you believe something needs to be said. It doesn't matter if it wasn't in the rehearsal run or not in one of the final slides." Seed planted. "Don't forget that these big CEOs are no different than you and me. They still put their pants on one leg at a time."

"That goes for their costumes as well!" Fink thundered.

Wharton reeled back from the unexpected burst of excitement that the reference to Halloween induced in Fink. After Fink had danced a brief Day of the Dead skeleton jig, Wharton returned his arm to pat Fink's shoulder. "Yes, their costumes as well," Wharton reassured, as if settling down a lost, and just as suddenly found, child.

He had half a mind to ask Fink if he would need a ride home from the Houston airport later, as Wharton knew K.K. would not believe his retelling of the day's events as she drove him home until she had actually met Fink.

• • •

Few issues, certainly not two straight fiscal quarters with losses and an outdated strategy, were as important in the zany carnival world of Dr Pepper as allowing the employees to express themselves on Halloween through costume. Halloween at Dr Pepper was a new experience for Wharton; never in all of his many consulting engagements had he ever dressed in costume for a final client presentation. Wharton stretched the cheap band of the eye patch as much as he could to flip it up so he could follow along. His skin needed no further reminder of why it despised Halloween than the swashbuckling pirate costume that was beginning to generate furious digging with his fingernails in all the wrong places. He continued to listen with diminishing hope for the swish of cool air snaking in through vents. For the last thirty minutes he had longed to stretch out his arm as his right rotator cuff had begun aching again this week, but he hadn't wanted to attempt anything that might bring on more perspiration. Each week back onsite at Dr Pepper had tested Wharton with a new trial, but all of the ordeals over the last three weeks were now drowned out by the joy flooding over him at Fink's impending consulting execution.

"Next," the CEO of Dr Pepper, dressed as George Washington, said. Wharton hit the arrow button on the keyboard to move to the next slide. He detected a previously unseen peevishness from the CEO that was not usually a part of his show-no-agitation demeanor. Turn on the air conditioner, Wharton restrained himself from yelling the obvious solution. Klay sat beside the CEO. Wharton worked his eye patch to flash Morse code across the table to Klay, who remained unreachable in a trance somewhere to the right of Ursula's shadow. Klay was dressed comfortably in a loose Aladdin outfit and not taking any notes as only a water-walker who reaches the position of chief operating officer at age thirty-seven makes a show of doing. On the other side of

Klay was Marles in a khaki Ghostbusters jumpsuit-and-boots ensemble, incidentally the only costume in the room Wharton felt worthy of what Ursula the night before had termed the absurd Americanism of Halloween intruding upon their client presentation.

Not wanting to draw the ire of Seymour and Stanley, who sat to his left, Wharton returned the eye patch to its role of obstructing his vision and gathering sweat condensation. Seymour and Stanley had flown up that morning from Houston dressed in suits. They had conveniently pleaded ignorance to the Dr Pepper culture upon arrival an hour before the presentation and were exempt by default from the one inflexible policy of the Cambridge Consulting Group: always dress onsite as the client dresses. The CEO had stopped by their team's room to insist the day before to Wharton that the presentation be carried out with the unflagging spirit of Halloween in the face of such hard economic times. Before Wharton had a chance to conjure up a religious objection to his team dressing in costume, Fink rushed in to congratulate the CEO and decree that such an attitude was exactly what was needed from the captains at the helm of industry in a time of war. Which reaffirmed Wharton's three-week assessment that Fink flailed around in his consulting death throes. In Fink's impaired vision of the world, he probably envisaged the CEO as President Franklin D. Roosevelt and Dr Pepper as essential to the war effort and an ambassadorial product of democracy. Soft power.

"Once you have divested," Ursula continued in her European-accented flawless English, making eye contact with the CEO during each address, "the freed capital needs to be shifted into the new energy and health drinks Dr Pepper released last year for which the margins are higher. A large-scale advertising campaign targeting the age demographic of eighteen-to-forty-year-olds should follow to increase your market share in these emerging markets. They are the future of the beverage industry. As outlined in this slide, several of these smaller competitors with a name brand already established in the energy and health beverage industry have to be acquired. The potential to grow in these markets is far greater than in the entrenched soda market, as my colleague Connor explained earlier in his analysis of your marketing strategy."

All beads and feathers, Fink sat as wooden as an Indian offensively caricatured in an old Hollywood movie next to Marles. The silent redskin's blank stare caused Wharton to titter into his fist. His intentional last minute "History of Dr Pepper Advertising" report request the evening before had provided Fink with the educational experience of his first consulting all-nighter. Fink's sleepless labor had found its way into a section of the appendix no one would ever read.

On the screen was a title slide reading RESTRUCTURING, a euphemism Wharton used to explain to CEOs that they were running their companies poorly and needed to cut jobs. It was a twist of the knife by Wharton to have a drowsy Fink endorse the necessary future layoffs by briefing what Fink believed was an injustice to the Dr Pepper employees. Fink had mumbled the words on the slide the day before in rehearsal, his fury surpassed by what Wharton perceived as Fink's humiliation that he would also soon fall under the layoff column.

"And now my colleague Mike Fink will discuss our proposed restructuring of a new and more profitable Dr Pepper," Ursula said as she transitioned to her seat on the other side of Fink. Though her Dorothy costume more closely resembled the ancestral dress of her native Switzerland than *The Wizard of Oz* because of her linebacker torso, Ursula had, as always, carried the baton well after Wharton's introduction and Connor's portion on marketing analysis. Wharton caught her eye and silently mimicked a golf clap that made her blush.

As Fink moved to the front, Wharton observed with his available eye the modified version of his costume, post–Seymour's morning intervention after arriving onsite at Dr Pepper. A horrified Seymour, upon sight of the wild native in his feathers and bone breastplate, had ordered Fink to return to his hotel and change at once into a shirt and pants—the health risk to others posed by a loincloth among the many reasons why being nearly naked for a client presentation might be inappropriate. Fink had committed the ultimate consulting sin of not knowing his environment. Hardly shocking when the man's lodestar was *Don Quixote*. This time, Wharton was taking no risk of there not being witnesses for the final undoing of Fink.

"Love the costume," the CEO said to accompanying laughter in the room.

"A note on the outfit," Fink said, doing a full turn for all to see both his warrior breastplate and loincloth now worn over an ass-covering pair of pants. "I am not supposed to be a Native American, but a riverboat pirate dressed up as an Indian of the kind the folk hero of my same name used to battle on the Mississippi River. This is why my loincloth is on the outside of my pants."

"Wear it however you wish, as long as CCG covers my rear! Next slide."

Wharton touched the right arrow on the keyboard. A black screen appeared, ending the slide show. He hit the left arrow, taking him back a slide. He jabbed at the right arrow key again twice with his finger but this time the black screen only took him back to the initial slide.

"Next slide."

"I think something might be wrong with the connection to the big screen," Wharton said.

"It's indicating that that is your last slide," Klay offered.

"It isn't our last slide."

"Here's the thumb drive you gave me," Ursula said, sliding across the table the silver thumb drive Wharton had given her before leaving to pick up Seymour and Stanley from the airport. Wharton held it up in the air as hard evidence of his team's presentation.

"I apologize for this. One second while I pull this up and resolve this snafu."

Wharton pulled up the slide show and gawked, as it listed slide sixty-two, RESTRUCTURING, as the end.

"Use your disk with the backup file," Seymour chimed in, the apprehension palpable in his phony effort to project calm. Wharton cringed as he remembered that the backup disk was on his desk all the way back in his Dallas hotel room.

"Pull up your copied file," Stanley echoed uselessly, as was the Snail's wont in times of pressure. On the other side of Wharton, Connor leaned over and puffed a sour, heated cottonmouth briefing breath so his nose could confirm the CCG anxiety. Droplets of sweat pooled at the inner base of his eye patch up to the downward curve of his bottom eyelashes.

"You want some honest advice not on this screen?" Fink asked.

"No," Wharton said before Fink made the situation any worse. Fink could leave the reservation and wing it all he wanted when the screen came back up and juxtaposed his rambling brand of idiocy with the bullets and statistics onscreen that the rogue was not adhering to.

The slide show file in the folder, Wharton noticed, was last saved four hours ago. He flipped up his eye patch, releasing the moisture there. Four hours ago? Four hours ago Wharton was on his way back from the airport with Seymour and Stanley in the rental car.

Fink was at it again, this time asking the CEO, "What about some straight talk?"

Wharton saw the machinations of a great duplicity with Fink as the orchestrator and Wharton cast as the rube.

"Yes!" the CEO shouted and slammed his fist on the table. "Hell, that's what I'm supposedly paying you for. Not that I ever listen to the advice of you showy know-everything consultants anyway. I'm like every other CEO out there paying you, because none of us ever got fired for hiring Cambridge Consulting Group to review and sign off on one of our new ideas."

"That's the damn problem!" Fink said, slapping the table with two hands for a louder effect. "Consultants have turned into a bunch of cowardly cosigners. We know what you want, and we give it to you. When jobs need to get cut, we come in and recommend it and play the bad guys for you as we reengineer and right-size it all. We had to burn the village to save the village. And when we're not providing you cover to move and maneuver as elegantly as a bunch of clodhoppers, we're trying to act like some yahoo idea we came up with is the result of us helicoptering it up to look at the big picture—the big picture that you guys are incapable of looking at since consultants are always the 'wis-est' guys in any room we occupy and you're too bogged down in the weeds. Then you further swallow the hook by putting us on a retainer basis to implement and manage the enablement project, at which point we keep commuting and basking in the sun like alligators on a mud bank at our five-star hotels and billing you out your covered asses. Is this who Dr Pepper is?" Fink leaned over with his arms bracing him up on the table a foot away from the CEO's face.

Fink had finally lost it. Mission accomplished within an acceptable Wharton timetable. Though his longed-for mental breakdown in public was also about to lose CCG a client if he dragged Wharton and his team any deeper into enemy territory. Indian country. "Sit down, Fink. Your own off-base personal theory of consulting is affecting the conclusion of this presentation."

Fink pushed off the table to stand up straight. "I have a little experience like your own William Marles in tackling an insurgency of the sort you're facing from these competitors of yours." The ghostbuster Marles rapped his fist on an anchored globe and bird emblem imprinted on the khaki boot of his foot that rested over his knee. "It's called counterinsurgency. And I learned the trade in the Green Berets." *Counterinsurgency*—Wharton bristled at the irony—would be what the far larger competitors of Coke and Pepsi would be engaged in to crush the market share of a midtier regional player like Dr Pepper.

Seymour, who had lost his jacket during Fink's tirade, clutched his navy blue suspenders as if they were ropes holding him back outside the ring from taking down Fink. Under his fogging horn-rimmed glasses, Stanley's face was the slick of a fleeing snail. For love of CCG, Wharton stood up. "No one here cares about counterinsurgency," he said to the insurgent Fink, while cinching down his slipping pirate pantaloons. "We're waiting on you to sit down and—"

"You sit down!" commanded George Washington. Seymour, with a look on his face that Wharton read as worrying more about how much could be lost beyond even the CCG client Dr Pepper, had sprung up from the edge of his seat to intercept Wharton. Seymour tamped the air with his hands so Wharton would sit back down before the CEO could rise from his chair. "I've had enough of your consulting-speak to last me the rest of my career." It stood to reason that Seymour, who no more knew how to handle this unexpected and unprecedented situation than Wharton, would hesitate to draw a bead on Fink. But the CEO did not, turning to Fink. "You don't strike me as having been in the military." Oh Christ on the cross, a prostrated Wharton wailed inwardly from his leather chair, did corporate executives ever torture your ears with such rubbish? "You were a Green Beret?"

"Please, Fink," Wharton begged, "we *need* to finish the presentation." If there was any chance of saving Dr Pepper as a client with Wharton's new "America Revisited" campaign for Dr Pepper, it would not come out of a digression on the culture of Special Forces.

"I was, which is why I'm going to level with you and tell you that what you don't need to do is heed the findings in this presentation you overpaid for." Fink's flat left hand chopped in the air like a tomahawk in the direction of Klay, who scrambled to write down this new information on the back of a napkin. Both Seymour and Stanley swiveled in their chairs toward Wharton, who had been responsible for billing Dr Pepper. He would have liked to pummel them almost as much as Fink. "Cut thousands of jobs? Take that suggestion along with our other chestnut about investing all your freed capital in new products and you will be bankrupt within two years. Hell, we need all hands on deck for this branding operation. This ain't the time to be feeding you the easy slop that you want to digest about new flavors and health drink fads that aren't sustainable."

"What do you suggest other than downsizing and investing in new products?" the CEO asked, shifting his wig forward to cover his flattop haircut. Forty-two years earlier, he had started at Dr Pepper on a truck route with the same haircut.

"Stop fooling with every new snake-oil cure and invest in what made Dr Pepper what it is." The grunting approval of Marles tipped Wharton off that Fink was recycling the workshop message of the veterans group. Also documented by Wharton in his fattening file containing the "Case Against Mike Fink" as: *Fink truly believed, lecturing me after missing most of the progress review at a "veterans workshop," that he had unlocked the quintessence of Dr Pepper as a faith-based product of quality in an ever-expanding market that was theirs for the taking.* That belief held up well if you spent your nights dreaming under the stars out in Plano, celebrating Halloween, and believing in Santa Claus. Not after a CCG progress review in which an analysis of the numbers deflated any such romantic ideal in a product.

"The drink Dr Pepper?"

Wharton accompanied the rest of the room by turning to Fink for his answer. Seymour might as well have been rubbing rosary beads the way his fingers traveled over his suspenders. What is Dr Pepper? The CCG brain trust had hired Fink to trick all-American clients, not to drag CCG's own team out on the high wire as to what is all-American. Wharton reveled in having a front-row seat as Fink overplayed his advantage.

"Couldn't have said it any sweeter myself. Dr Pepper *is*," Fink said, gesturing beyond the room, "Dr Pepper!" Fink grabbed his neck skin at the gobbler, beating out an envious Wharton, who had been waiting to wring it. "The only soda that gives that good burn in the back of the gullet going down." Fink's hand now pointed at the Dr Pepper clock. "The one prescribed by doctors, taken at ten, two, and four," resurrecting the slogan from the history of Dr Pepper advertising to amplify his delirium. "What kid wouldn't choose Dr Pepper over milk? Dr Pepper is what America drinks. And it's definitely the one drink required when stranded on a desert island or in Iraq after a day of missions. Show some belief again in your product." Klay swiped his flat hand back and forth across his throat for Fink to see. "Because we're going to need to double down with an initial surge of troops and money and a maverick marketing strategy that separates the Dr Pepper brand from the enemy. We will target each demographic until we win the consumers of village after village and our Dr Pepper oil blot stains the entire country."

Short of spontaneous human combustion, Fink's meltdown—complete with military analogies—was of the kind of supreme annihilation that Wharton could not have matched with his original presentation trap. He had been wise not to cut Fink off. Since it was safe to presume CCG had forever lost Dr Pepper as a client, Wharton went in for a few licks that otherwise would have reflected poorly on him as Fink's superior: "I believe you recommended applying that same failed strategy, word for word, last month to the frozen food industry. In the context of Dr Pepper's current situation, it is an even more preposterous branding strategy when the goal is maximizing shareholder value." Wharton only wished he could have taken bets in true CCG fashion as to whether Seymour or Klay would kill Fink first afterward.

"It is like a counterinsurgency, isn't it?" the CEO asked Marles, who smiled at Fink and let out a Marine *ooh-rah* groan.

To give credence to the question hanging in the air was to accept an axis shift in Wharton's world. That there might be multitudes behind CCG's Don Quixote, who had only accomplished demonstrating—at the expense of a client and Wharton's career—that he would recklessly risk it all if he believed madly in something.

"Of course it's a counterinsurgency dogfight!" Fink exclaimed. "Viewed through this prism, we've got all the technological advantages over our smaller rivals, but we're losing because we concentrate too much on that aspect rather than drying up the sea our rivals swim in. The only way to win over the consumers on the fence is through a more agile Dr Pepper brand. A brand that can have a smaller, subtler footprint while also strategically engaging behind the scenes with the influencers from a position of strength. Branding ain't going to be easy or risk-free or quick, but it's the only shot we've got at waging a successful counterinsurgency across this market chasm when we're getting outright licked like this. Folks have to remember again that it's that unique Dr Pepper flavor that makes them dance." Fink started to bend his bowlegs and whistle a classic jingle from deep in the archives of Dr Pepper advertising. "'People drink Dr Pepper because that beautiful odd soda makes them feel like being a Pepper again, that original person that you wanted to be, not some bottom-line turnkey,'" Fink sang, stopping on an improvised lyric about clones to stomp his feet and wave his hands at Wharton. "The Dr Pepper brand is individuality—and that is America. Isn't that what makes Dr Pepper the best damn soda out there? It's a drink so original that you can't even describe it to anyone else by referencing other things, as it doesn't taste like any known flavor."

"We should put him on the commercial," the CEO said. Wharton laughed uneasily to go along with the hilarity rattling the room, because next to him Seymour and Stanley laughed as if a method for retaining a client were to laugh like they had heard the funniest joke ever.

Wharton was not alone in waiting for the room to fall silent. Fink addressed the other man standing, the chief executive officer of a Fortune 500 company. "In a land of eternal reinvention, sometimes you re-create your brand by not allowing the terrorizing winds of the marketplace to rebrand you. Rather redefine the brand through rediscovery." *Was he really going to say it?* Fink answered the question by smiling at Wharton and looting the campaign catchphrase on his hanging tongue. "Let's revisit America and Dr Pepper."

The CEO fingered his George Washington ponytail as the whole room waited. He walked away from Fink and the front of the room as if he carried the cross for the entire group. The CEO circled the table until he reached where Seymour sat and said for all to hear, "We're all in." The CEO raised his hands to simmer down the cheers and pointed at Fink. "But on the condition that he stays on next month to advise me and a team on how to conduct a counterinsurgency."

Fink said, "Won't be the first time I've been embedded and turned loose as an advisor."

During the CCG celebration that followed back at the hotel bar, Wharton was forced by Seymour to raise his glass and toast the virtually nude dancing Indian Fink (restored again to only his loincloth and a pair of moccasins), who had not only saved the Dr Pepper relationship but also generated new business for CCG. There were several other patriotic toasts to the hero before Wharton was able to slip away and flip up his pirate eye patch, where red bumps had begun surfacing around his right eye. He ducked in the lobby restroom and buried his face in the white warm towel offered by the bathroom attendant. The lemon scent in the towel transported Wharton back to the soap his nanny used to bathe him in as a boy at their Galveston beach house. Wharton and K.K. had gone all the way to Africa on their honeymoon but had never once traveled to Galveston, a simple forty-mile journey, its ruins of another age from its days as a pirate haven, instead always opting for the bluer water of K.K.'s family island in the Caribbean. To dine out, freshly cleaned along the grimy Galveston seawall in the salty sulfuric air . . .

"Ooooooooooooh-rah!" the stampede violently sounded, seizing Wharton and bitch-slapping him out of his nostalgia. "Call-out to our loyal Marine Corps."

"Mr. Fink, what's up?" the reserved Hispanic bathroom attendant howled, breaking out some sort of complex street handshake that a juiced-up Fink matched instep.

"The girls in this bar, Jesus! It's like a goddamn petting zoo," Fink demonstrated with his upturned hand at waist level, fingers nibbling the air. He joined Wharton at the counter and put the towel the bathroom attendant tossed him around his neck as if he were a winning prizefighter post-knockout. "Looks like Mike Fink's in the lead after a little unconventional warfare. Me personally, there's no one I would rather see up on that tightrope. And I didn't have a hundred ladders to help get up there or a hundred safety nets below to catch a fall."

Nothing agitated third-person self-referencing psychotics more than treating them like they were normal, Wharton had surmised from his hours suffered in the company of Fink. Wharton soaked the towel in cold water and dabbed the rash under his eye with it. "Congratulations on getting your first assignment as project leader," Wharton said into the mirror at Fink, who rocked back and forth on his toes. "The novelty wears off quickly once you get your cherry popped."

"Whoa," Fink said, halting his bantam footwork, "what's with the locker-room language?" As it was important to not display a reaction to this tease, Wharton stuck to splashing water all over his face. "You think I liked it any more than you did when the partners imagined they'd use me and my military experience to profit off a couple of contracts?"

"You should tell them to hold your salary if you think it compromises your integrity."

Fink laughed and threw a ten-dollar bill in the tip jar, grabbing a trick-or-treat handful of condoms from the counter basket, and, exiting, paused to smile and dispense a free consultation. "Speaking of compromise, you need to encrypt a file so your slides don't get ambushed. A lack of situational awareness, really. How I wish I had had my phone so *I* could've taken a picture."

The hubris of Fink to believe his street smarts and dirty tricks would triumph over a lifetime of doing everything right. That Wharton had mismanaged all his time in a wasted effort. With the edges of Fink's hairy ass cheeks mooning him in the mirror as he exited, Wharton cursed and cast off his eye patch.

PART TWO

4.

THE GOLDEN AGE OF TERRORISM

"He's a terrorist."

"I thought he killed terrorists."

"I think he could be trying to kill my career."

"Diamonds or pearls?" K.K. Wharton asked her husband, holding up an earring from each set in front of their bedroom dresser. Her small hands had fortunately never been in danger of performing manual labor, or anything they did not want to do. After six months as an associate in real estate practice upon graduating from law school, she had retired from her legal career to manage her family's ranching fortune (stolen from the Indians, of course, who never understood when to lawyer up in the Wild West). Pretty to a degree—the sort of pretty that comes from generations of paired similar genes reviewed first by a board of underworked trust-fund parents ("A two-goal handicap rating," her father was fond of clarifying, regarding his job as a professional polo player)—K.K. Wharton wore her long, brown hair well around her fair but equine face. Unusually, Wharton had been attracted not to her looks but to her confident nature first, a sureness that most other girls thought largely unearned and an irritating mark of her insular upbringing among the incestuous South Texas ranching royalty. Or so he told himself about the order of his attraction, as there was always the great attraction of joining her dynastic family. *Professional* polo player, the competitive Wharton still remembered exclaiming after throwing down his own silver spoon that seemed instantly to be tarnished pewter: who knew they even existed?

"Diamonds. I need you looking hotter than anyone else there tonight."

"Not so easy when you're five months pregnant."

K.K. turned her back to allow Wharton to zip her sequined dress up. The science-project magic of her pregnancy had begun to wane. What had replaced his amazement at life was an unpleasant recognition of aging. Her triple-A-rated skin now had a thinner, rubbery texture that he had to downgrade below that of his own troubled skin. The glimpse of his wife's black bra as he zipped aroused his dormant disappointment that his wife's small breasts had yet to correspond with the increase of her waistline. The much-vaunted milk fund would probably underperform. His wife was slipping in the rankings. Their appearance at the CCG holiday party tonight would have to be an in-and-out operation. Wharton hypothesized that while her family might endlessly boast about their thoroughbred racing horses and knowledge of bovine breeding, his wife's lack of any tits exposed that more ranching resources needed to be devoted to human breeding. And what was the point of having a fortune that size if not to buy a set of nice . . .

"Did you invite him to our Christmas party?" K.K. asked the image of his puckered face in their dresser mirror, interrupting Wharton's Breast Genome Project.

"I do not want to even picture how obscene all our guests would find him," Wharton said, squeezing a handful of his wife's burgeoning behind. The cost of the annual Wharton Christmas party next week had already ballooned to eighteen thousand dollars—prior to insuring for terrorism. Then there was the opportunity cost of all the hours Wharton had logged since he was twenty-seven years old, strategically altering the revolving invite list of friends each year to best serve his career rise instead of hours spent billing a client. "I would invite the analysts and support staff before I would invite him. Think if your family met him." Though not a bad idea if that meant they would visit less thereafter, Wharton thought. "He'll only be at the CCG holiday party because everyone is invited and he finished the Dr Pepper engagement yesterday."

"You brought that company to CCG." K.K. turned around to face him with the icy stare that had sobered many wise South Texas suitors before Wharton came calling. To his distress, the hormonal pregnancy had dramatically increased the frequency with which K.K. pursed her thin lips to bring about a dead calm that caused near hysteria in Wharton. "You're still CCG's starting quarterback, right?" Could she be aware that such pursing recalled the steeliness only seen during their prenuptial agreement conversation?

Wharton imagined dropping back in the pocket to throw a long pass downfield, but this ended with him being sacked savagely into the dirt for a loss and not the floating touchdown toss in slow motion. He had been benched by CCG, if the last six weeks tagging along to perform due diligence down in Alabama for the blue-collar leadership of Wallymart were any indication. The infamous Wallymart itself: consulting blue-collar leadership for "wage-earning workers." Why did this not-part-of-society element hate the Brock Whartons? Because of his wealth? His values? His WASP jaw? His winning record in life? "He has momentarily pulled the wool over CCG's eyes with his voodoo and war stories. His 'integrity' is somehow above questioning because of his military service."

"Do you want me to call Kenneth?"

"No." How he longed to smite her ignoble Judas of a cousin, who had risen to initiate the standing ovation for Fink after the handshake with the CEO. For a traitor-to-his-class encore, cousin Aladdin had glided in on his culturally appropriated fast-tracker magic carpet to suggest CCG be put on further retainer in the spring to advise product development. Kenneth Klay, from beloved cousin to patron saint of Wharton's enemy, formally relieved Wharton from all future Dr Pepper engagements by passing on that Dr Pepper had decided to go in a different direction with its branding as envisioned by Fink. Even having the gall to act as if Wharton and Fink worked at competing companies. Branding. Succumbing to his one weakness, self-pity,

Wharton dreamed for weeks that a scarlet *L* for *loser* had been branded on his victimized noble forehead for all to see.

"That's my favorite of your ties," K.K. said, patting his Ferragamo pastel-green fox-patterned tie. The softness of K.K.'s touch on the silk was a reminder that beneath her legal exterior: love! Or an aquifer of love, and quite a bit more affection when love periodically rose to the surface than had ever been available from his frigid mother; despite the age difference between them, both women had indistinguishable hands, the underuse of the aristocrat's hands serving Wharton's mother well. "You know what I know?"

"Maybe he has a particular strand of PTSD causing him to fight for al-Qaeda against America," Wharton mused, shepherding his wife out to the garage.

"I thought we were fighting ISIS?"

"ISIL, yes."

"No, you mean IS."

"IS is ISIS," Wharton said, tutoring his wife on the Islamic State's ongoing identity crisis as he reversed down the driveway. Foreign policy today, Wharton had discovered, was no joke.

Ten bayous flow through Houston, but it is said only the biggest one can cut the city in half. In a hurricane deluge, almost a bath for this body of petrochemical gumbo, the Buffalo Bayou boils over into potholed streets and civically washes away attempts at public art. Though all the alligators large enough to wrestle were long gone from the big bayou and the buffalo it was named after were now another myth of the frontier, Wharton never forgot that the historic battle for Texas independence had once been fought on its banks. In the excitement afterward, expectations high and combat fresh, the men erected a capital on the humid coastal plain but failed to consult the settlers of the republic, who quickly relocated their victory monument to a more hospitable city inland. And so as Wharton neared Allen Parkway and the legendary Buffalo Bayou in his German luxury car, his pulse spiked at the sight of the darker and dingier bayou-area backstreets.

Indeed, any time Wharton stumbled on a street of banana trees and sunroom houses in his hometown he had not explored, the high of discovery surged through him like a narcotic. In many ways the heightened sensation from these rare forays in slum tourism also triggered the resultant downer of self-consciousness when he returned to their home. For a "wedding gift," his parents-in-law had bestowed a two-million-dollar house on them before he had saved any real income professionally. Wharton had lobbied for a half-million-dollar starter home for the first year of marriage in such a newlywed neighborhood as the one he cut through. He would wake up and run the bayou trails, sit on the front porch swing at night ("But the darker the streets, the easier it is to see the stars!"), before his then-fiancée K.K. made it known that pursuing this bohemian fantasy constituted a deal-breaker as per their relationship. Yet here it was, the second week of December, and the humidity had dissipated while holding off the cold, the gulf clouds above weighty and lingering, mosquitoes still buzzing with joy.

Next door to the winding cemetery where the city's celebrated eccentric Howard Hughes was buried, Hughes Hangar along the Washington Corridor had been a neglected, old airplane hangar overlooking the bayou. It had been recently converted into a speakeasy, and its centerpiece was the propeller and cockpit of a test plane purported to have been flown by Howard Hughes himself. Wharton passed on the valet service, recalling a Fink story from his training week about his high school job as a valet. He dropped K.K. at the entrance and searched for a parking spot. After two passes, he returned to the twenty empty spots at the back of the lot marked with orange cones.

"What are you doing?" the high-school-aged valet asked Wharton, who was stacking one cone atop another orange cone in the spot next to it.

"What does it look like? I'm moving this cone over so I can park my car."

"Sorry, but all of these spots are reserved."

"I'm with the Cambridge Consulting Group party. I'm one of the consultants."

"What's a consultant?" the valet asked with new interest. "Is that like a counselor?"

"A consultant diagnoses problems and prescribes solutions. Let me demonstrate. If I were to park here in this empty space, I would be able to attend my party inside."

"But I am under orders from a gentleman inside who said that no one parks here who doesn't support valets. From your director." He handed Wharton a business card.

MIKE "KING OF THE MISSISSIPPI" FINK, CAMBRIDGE CONSULTING GROUP, read the soulful plastic card. Was this tacky nickname on the business card an obnoxious veteran thing? Wharton had once known an insufferable Houston investment banker who had been an armored cavalry officer for a few years whose business card also included his self-appointed nickname of "Lighthorse." All Wharton's colleagues had laughed at Lighthorse until one day he was killed after being thrown from his mount during an equestrian competition in River Oaks. It was said that Wharton's floral arrangement had been the largest sent to the family.

"Okay, valet it," Wharton scoffed, handing over ten dollars to the valet.

For the little luck of Wharton's that remained in the year 2014: Piazza was not among the crowd gathered inside around the bar and the storytelling Fink, as Piazza lived to retell other people's funny stories over and over again at work. In the one retro décor setting in Houston where Fink's navy double-breasted suit was appropriate, Fink appeared to sport a nearly identical charcoal pinstriped suit atop French cuffs matched with the same Ferragamo pastel tie to mirror Wharton. His hair had been cut short, neatly groomed with a sharp coif on the same break as Wharton's. *Trying to out-Wharton Brock Wharton?* seethed the real Brock Wharton. Though, to be fair, they all had the same look to any outsider.

Wharton located K.K. by the plane and came up behind her. "Here's my sexy copilot. Already desiring to fly away from this party too?"

"Is that him?"

Wharton knew who.

"The one at the bar with the two skanks." He felt a tingle, the arousing kind, at hearing his proper wife hiss *skanks*. Was it really all that long ago when good-girl law student K.K. had thrilled at being a bad girl? His secret skank to spank. As he had had to best her then-fiancé, who was from a far richer old-money Texas family. It wasn't until after he had stolen the little tart away that he was seized by the notion that he had been *her* mistress; irrespective of past roles, she now made her husband compete for sex against her social schedule, which had a way of taking the naughtiness out of the mix.

Wharton smirked upon sight of the two blown-out blondes of Fink's same social class. All three took shots at the bar. Fink's two front teeth carnivorously clamped down on the shot glass to overturn it in his mouth. The cocktail waitresses were in identical strapless satin red dresses from some streetwalker Christmas catalog, their aggressively propped-up breasts ready to take aim at their target. At the moment—Wharton did not need to be briefed—their intended target appeared to be his ego.

Wharton did not have the curiosity to stick around for the act that would surely see Fink take to the skies and autograph with a marker the girls' fully revealed, waiting fake boobs as he climbed down from Hughes's cockpit. Though where had voluptuous girls like this been when Wharton's college was selecting the homecoming court and he had been the coolest student on campus? It must actually be the hormones in the beef. From behind, he looked down his wife's dress at her small nipples that seemed as if God in an afterthought had thrown two after-dinner chocolates on a wooden cutting board. Again, was this the breeding her ranching family was so proud of? *Ranching*—Wharton snorted in disgust at the delusional image her family pathetically grasped at—was that what you called allowing Exxon to frack every acre of your property with gas wells? It was best that Wharton not linger on K.K.'s natural beauty, or all he would want for Christmas would be to frack the shit out of both waitress skanks in the cockpit.

"I'm ready to go, K.K." Any more ready and he would swap her and her overvalued confidence and "good family" background for one night with either skank. It wasn't like K.K. allotted him any bonus points for marital fidelity anyway.

"We just got here."

"You devils just got here!" Nathan Ellison said, walking up with his twin of a wife.

"You'll have to forgive him," Kim Ellison said. "He was playing some kind of drinking game with wild Mike Fink and he's not used to drinking. Come on, K.K., let's feed you and that baby of yours and let the boys be boys." Yes, everyone loved wild Mike Fink and his larger-than-life tales. Must be nice when all different kinds of people wanted to hang out with you and cheered you on. It stung Wharton that Fink's shape-shifting and stretchers about his past held no consequences. Had his fellow disconnected citizens so mythologized Afghanistan and Iraq veterans that they were allowed to exaggerate without accountability? It bothered Wharton even more that he himself coveted the applause they expected, for those like Fink who had survived seemed charmed, still sprinkled in a magic dust from overseas as they floated about without the burden of the same anxieties.

Nathan did not wait for his wife or K.K. to be out of earshot. "Did you see the carriages of those little Santa's Helpers who've been chatting up Fink? To get behind one of those would be like driving a chariot!"

"Client development for him, no doubt."

"That tomcat really believes he has the power to heal"—Nathan laughed—"with his dick."

Fink, as if sensing their debate on his mental sanity, lifted his hands from the lower backs of the waitresses and presidentially waved with two hands to them across the floor. Wharton ignored the cock redeemer's megalomania. "He has no filter. The way he talks—this isn't the military. It's only a matter of time before CCG gets slapped with a sexual harassment lawsuit. You should hear him making light of his string-bikini fetish. Something sick about how after sex he resurrects the erection by having the girl put on a bikini, the framing and unwrapping of the bikini strings being like a present. Why would you make a beautiful woman who is naked put on clothing? Macroaggressions."

"Microaggression?"

"But greater."

"Let him enjoy it while he can, because he'll be staring at ankles come Sunday in Saudi."

It was no longer just in his imagination that he was being tackled from every direction: Saudi Aramco was CCG's second biggest core client and the world's most valuable company.

"This is not a game of craps, Nathan. He can't fill the role of a senior partner."

"They want a no-bullshit assessment regarding their risky strategy to keep the spigots open through this price collapse to protect their market share. After Fink's grand slam at Dr Pepper, we know he's got the swagger of a rainmaker that makes it happen and won't mince words with the Saudis. Plus, he's an old Middle East hand who knows what's what over there."

CCG's half-ass Lawrence of Arabia, 007 himself, crossed the floor to join them. "Glad you could make it, Brock." Fink's grubby hand extended out from a monogrammed cuff to grab Wharton's. Ice must have been applied to his gums, as the color was a healthy pink. His elongated neck, however, remained and continued to crane toward Wharton. Though it was difficult to prove, the foxes on Fink's tie had been altered, enlarged to be wolves. "Did your wife come?"

"Happy holidays. What about your date, did she stand you up?"

"'Tis the season," Fink said, dropping his hands to his groin at Wharton's kick there. "Let's hope not. You might even know her, she's from Houston." Wharton was laughing at the idea that their social circles had any intersection when Fink yelled, "*Inti jameelah, sadiqati!*"

"*Shukran, habeebi*," a soft female voice behind Wharton said. "Aw, thank you, Mikey."

Whatever blow he had just landed below the belt to Fink, it was the sensation of a metal driver connecting with his teed-up testicles that Wharton experienced at the sight of Leila Berger. The pulsating jealously announced its arrival with all the warning and force of a flash flood.

Tan and with the dark, silky hair of a shampoo advertisement that doubled to market a jeweler's finest pair of circle emeralds that were her eyes, Leila Berger at age thirty was God's proof—in only the way the offspring of a Lebanese heiress and an Austrian count can produce—that perfect symmetry existed. Minus the crescent scar from a childhood dog bite on her right hand, the Houston-born-but-exotic Leila Berger was so much the model of perfection that the mothers in River Oaks like Wharton's own used to teach their sons manners with the preface, "Now imagine that Leila Berger is sitting across the table from you." Her black velvet dress showed off her long legs and, unlike the waitresses, she allowed for a tasteful peek at breasts that actually jiggled with holiday spirit. *The* Leila Berger: ex–homecoming queen/prom queen/head cheerleader/high school girlfriend. Wharton hadn't even been there for her senior year achievements (she was only a freshman when he dated her for five months during his senior year of high school) but had read about them. The *Houston Chronicle* had featured her and her two legendary older sisters, who had also been the homecoming queens of their high school classes, alongside a photo of all three of them in their tiaras under the headline "The Fabulous Berger Girls." Like many of Leila's ex-boyfriends, Wharton digitally stalked her every six months or so, often discovering new photos of her in the glossy society-pictures sections of Houston publications. Wharton hypothesized he was held hostage by these masturbatory photos more so than her other ex-boyfriends. It was his belief that he was probably the only ex foolish enough to ever hold the post of class liaison to the guilt-tripping Christian Young Life adult leaders, who had a degree of access out of a molester's wet dream to their high school to prolong the virginity of easily influenced Christian youths who became bitterly regretful haters. Especially those who were morally stranded in scoring position between second and third base in the aftermath of that initially lustful squeeze of a creamy colossal Leila Berger boob more fit for an ape's wider palm.

"Hello, Brock, it's been some time."

"Leila, but how do you know . . ." Fink turned his body slightly toward Nathan more—and Leila followed suit—as Fink had attached his arm to rudder the beautiful backside of Leila Berger. Not just Wharton's insipid penis, but Wharton himself, beheld Fink and Leila Berger with the wonder of a baby tossed in the surf. The savage must have ascertained that nothing was ephemeral about his glory, having raided Wharton's work and wardrobe to ride off with the biggest crush of his life. The totality of this raw daring pushed to recast Wharton's very existence as a rejection, a captive of the immensity of all that he did not know about life. What could his Leila Berger, his once-and-true Leila, feel toward Mike Fink? What was Wharton failing to understand about the wider world Fink had kicked him into? Time, yes. Fink rode its turns with all the leaning mastery of a veteran jockey. For a moment unto himself in the segregation Fink was so adept at creating, a proud Wharton prepared himself to offer his shriveled sword and signature as part of the unconditional surrender.

Until gold jingle bells—sewn onto an intentionally ugly red Christmas sweater with a pattern of brown reindeer dancing under a disco ball—rattled as Phillips-Goydan skipped across the floor in skinny jeans. Wharton wanted to trip CCG's own court jester and kick his heinous sweater down his throat, but energy needed to be conserved for the fight against the A-game of Fink. "*Ahlan wa Sahlan!*" Phillips-Goydan greeted her in a welcoming shriek. He kissed Leila on each of her cheeks and asked her and Fink, "When are you two lovebirds going to teach me more Arabic? It pleases me to no end that I introduced you two." Were it not for the fact that he might be charged with a hate crime due to Phillips-Goydan's closeted homosexuality, Wharton believed he now had sufficient legal authority to ignite Phillips-Goydan's flammable sweater.

"The greatest consultants speak the same language as their clients," Fink reminded the boys and girls and half-halfs like Phillips-Goydan listening. "Leila, this is Nathan Ellison."

"Pleased to finally meet you, after hearing so much about you from PPG," Leila said, sticking out her right hand for Nathan, who started to speak but was too busy breathing through his mouth like a fish dropped into a new aquarium. He rotated her hand around from a handshake to kiss the top where the sunken skin traversed the hand. It had been Wharton who had taught her not to shrink from the scar she liked to hide in her jeans pocket, educating her that every supermodel had a famous imperfection. "The free hours that CCG has been able to give our nonprofit over the last two months has made such a difference at this crucial moment in history. I have emailed my other friends in the nonprofit world who are also directors about what an amazing experience it has been working with CCG." Wharton vowed never to turn down another pro bono social impact engagement until Seymour had first shown him a picture of the director.

"And I believe you know Brock Wharton," Fink said, smiling at Wharton.

"We've known each other since high school. We even dated in high school." Wharton felt his dick trying to do a curl to his heart. Where was K.K.?

Fink's eyebrows danced and he reared his head back like he hadn't expected this lighter fluid to flare up the lit logs of the bonfire he had constructed for his lampoon of Wharton. "*Dinya saghirah.* Arabic for 'small world,' should you ever wish to learn, Wharton."

Bells jingled as Phillips-Goydan, in jester costume, reached out and grabbed Leila by the arm. "Gentlemen, excuse us for a moment, but I need to borrow Leila and Nathan for a second. I want her to update the seniors in person about how impactful our pro bono consulting has been for the Iraqi Refugee Project Now. I don't need to tell Mike this, but there is an urgency to help the Iraqi interpreters who worked with the U.S. and the others who are in life-and-death situations in the face of the Islamic State's advances. It doesn't matter how you feel about the Iraq War, which I was personally against, because this Middle East refugee crisis is a human rights issue."

Phillips-Goydan's involvement aside (he had been eleven years old and probably still wetting his bed when he apparently was not out protesting the invasion), here was a charity to never donate to. Not that Wharton had any fondness for any of the charities in town that did not bring with them social benefits. But this charity had as its spokesperson Leila Berger, who was not Iraqi but half Lebanese—and even then about as half Lebanese as his hairy asshole—and Fink, whose specialty was not helping people in danger but rather endangering people. With these three doing the saving it would be a full-on genocide of Iraqis. Wharton shook his head as Phillips-Goydan led

Nathan and Leila away, horror-struck not so much by the information that a lot more Iraqis were going to die but with the sickening feeling that a charitable donation to the opposing side of Fink in this circumstance would more than likely land Wharton on the terrorist watch list.

Wharton could not bear to picture how Leila probably lived in a renovated 1930s pastel bungalow in Montrose and took weighty walks at dusk, a life of happiness off the treadmill of outperforming. Another life entirely. But Fink was eager to help him fill in the rest of the canvas, reflecting, "Breathtaking, isn't she? For my birthday last week, she wore this matching sea green outfit, if you know what I mean. It's like I'm coloring again with all my favorite crayons. Best yet, that little minx has a real gift for narrative."

"You might be a good saboteur, but try faking the rest."

"I rather delight in this developing awareness of yours to the change that is all around. In this new paradigm shift, do you have the bandwidth to be a guru of white-space opportunity? The obsolete ways and models of the past are being replaced by more effective designs to change the flow. What us consultants might term a 'value migration' is sweeping the land in this epoch of change management. Do your core competencies exceed the new hurdle rate as set by the leaders of our generation? Can you communicate in this new language of awareness that you could get by without in the old world?"

"Erase a few slides of a presentation and you think it's your company? I've earned it."

Fink took some time to mull over this analysis, exaggerating a turn toward a graver approach to their feud. "You need a framework. A Balanced Scorecard that translates your vision of taking yourself very seriously into a set of performance indicators. But beware of scope creep if you engage in guerrilla warfare. This blank slide is not a game of convergence with four quarters, out-of-bounds lines, and a referee to blow the whistle once you start. If it were a game, a quick back-of-the-envelope calculation shows I'm winning." Fink's eyes never strayed from his during the taunt in Consultingese. "Let me play this back. You, in reality, thought I would lose to some soft overbred scrub like you whose weight I carried over there when I was the one staking it all? Boy, you're mistaken in thinking I want a country club seat at the table of robber baron self-satisfaction. Upon coming home from that goat-fuck overseas my platform was this crisp: Leave No Douchebag Standing. So it is that I intend to close the loop by winning while concurrently instructing you in all the lessons your scion father never taught you about life and death, all at the chargeable CCG premium."

Wharton stepped back. "Why me?" he asked the sociopath, confused as to why Fink hated him—even if he were a douchebag. All his father had ever done was berate him. There was the hateful moment when his father caught him skipping football practice in junior high to read the novel *Of Mice and Men* in the library, pronouncing that there were only Three Types of People Who Read: "fat people, gay people, and nerds," none of which Wharton believed he was. *How am I supposed to be top of my class if I'm not reading as many books as I can?* And how did his father exempt his own reading of Winston Churchill biographies from this cataloging? But the old man never lost his withering arguments. How was Wharton supposed to debate with someone like Fink whose declared mission was to destroy him, who was actively gunning for him? He would have been lucky to only have had defensive linemen out for him on this muddy field.

Fink thought about Wharton's question for a moment. "When you want to end tyranny, you chop off the head of the snake." Then, diffidently, as if they were like-minded friends and he could trust his target Wharton and bare the part of his soul he had not bartered to the devil: "Don't you want to do the same in the Great Game of Life?"

He was the head of the snake? Wharton did not have an answer but rather questions: *How am I going to stay sane battling this nut? Is it even worth it?* "I don't believe I've been properly introduced," K.K. said, walking up and handing a champagne glass to Wharton. "K.K."

"The esteemed Miss Longhorn of legend who let loose a thousand keelboats in pursuit. My good friend, Kenneth Klay, never stops talking about his favorite cousin K2. Mike Fink."

"And Brock never stops talking about you either." K.K. blushed.

"Did you two meet when he was the quarterback? Quarterbacks. I for one never did understand how a heterosexual man can put his hands down in another man's crotch. Unless, of course, his friend had been shot and he had to plug a femoral artery bleed."

"When I was a 1-L at UT Law and he had just earned the captain's position on the team."

"I admire earning it. Nothing's worse, Brock, than one of those legacy deals where one horse-trades all around town off their family's fortune." Was that what Fink thought he'd trafficked in to arrive where he was? His wife's affluence was more like a restrictive horse collar, Wharton never receiving his fair due for achievements from naysayers who linked any success he had to his in-laws' fortune that he could not outrun. "K.K., can I get you anything to drink?" K.K. waved off Fink's offer by tapping her pregnant belly. "Dr Pepper?"

"We're calling it a night," Wharton said. "Enjoy New Year's in Saudi Arabia."

"Ain't it a shame I won't be there long to savor the shifting sands of Arabia?" Fink asked in a voice laced with an undercurrent of teasing that whirled Wharton back around. "The good news is CCG wants me to vet the summer internship interviewees with you to reel in a few."

Outside, at his wife's insistence, Wharton fished in his wallet for a few dollars to tip the valet and further contribute to the valet racket he was sure Fink was running. "I should run my own business."

"Wouldn't you want some leadership experience first, babe? What's your business idea?"

"I don't have one. But you don't need one. I have some leadership experience."

"Well, you need an idea."

"You don't have to have an idea. There are no rules. There are risks."

"Without an idea you cannot have a company."

"I could buy a company. Run it. We have access to the money. And I've invested my earnings wisely. We could move into a smaller home. One overlooking the bayou."

"The bayou floods."

"Part of the adventure. We don't need our giant home even if we have kids."

"If? We're already having kids! Run a business? This is the first I've ever heard of this. Why would you want to leave CCG if you're still the star? You're at your best when you are finishing ahead of your colleagues. Banking, business school, consulting. Not leaving the team behind and striking out alone and doing your own thing. How would you measure yourself then? Against other entrepreneurs you don't even know? You would go crazy."

Wharton hated to think he had anything in common with Fink. Though he was beginning to feel like he needed to wise up and stake something if he was going to keep his head as the snake.

• • •

With work emails sent and Wharton forever done with Leila Berger Internet searches, the plane's wireless connection was of little value to him when the only news was about the chaos in Afghanistan. Were there days when there were not attacks, political chaos, earthquakes, corruption, and starving people in Afghanistan? Oil was at forty-six dollars a barrel in the third week of January and falling faster daily than the energy companies could lay people off. Nor did Wharton understand how Afghanistan was still making the headlines in the new year, when America had ended the war in December. Now it was Syria, Yemen, Libya, West to East Africa (nor did the Horn of Africa and North Africa wish to be left out), and Iraq *again* (was there now a strategy for Iraq this time?). For the first time in his life, he had checked the terror alert level, only to find out that the color-coded Homeland Security system had been replaced. The world would go on, as it always had, if the Whartons kept their vigil at the helm, with rationalism, not extremism, steering the course.

He twisted the knob above his head for full air and the gushing sound it produced to drown out the heavy dragon breathing of the sleeping terrorist next to him. Wharton nudged Fink's drooping head and greasy mane off the shared armrest area a sleeping Fink had hijacked between their spacious first-class seats, reaching over to close the window cover Fink had left open. At least the pestilent Fink was not still chattering about his engagement with the Saudis of the past four weeks, though his soldier's facility for immediately falling asleep anywhere did not help a sleepless Wharton moderate his envy.

Only forty-six thousand frequent flier miles until Wharton entered the gates of the One Million Club. All miles logged in just five years of consulting, the insides of most airports and planes being as familiar to Wharton as his college football playbook had once been. He invariably knew them better than the cities he traveled to. Every Sunday or Monday and every Thursday or Friday, he shuttled through the hurdle of airport security to and from an onsite consulting engagement. At first he had enjoyed the glamour of traveling, a life on the run in suits and expensive hotels with a high per diem. But lately Wharton had grown hungrier for the day when he would be the managing director in charge of bringing in clients and not out on the road consulting, always in some place other than his beloved Houston kingdom, bending over his laptop in an airport after searching anxiously for a reliable electrical outlet to plug into for a hurried hour of work. Consulting hours were night and day from those in energy. The balanced hours on the clock of work were one thing you just could not beat about the family-oriented energy industry, an industry by its nature opposed to young Brock Wharton's own goal after college of limiting time spent around his family. And any offer to work under or alongside his father in their own family energy business had not even received a hearing from Wharton, who wanted these advantages in life even less than more mentorship from his father.

Fink slept until the wheels of the plane touched down in Boston. During the taxi ride to Cambridge, Wharton did not exchange a word with the driver, who was obscured by a giant yellow "Don't Tread on Me" sticker of a rattlesnake on the glass between the Colonial cabbie and where Wharton sat behind him. A rested Fink conversed with the equally loud driver about health care premiums and the history of the area. Happy to have Fink distracted by a working-class compadre and his version of the local rebellion igniting the American Revolution, Wharton gazed out of the cab window at the familiar snow-covered sights of the region, occasionally drifting back to the triangular-headed snake in front of him.

The taxi dropped them off near the main quad for their march. Wharton led as they crossed the bridge over the Charles River to the tallest redbrick and white pillar building, the soft insect crunch of melting snow under their black shoes. Good old true HBS, or as anyone who was anyone in the business world would leave unspoken: the Great Filter. Where the country separated its studs from its scrubs in its admissions office, a process that transpired long before an application ever came over the transom with official university emissaries like Brock Wharton serving as unofficial gatekeepers. Only an amateur networker relied on authorized channels at HBS. The degree was the essence of time management. One entered here in the first-year fall and left in the second-year spring with a spooned seat in a business world catapult for the rest of his life. Though its business adherents would have been even more plentiful in the world of investment banking or private equity, the sacred text of CCG partners could have been called *The Book of CCG: An Account of Unshakeable Faith in HBS to Nurture Business*.

"They say there's some talent in here," Fink said on the last of the icy stone steps.

"The best," Wharton responded a little more passionately than he meant to as he slid out of the cold and into another America. The light that lingered on reverential objects stamped Wharton every time upon entrance. "It's my alma mater."

"I wish I had gone to another college. You ever wish you had gone elsewhere?"

The question surprised Wharton. Could it really be the first time the question had been put to him? His father, who had chosen UT for him, had never asked. Perhaps a heartfelt, honest answer was something Fink could respect, as he had to have been ordered on his share of forced marches while in the military. "I can't say this to any of my friends, but what I wouldn't give to have transferred. The best day of my UT playing career was the day it ended and I stopped getting criticized by people who couldn't even throw a football. I laughed at the offer then, but I should have gone to Rice. Received a better education, hung out with nonjocks. Anything I would have done on the field would have been a bonus and far more appreciated. I could've been a hometown legend."

"Rice, huh? Something about underdogs in life. You can't quantify grit."

After an exchange of new brochures with the Career Management Center personnel, a staff member showed them to a room on the second floor that they could use. A large, square white table was in the middle of the damp and poorly lit room. Because of the overcast day outside, the single window failed to produce enough illumination to aid the electric light above the table. Wharton did not remember the room from his time at school, when he and his classmates occupied every room in the building at some point for their team projects. He rearranged the seating so one of the chairs faced their two chairs across the table and sat down next to Fink.

"How was Wallymart?" Fink asked, after sketching a picture of two crawfish wrestling with claws locked on the cover of the HBS brochure. "That looked like a pretty cool engagement. My father sent me an interesting article once about how Wallymart founder Wally Bailey lived in the same one-story house even after he was worth billions."

Wharton was unsure of Fink's agenda with this inquiry. A schema of his mind had yet to present itself to Wharton. Friendship could be ruled out as a possibility. The little that he did know about Wally Bailey of Wallymart was that while the business visionary was alive he had gouged his non-union employees and his demographic of lower-class customers—along the way burying so many mom-and-pop businesses across Main Street America that he probably could not afford to move out of his one-story home and chance the corpses that would be discovered there by the new homeowner. At least in China, where Wallymart was considering expansion, they were used to disposing of their dead in backyards. "Fine."

Fink stopped drawing and beheld Wharton with a wounded look. After a while Fink grunted, breaking the silence that had ruled after Wharton's refusal of small talk. He contemplated offering up one of Fink's celebrity apologies: not really apologizing so much as apologizing if he had offended anyone. Fink broke the new awkwardness that had followed his grunt to ask, "Where are the students? Do I need to go out and gator-rope us our first applicant? I came here to see what a *master* of business administration candidate walks and talks like."

For almost four hundred years the institution of Harvard had kept the barbarians, to include alligator-ropers, outside the walls. Wharton assumed his place on the wall and spoke to Fink: "Know that our actions here will get back to not just the CCG Texas office but also CCG headquarters. This is our company's primary recruiting ground."

"Hence why CCG is ineffectual. And we're a company that advertises intellectual uniqueness. So shouldn't the Hemingway gene trump the Harvard gene? I know I'm biased, but a more diverse recruiting pool would be combat veterans. Extend them jobs. A real *thank you for your service*, and one that actually adds to CCG's arsenal of attack weapons by utilizing their varied experiences. Everyone wins. Still recruit from HBS, but bet on a vet some of the time."

"The few veterans in my business school class had on average a GMAT score seventy points lower than the nonveteran students. This is indisputable."

"Look at me." Wharton refused to. "Oh, don't you see? Any test that you take on a computer can't test that much."

"Does that make any sense? We live in a world of computers where every workday is a test on a computer. If they weren't veterans, they probably wouldn't have even been asked to interview at a Top 25 business school."

"That weekly Princeton Review GMAT prep class you enrolled in is a tough commute from Kandahar. And amazingly, improving their GMAT scores wasn't the top priority of the soldiers I knew who were getting shot at over there. Level the playing field some for the nonhomogenous. As Gertrude Stein said to Ernest Hemingway in her Paris salon of the world's most innovative minds, 'Talent is talent is talent is talent.'"

"Use your influence to bet on a vet, then. I use my influence as the leading donor from my class—"

"I stand corrected." Fink passed the open brochure over to Wharton. "Your family's money, or your wife's family's money?"

Beaming at Wharton on the first page in a halo-like glow of backlighting superimposed on a gold trident was a photo of an ex–Navy SEAL student who was president and co-founder of the Veterans in Business Association. On behalf of the HBS veterans, he thanked the generous donors of Wharton's class for endowing the most generous military scholars program in the country, along with a series of annual veteran speaking events that had resulted in attracting the highest number of veteran applications in school history.

"You should keep leading the way with your influence to fund this great cause. Jimmy's a great dude. He's an old Quiet Professional buddy from my SOCOM days. You'd like him."

Ten minutes elapsed with not a word passed between the Quiet Professional and the Quiet Hater, who plotted to retract his large scholarship donations and have the director of development fired. Already an army of would-be Finks trained in Wharton's halls. Next to him, Fink tilted his pen at a lower angle and shaded his drawing. Wharton noticed that a third larger crawfish helmed the plow rudder of a keelboat manned on each side by four smaller crawfish with long wooden poles. The boat in the drawing barreled downriver head-on toward the wrestling crawfish. The entry into the room of a student candidate halted Fink's sketch and Wharton's window into the mind of his combative colleague.

"Hi," said the trim student in a black suit and silver power tie. His straight black hair was parted an inch off the middle and worn just long enough to fall on the sides like a movie star's. "Is this the room for the Cambridge Consulting Group summer internship interview? The directions I received in the CMC weren't smartphone compatible. I'm J. Michael Ziedman."

"It is. I'm Brock Wharton and this is Mike Fink." Fink shook hands with Ziedman. "How many more interviewing applicants for CCG were waiting in the CMC?"

"Did Diana not ping you? The other three accepted offers from start-ups this week and withdrew. This app economy is blowing up." To break the ice, Ziedman fist-bumped an imaginary fist and then blew open his closed fist. Wharton thought he could see Fink mentally note the explosion behind his own exploding sapphire eyes. "I'm the only one."

"Please sit down. I'm thrilled we'll have extra time to get more acquainted. Why CCG?"

Fink was quiet throughout it all. Ziedman was not. He was from Kings Point on the North Shore of Long Island, smart, short, and tanned bronze. He had checked all the right educational and professional boxes, memorized the consulting practice books, and liked to talk about himself, particularly about being told he looked like a Brazilian Richard Gere when he worked in Brazil for a year. When he brought it up a second time, Wharton thought that Ziedman might have Gere's nose but could never pass for a Brazilian.

What Ziedman lacked in awareness he more than compensated for in intelligence, providing a virtuoso analysis of the Swanberry case. In every way that Fink had failed to do during his interview, Ziedman laid out the pros and the cons of investing in the new technology before arguing against investment, advocating for a new short-term strategy that would boost profits and proposing a reevaluation after a year of a new go-forward strategy incorporating factory retrofits and automation to cut long-term costs. Wharton looked over and chastised a silent Fink with a noting finger after each point hit by Ziedman. J. Michael Ziedman would not have been who Wharton would have picked to embody Harvard, but he was nonetheless a fine credit to the quality of America's oldest and most selective institution of higher learning. The first peep from Fink came after the conclusion of the case and was not verbalized. It was on the evaluation form he passed to Wharton. Wharton looked at the handwritten declaration in the left margin of the otherwise blank evaluation form: THIS KID WILL CRACK WHEN THE BULLETS START TO FLY.

Wharton printed with his fountain pen YOU ARE WRONG. Fink rose abruptly and mule-kicked his chair into the wall behind him, startling Ziedman but not Wharton. The mission had fallen on him and Ziedman to debunk the great myth of Fink: that a pair of balls was *not* in fact the ace of spades over talent in America.

"Do you even want to be a consultant? I might not have one of 'em two-hundred-thousand-dollar MBAs, but I've been downrange in the suck!" Fink yelled across the table at Ziedman. "You think CCG gives a rat's ass about your leadership as president of your fraternity or that you *served* a year in the White House as a deputy associate in Homeland Development?"

Wharton believed this outcry hypocritical by the one who listed "high school senior class president" on his résumé but nevertheless admired Fink's opening salvo to rattle Ziedman and prove his point. There was a bizarre nobility in Fink's deep care for those who had served that conflated any issue not related to veterans with a test of his commitment to fight for underrepresented veterans. Fine. As a consequence he could try all he wanted to not reward Ziedman for his superior résumé, but how could he punish him for it? At any rate the science of reasoning was not behind Fink's "logic," but if there had been a flimsy rationale to it, then this same illogical thread would have Ziedman as Wharton's underdog.

Fink continued to direct his rant at Ziedman. "Or that you're prancing around as a social entrepreneur and pitching executives at top companies about this charity organization that you founded and will just as surely let die the moment you resume working full-time? Hell, I can see it makes you feel good about yourself and allows you to feel self-important. Raising awareness about raising awareness to organize your community connections with Daddy's funding."

"I only cited those because you asked for examples demonstrating leadership ability."

Fink wheeled around to Wharton and asked, "Is that what they teach you at Harvard to cite for *leadership*?" Harvard could hardly be alone among universities in not testing Fink's Law: the value of leadership is proportional to the square of the number of bullets flying.

Wharton was nobody's fool on the study of leadership. "They are fine examples of leadership experience." Wharton stood up to physically demonstrate for Ziedman his task, not that this was even about Ziedman. Jesus, Ziedman, serve a cause beyond yourself! "What would not be a fine example of leadership ability would be to back down from your original statements because of Mr. Fink's outrage. To waver, or shall we say *crack*, under an assault. Reading your résumé and listening to you today gives me faith that that is not what would happen if we brought you in as a CCG summer intern."

Ziedman looked at the good cop Wharton and mumbled, "You can count on me."

"I ain't convinced, Wharton," Fink said. "I think he likes the idea of being a consultant. A well-paid advisor who gets to walk away from an engagement at its declared end without the burden of any unintended second- and third-order consequences."

"Your bullying and outrageous theatrics have failed you," Wharton said, smiling at Fink's botch in identifying a fourth-order impact. Wharton had to get civilian Ziedman, culpable only of his own douchebag nature, out of this crossfire. "Well done, Ziedman, well done."

"Am I done?" Ziedman asked. Wharton felt a prick to his skin on the collar line at this plea; he noticed that his proxy Ziedman seemed to be avoiding any looks in the direction of Fink, who now circled the table and the sitting Ziedman.

"You're done when you can tell me how you would lead a consulting team after you lose three of your men," Fink informed Ziedman. "And you're taking indirect fire."

Wharton prayed almost audibly for Ziedman to stay calm and let his business school leadership training take over unconsciously. Muscle memory. *You founded your own nonprofit.* Wharton attempted to reassure him by a stern look across the table. *Steady ho, lad. You are not playing for the conference championship in front of a stadium crowd of eighty thousand fans who want to see you on crutches by the end of the play. Be a CCG man. Be king.*

"Did I also tell you that commo is down, the truck in front of yours is charred and flipped on its side, and your best friend in the seat next to you has no fucking legs?" Fink came around the table and shouted next to Ziedman's ear, "We're waiting! We're fucking waiting and dying while we wait for you to do something! Say something, Ziedman. I'm sorry if my language is a bit rough on your manicured ears, but people are fucking dying because you aren't fucking leading. Consultation, please! What are you fucking doing, Richard Gere?"

"I don't know! I got nothing . . . I haven't been in a situation like that before."

Neither an officer nor a gentleman, Fink kicked the leg of the table supporting Ziedman's elbows. The table and Ziedman shuddered.

"Of course a taker like you hasn't been in a situation like *that* before. Yet you want to lead and be part of the self-licking ice-cream cone of consulting? Take, take, take. I must be crazy to have expected you to have actually served and done your part for your country. Congratulations, Ziedman, you just got your whole team killed. Quick sniff test indicates your quarter-of-a-million-dollar MBA is fucking worthless because your whole team is dead."

"Consulting team?" Ziedman asked meekly.

"Yes, your consulting team. And your excuse of," Fink said, now pretending to break down crying like a baby, "'I haven't been in a situation like that before.' Guess what, genius? No one has ever been in a situation like that until it happens! You want us to entrust you in some foreign country with a consulting operation with none of us there to oversee you? You can't even hypothetically lead in the case I gave you. Go back to the womb of your congenial Harvard classroom and prance around like a special snowflake and let your mommy and daddy think of you as the Good Son."

Ziedman cried, "You don't—"

"You don't think I know you?" Fink interrupted to finish the thought. "Where you come from, how the Ziedmans pampered you, what fires you weren't forged in?"

"He led peerlessly during the case portion," Wharton said, seizing the opening that Fink had not technically run Ziedman out of the room. "And when under pressure with situational questioning, you never quit, Ziedman. That, more than anything, is the sort of talent we are looking for in a CCG consultant." *It's all a test, Ziedman.* Wharton waited for Ziedman's eyes to search for hope.

Gradually, Ziedman looked up childlike at Wharton across the table for affirmation of the mental toughness fully pilloried by the demons of Fink and shown to be nonexistent under scrutiny. Wharton held his gaze to buoy Ziedman and convince him they were in this together, two lads interested in consulting, on the other side of the inner war Fink fought with himself. There was no overvaluing of Harvard privilege in the great race of time, Wharton wanted to explain to Ziedman. But before they could cross the finish line, Fink's leathery head came between them.

"Speak for yourself," Fink said, examining Ziedman's face a foot away. "I'm looking straight into the silver-spoon soul of weak genes here and I see a whole lot of quit."

Later, thirty thousand feet up in the air on the flight back to Houston, Wharton thought of Ziedman's tearful exit. It was not the defeat suffered from Ziedman's unmanly retreat that lingered in his mind, another notch for Fink. What occurred to Wharton was that he had not completed his due diligence on the case of Fink, to whom Ziedman had directed his exiting cry, "Self-hating Jew!"

5.

COUNTERTERRORISM

Wharton's right foot narrowly landed to the side of the crater, avoiding a twisted ankle as he crouched into an air squat before he dropped down to do a push-up. Designed to represent the Moon's Sea of Tranquility and its cratered lunar surface where man first landed, Tranquillity Park in downtown Houston was built during the previous big oil boom. Born of the swagger of that era (including the deliberately imperialistic misspelling of its name with a double *l* to mirror the Apollo 11 mission), the modern park was a two-block-long space of treacherous steel craters, phallic pillars, concrete Native American burial mounds, algae-infested waterfalls, and the occasional lost tourist. It held the distinction of being the park with the highest bum-per-square-foot rating in the city, according to a joint study tracking homeless people's effect on business as conducted by the City of Houston's Performance Improvement Division and Rice Business School. But consultants Brock Wharton and Mitch Piazza were agents of change, taking one small step for mankind by relocating their Consulting Bowl training session to the park.

"Only four more sets," Piazza yelled from the steps he was running up and down. He had cut their workout down from twelve circuits to ten because of the NED Talk conference.

Wharton did not reply. His concentration alternated between his right rotator cuff pain from the kettlebell swings one minute and investigating Fink's background the next. The rumblings from his stomach complicated the dizziness from his back-and-forth swapping of focus, and he scolded himself for drinking coffee beforehand. Wharton pushed on, though, for in a few more months he would be a father to a little girl and would long for times like this, when he had all morning to induce vomiting through a workout. Secretly he hoped a daughter would bring about a sea change in this sort of masculine mentality, surely a holdover from his father's parenting. Maybe an alternative way to raise his own children, daughters or sons, would be to not heap expectations of being the best on the kids.

Down the stairs to an entrance that led to the tunnels, a catatonic Father Time variant of a homeless man lay wiped out. If performing due diligence on Fink uncovered a true great-great-great-great-grandfather, here he probably was, another wilted leaf on the scrub oak of family trees. Poor Fink probably had a father nearly as awful as Wharton's, in his own way, if presumably that was from whom he had inherited his boisterous machismo. The man's unruly and uncut white beard would grow until tickled by that final guttural TB-breath. Wharton incorporated stepping around both the puddle of urine and the empty whiskey bottle into his plyometric workout as he ran up and down the stairs. Wharton's penultimate set of stairs roused the pale man, who shrieked at the huffing and puffing Wharton springing down the stairs at him.

"Only one set left," a frightened Wharton begged.

But the uninformed homeless man—not having been consulted that the point of the exercise was precisely to get one's heart rate up—vomited violently. The added third obstacle of vomit stopped the workout. A lull in the shrieks allowed each to take in the other moon creature. Wharton searched his pockets for money to bridge this brave new universe he found himself in, wishing that it were as simple as pulling at a tether to end his hallucinatory spacewalk. No money in his pockets, Wharton flashed a Longhorn sign with his right hand to stay the bemused man.

"Did you find what you're looking for?" a faraway call by Piazza transmitted from somewhere up above and across the lunar landscape and scrambled through the homeless man's sneezing fit. The horn of an early-morning freight train in the distance washed over them, and Wharton turned away and ran up the stairs to street level.

After he had showered and was safely ensconced in Piazza's office, territory of the near enemy, Wharton gathered the most recent information on rumored engagements before attacking the root of all his nightmares: "What's the name of that private investigator you used?"

Wharton chanced another future betrayal by his closest CCG friend, disclosing to Piazza the ending clue from yesterday's HBS incident and the further suspicion it cast on Fink's story. Idea Man let a moment pass first, as if he were leaving Wharton alone to stew in his own paranoid ideas. Then he dug through his desk drawers until he found the private investigator's card. There, in his moment of defenselessness that even Piazza must have been conscious of, Wharton's friend refused to sandbag him. "Thank you," Wharton said as he pocketed the card, the closest to a treaty that they had ever brokered in their own competition. He stood up to rotate his right arm in small circles.

"You should really get that arm checked out. We need you for the Consulting Bowl."

Consulting Bowl X: CCG vs. McKinsey. The Consulting Bowl was an annual forum to demonstrate Wharton's unmatched athletic prowess in the world of consulting, where such ability by a man in his thirties counted for more than it would have in most other respected professions. Wharton maximized the points racked up with his annual dominating bowl performances by both feigning an obliviousness of his talent and denying the training he did for months preceding the game. All in a sport he had never cared that much for.

He mimed a football pass to Piazza and exited. In Seymour's office, Wharton walked in on his boss twisting around to no music. "Signed a small engagement with Phoenix Energy." The dinosaur's suspenders were of a gaudier red than the dye job in his limited hair.

The whole shale boom of the last several years had been one big value-creation event that lifted all ships on its rising tide. The bust would see most of the parasitic rats jumping ship incinerated by the dry powder private equity money on the sidelines waiting to acquire at the bottom. There were many theories of how and why it had happened, and what was still to happen. Perhaps the strangest theory was the one beginning to percolate through the conspiratorial mind of Wharton: that the trading price of oil paralleled Wharton's freefall. Over the course of his whole life he had believed himself apart from oil, the traditional lifeblood of Houston, which had enabled his talent to win life's races with the time to beat. Then along came Fink, who had tied Wharton to oil as if self-ordained to upend the claim of Secretary Topper Musgrave II: "Oil is a commodity you own, not something that defines you." It was not conceivable that the life of fast-tracker Brock Wharton could mirror a commodity. If Wharton could be bought and sold in the marketplace, he was expendable, no better than cannon fodder, a common foot soldier tied to the unfeeling chaotic universe. With Fink out there claiming to be representative of the zeitgeist, time had come to champion whatever would once again make Wharton champion of Houston. "What's the project?"

"The majors want to be like the wildcatters."

"That idea had sex appeal when oil was worth twice as much and it was okay to be overleveraged in high-cost acreage. I want to talk to . . . I want it."

"Look, Brock, I'm sure everyone will want to be on this project since it's brief and here in Houston. You know the process, go talk to Katie and pitch her on capability, interest, and why you would be a good fit for being staffed on the project."

"Spare me the 'black box' nonsense. I already had Dr Pepper stolen from me, and rumor has it that the new strategy there isn't going so smoothly. You need your top performer for this."

"I agree with you. We need the best person suited for this. Case in point, Fink has a bio perfect for this assignment." Give Wharton's private investigator a week and they would see how suited Fink's "bio" was for anything. "You've done a great job mentoring him."

Wharton stared at Seymour, who tried to escape eye contact. "I need this."

"Well, I need not explain to you that we eat our own here. At the moment I'm more curious to see what summit this new generation of leaders like Fink will take CCG to."

"We're the same generation! I will guarantee an enablement project."

"Guaranteeing an enablement? Bold, even for you." Seymour fondled his suspenders with his thumbs. "All right. Make CCG proud—but the expectation is an enablement."

• • •

"The data shows that women, *women*, just do not swing away. How can our daughters smash the glass ceiling if they don't swing away? We have to get women to swing away. And the only way we can do that is by having the courage to start rejecting society's labels. Don't judge us when we courageously lean forward, when we have the courage to swing away."

Of the large CCG group in attendance, only an aghast Fink, who thrashed about more than Wharton at the Silicon Valley tech executive's rapacious invoking of valor for her summons, also displayed signs of revulsion. The rest of the NED Talk conference audience gathered in the downtown Hobby Center for the Performing Arts dreamed the impossible dream, as they had all morning, NED Talk thought leader after thought leader passionately spouting change through the thin silver claw of their headset microphones. All of which was inflicted upon a persecuted Wharton (under the auspices of CCG professional development) from his perch onstage. Up onstage he sat in a section of twenty chairs that were set behind the speaker and to the right of the radioactive glare from the football-stadium-sized video screen. Each time Wharton looked at the screen, it changed hues like an acid-rock concert projection. Wharton had protested his seating with the NED Talk director but was curtly rebuffed: "Often NED likes to experiment with stage design, because NED is like all the curious souls here, mixing it up to most effectively engage." Wharton had nothing against smugness and superiority. But in the name of saving the world,

Wharton found it positively distasteful. Onstage, the rest of his colleagues became strangers to him no different from Fink in this new-age professional development. Where there should have been rioting there was swooning worship.

"Men, have the courage to stay at home and support your wives' careers! Yes, I said it. I went there. Did that one hit? Swing away! It is tragic, truly tragic, that men are viewed as weak when they exhibit the courage to play mommy—but this is exactly what online data collected from BaboonPolls tells us." The female executive pounded on, Wharton having tuned out the usual statistics she raised about the percentage of women who failed to make CEO (she was only a COO) and negotiate their initial job salary. He hated to consider how much of a speaking fee she had negotiated from the have-the-courage-to-be-vulnerable NED (Necessary Enlightenment Delivered) to molest to life this dead mare of women's suffrage (at a confounding seven thousand dollars per person to attend the NED Talk conference, her commission was probably enough to fund a few new chapters of her Swing Away cult). Time, Wharton felt with NED-like conviction, would prove him prophetic in leading his generation away from fascination toward bafflement and hopefully loathing for anything NED-like. Until they were ready to listen to their Hating Moses, Wharton understood he would have to suffer this opening trial of persecution stoically. For he still had his parents' anniversary dinner later, its own succession of challenges borrowed from the Old Testament to test forbearance on a biblical scale.

A few seats over from Wharton, an audience member in the front row dropped a cell phone. Katie Kidder. Had she been attempting to discreetly text to avoid participating in this regressive professional development? Wharton hoped so, moving to help her pick up the separated pieces when no one else stirred. "*Really?*" the female COO asked, prior to flashing a smile to show she had pardoned her fellow sister and given the audience permission to laugh. Not even a smartphone shattering would prevent the promiscuous flow of inspiring NED ideas from spreading like a venereal disease. "I'm guilty too. Not that long ago, I was asked to speak at Harvard's commencement. Yet there I was at an exclusive party hosted by the president when I found myself all over the leaders—both men—of the top two private equity shops in America, rather than conversing with the women in the room—which I obviously care about strongly—when something embarrassing, but I think important, dawned on me, 'Wow.'" At this point even Wharton was guilty of leaning forward. His anticipation diverged from the rest of the audience, unless their prayers had been for a wrecking ball to swing toward the female COO and lay bare her vainglory hidden beneath the veneer of confessional social media idiocy that had launched her into the realm of male leadership. "Wouldn't it be nice to live in a world where half of the CEOs of the best private equity shops were women? I have a six-year-old son. And I have a brilliant and creative two-year-old daughter." She paused, both to accommodate the eager audience with an opportunity to applaud and to signal to Wharton that his abhorrence could be boundless. "It is my favorite thing in the world to take pictures with my daughter and post them on social media. God, how I wish I could post a picture or a chart that explained to her that she has the same shot as her brother at becoming the CEO of the other top PE shop. Swing away!" The COO left him to think of his own impending fatherhood to a little girl and how he would refrain from ever trading on his future daughter for extra credit in life, even if Satan could guarantee Wharton that a NED Talk would never find another working microphone again.

Dressed in what could only be categorized (if NED permitted categorization) as skateboard formal, the NED Talk director, who Wharton avowed was Phillips-Goydan's older brother, skipped onstage. "She really unpacks it, doesn't she? The accessibility of new ideas to fuel the possibility of change is what NED caters to. Speaking of which, NED doesn't believe in a world of catering unsustainable, poor-tasting food."

Sustainable or unsustainable, the lunch was an epicure's delight. Houston's rich and famous encountered a diversity of rich people from all over the world over a selection of catered food from Houston's four most modern American fare restaurants. "What is genius?" Phillips-Goydan posed the question to a tech hipster CFO from London.

"There's new research," Seymour informed a renewable energy CIO from Portland. "We have to transcend government to create an uncorrupted business world devoid of society," a utopian venture capitalist from Silicon Valley, who had made his fortune because of regulations, proselytized to Nathan. Piazza was on the jock of an ex–NBA player from Indiana who had started a nonprofit to bring quality basketball shoes to famine-stricken South Sudan. Wharton ran into a Houston friend whose new entrepreneurial venture he and K.K. enjoyed bragging about after a few drinks when impressing dinner party guests: "Let's just say we invested a not-insignificant amount of money in his company." But the friend's unadulterated adoration of the talks infused Wharton with all the assurance of a no-confidence vote in his investment. "I've never experienced perception such as this, Brock. I am changing everything about the way I run my life and business."

"Can we continue this conversation in a minute?" Wharton interjected, saving himself from the first-degree murder he was planning in order to recoup his investment. He walked over to a quiet spot in the lobby of the theater to join Katie, who stood alone at a window.

Katie took notice of him before returning her stare to the downtown rail. He was hopeful the espresso fumes from her latte would awaken him from the nightmare of the NED Talk conference. "I was unaware the Metrorail went by here or that the new line goes all the way to East Downtown and through the Museum District. I don't know if it's because of the absurd no-zoning thing, but there can't be another city that changes this fast. Did you walk here?"

"This is Houston. None of these one-earth hypocrites carpooled either. We can't leave our carbon footprints fast enough in bailing. You should first ask for forgiveness from NED for dropping your phone, and also atone for allowing Fink to scare away our HBS intern class. You would think one of these assholes would address ending homelessness. Too real a problem."

"Necessary. Enlightenment. Delivered." In heels she was an inch taller than him. "Kill. Me. Now." She shooed his offer of a phone away with her hand. "I'm mad at you. Screwing up my system just so you can get on the Phoenix engagement. You and Fink are like brothers from another mother. Always scheming. Both in need of constant praise and an audience. I'm glad I wasn't born with a small penis."

"Although I find your comparison appalling, I'm glad someone has finally detected that scheming is what he does in lieu of consulting."

"He should have stuck with acting."

"Acting?"

"CCG's thespian. He tried the theater after the military for six months, but it didn't go anywhere professionally and his then-fiancée, a corporate lawyer no less, explained to him about the danger of having a 'gap' on his résumé." Wharton concealed his desire to text message the private investigator this lead then and there. Katie laughed and took a sip from her coffee. "If you had seen how he begged the partners in Seymour's office to be a part of the HBS recruiting trip for doing the Saudi gig, you would have put him in for an Oscar. Probably more like a Daytime Emmy, but he has some acting talent. Not that I would have staffed him on either assignment had I not been overruled. Does that make little Brock feel better? I spied him talking to the NED director backstage when I tried to find a place to hide, and he was at it acting out something. You two are a lot alike. But I think you're the better actor."

How to explain his upbringing, where the idea of premarital sex was equated to a gateway drug, and the actual act somewhere between crystal meth and heroin on the immorality drug chart. Wharton leaned back slightly as if to take all of Katie in. K.K. too had once called him out on his talent in the theatrical department. Not long after they openly started dating and had been having sex, she had confronted him about the Christian conservative image of a waiting-for-marriage virgin he wore around campus. To reduce her anger at him by way of sympathy, he confessed that his actual virginity had been stolen by an eager sorority girl who had taken advantage of him after a night of drinking. But with her law school training, K.K. had been quick to point out that his dubious claim of rape by a female did not, unlike his erection throughout the act, hold up legally. Without knowing it then, that had pretty much been the curtain call for his sanctimonious-Christian act. Wharton thought it too late in the conversation to compliment the bangs of Katie's new hairdo. She would not care that he always failed to notice alterations in K.K.'s hair. "Why did you drop off from the partner track?"

"Because some of us are in danger of having a 'gap' in life from plugging our résumés."

He thanked her for the intelligence tip. Fink, Fink, Fink. In a bathroom stall, Wharton reviewed the schedule: a novelist on eliminating AIDS in Vietnamese mountain tribes, a neurosurgeon on the future of the Internet, and the closing keynote address by the inequality economist Adam Foote forecasting on the topical "Wealth in the Twenty-Second Century," followed by a cocktail reception of ideas. Only the cocktail reception of ideas left Fink any room for havoc. And not much room for a failed actor. What was Fink thinking? As luck would have it, NED had already wanted to start a dialogue on that very subject, "Seeing It from the Mind of a Terrorist: A Militant Monologist Rages," featuring a magnetic jihadist. Wharton added to its number of views by using his phone to tap on the third-most-watched NED Talk.

He finished the mercifully brief—two qualities usually absent in Wharton's era of post-9/11 terrorists, where they insisted on pedantically reciting the whole Qur'an at you before finally beheading the innocent, in case you had missed the previously posted beheading lecture—video and scanned the headlines. The last forty-eight hours of non-NED news had once again been subjugated by terrorism: a hotel bombing in Jordan, a suicide attack at the capital airport in Pakistan, a siege at a university in Kenya killing over a hundred, and gunmen had killed thirteen tourists in Indonesia. All spectacular attacks designed to attract as much attention as possible.

The cocktail reception of ideas, in his intelligence analysis, provided Fink with a possible platform for publicity—but not if the surprise element of terrorism was stolen by Wharton. At the front line of optimism and innovation, NED implored followers to neither condemn nor condone terrorism, but in the words of one of NED's most beloved heroes, albino Austrian part-time hacker of freedom and charged rapist Julian Assuage, to "allow terrorism and ideas to engage in a safe space." Back in his seat, Wharton weighed ideas of how to neutralize Fink at the cocktail reception during interludes between speeches. Because throughout the actual speeches, the nauseating NED creativity incited a terror experienced by both Wharton and Fink. They competed in an innovative dance-off of the Worm from their onstage chairs backed by the squirming NED rhythms. The NED Talk director ended their dance battle by asking everyone to stand up and stretch before he introduced the final speaker.

The NED Talk director now paced the stage as if he were one of the genius twits advertised. "It is NED's regret to convey that due to inclement weather while flying from the Aspen Great Ideas Festival, Adam Foote will be unable to make it in time." Even the conditioned NED Talk conference reeducation campers failed to repress their disappointment. "However, there is nothing NED is more moved by than conference attendees so motivated by the talks that they want to spread their own ideas to change the world via talk. So if it's all right with you—and it's already all right with NED—do we have any volunteers for our NED Talk stage?"

The hum of NED-style connectivity emanated from Wharton's section. Seymour and Phillips-Goydan were volunteering a not-very-reluctant Fink, who had already risen before the director noticed him. The ceremonious passing of the director's headset microphone, which Fink slapped on like a piece of combat gear, completed Fink's transformation into one of those giant plague insects with a silver appendage in front of its mouth to help feed it fawning crowds.

"My name is Mike Fink, and I'm attending today as a consultant for Cambridge Consulting Group. I must say that despite having served in the Special Forces during our wars, being thrust out on a stage is more nerve-racking than any mission." Priming his audience, Wharton thought, with a little of his unconventional humility. Like a trained actor.

Fink bowed his head for a moment to overemphasize his quest for a topic. He held up a finger, then added a smile Wharton recognized as one tagged to feigned Fink spontaneity, and proclaimed, "How to be a good consultant in life by not being a consultant."

A breathless Wharton turned to Katie, who shrugged her own surprise. Nearest to them, a transfigured Seymour, Nathan, Phillips-Goydan, Piazza, and the other CCGers beamed at one of their own being a trailblazing global thought leader, ready to lean in and swing away.

Fink cavorted around the stage like he was about to unveil a new technology that would correct not only the entropy of the conference but also of the universe. "A good consultant is taught from day one on the job that being a good consultant consists of having an intellectual disposition. This enables the consultant to objectively and unemotionally analyze large swaths of data and complex problems. The idea behind this being that a good consultant employs such a disposition as the best method of solving problems and adding value to a company. Wrong." Here, the audience members aside from Wharton turned to each other for guidance in seeking a deeper understanding of Fink's bearing. "That's the exact opposite of a good consultant. You want to kill creativity or an imaginative way of looking at the world, go be a consultant at CCG or McKinsey. They will train the creativity right out of you. No coincidence that consulting is where artists go to die. Scan the data if you don't believe my theory." Fink jumped forward and landed with his arms above his head and his two legs together paratrooper-style. "The only way to save our future on this earth and avert this fate is to do what I am proposing: 'Jump in!'"

It was in his voice, his posture, his soulless chameleon body, his salting of Wharton's planet with his seed. The way he relished staging his mocking for Wharton's instruction, letting only him in on the joke by making his whole life the butt of the joke. His ridicule spared no one, not even their employer, nor the venue or audience provided to him. Here was a camp performance for a crowd of Don Quixotes who would salute and march in his parade. But Fink himself was no Don Quixote madman, as Wharton knew he believed in none of this. Fink would watch them all walk off the cliff from his perch on the edge, in which anything short of war was not taken seriously.

"Jump in! Hearts and minds, with our money all on the former. It's the same reason Martin Luther King Jr. scrapped the speech title 'I Have a Strategy.' You only have one chance tooooo . . ."

"Jump in!" the audience chimed in unison. Wharton yearned for the female tech COO and her utterly asinine seventeen minutes of "swing away."

"Jump in or get out! Life is about taking risks. Hop a freight train. Go down to Buffalo Bayou and grab an alligator by the tail. Join a keelboat race down the Mississippi and take a shot at being king of the river. Because this is America. It doesn't matter if you come from working-class coal miners or married into a family of kings. It is about backbone. I once had a wealthy friend who had a gentle father who would only coach his son in football if the son asked, but the son was too uncomfortable in his own skin . . ." From the beginning of Fink's tale, Wharton understood that Fink had beaten him in the race to investigate the other's background. His gross misrepresentation of Wharton's relationship with his father was an intentional red flag unfurled for Wharton to make a pass at the bullfighter. One was kicked less in front of a chorus line.

After pissing on Wharton with a five-minute parable about grit that doubled as a grand golden shower, Fink warped his public declaration of war further by ending on a note of peace. "Because each day the rules are being invented anew. When soldiers wage a counterinsurgency, they have to sometimes work with their former enemies," Fink said, holding his hands out Christ-like. "Even making friends with them. You'll have to put yourself out there to initiate breaking the endless cycle of fighting. So cast aside your fear and terror of the other. Connect over common ground. True innovators take time to observe. And then they take risks when the rest don't. Don't worry about your salary, worry about creating value. The victories follow that. Jump in!"

The sick genius of the thespian Fink was his ability to veil his animus toward Wharton in a fable, preaching empathy for others less wise than him to swallow. Within that was Fink's lure of peace; who knew to what nadir that truce would lead Wharton if he accepted. The NED director prohibited Fink from leaving the stage until he took a bow acknowledging the audience's standing ovation. After performing several tandem jumps onstage with Fink, the director harangued the masters-of-the-universe audience with a warning: "Jump in to our reception. I strongly encourage all NEDsters to attend, as it's designed to avoid 'NED-crash,' that unavoidable letdown feeling after being mentally exhausted by so many luminous ideas."

Little wonder ISIS hated us. They had something, Wharton submitted, looking around at the NED audience. Call in the airstrike. He would gladly direct the terrorists as to which groups they should round up if they arrived in country. Even volunteer his own nonbeliever ass for execution first for having no emotional core and being part of this unreflective herd.

Wharton risked "NED-crash" and skipped the cocktail reception of ideas. The wheels in his head spun maddeningly as he left the downtown parking garage. He could not afford to wait on the private investigator's report. Fink's terrorism, which fed off the broken arrow of time, had to be countered now. Counterterrorism. Onstage, Fink had most likely called for a coded cease-fire and empathy only as a means of driving a future stake through his exposed heart.

Halfway home in his car, Wharton decided to head back to his office to map out a strategy rather than go home early before his family's dinner outing and hear his pregnant wife stress about the Triple Crown: acquiring a "night nurse" for their unborn daughter (wasn't mothering the baby the point of his Ice Queen not having a job?), getting her yet-unknown name on the waitlist for a summer camp slot at the prestigious Camp Wildenbed for Girls in the Hill Country, and reserving her a mat at the thirty-grand-a-year pre-preschool The House of Tigger Corner. He texted K.K. to instead meet him at the River Oaks Country Club for their dinner later, relieved to have some momentary peace currently unattainable in his mansion. Compounding domesticity, K.K.'s stress had also lately provoked her dormant eczema, her hands so scaly and rough that the Once-a-Week Handjob solution—which had replaced sex at this stage of her pregnancy—evoked the undesirable sensation of being jacked off by a crocodile.

Along Allen Parkway, where engineers had just rerouted the flow of the bayou, the female joggers in their venomous-neon, Please-Stare-But-Don't-Dare-Touch jogging bras seemed to only highlight Wharton's neutered state and flaunt how much less sex he was getting than the animal Fink. Wharton's circuitous, scenic drive through his city was halted by a group of fifty bully male cyclists that pulled out *into* the road. Their bicycle-shorts neon, however, dared Wharton to run them over. Into the road: when had bicycles attained the status of luxury sports cars? Gangs of these spandex-wearing, high-tech outdoor lovers who Wharton suspected of being homosexuals (or maybe these were the transsexuals who eluded him?) had been moving from the country's coasts to the boomtown of Houston over the last few years at the rate of over a thousand a week. If it was not cycling on roads designed for cars only, it was their food trucks (yes, these people eat food from trucks, Wharton would tell listeners in astonishment at the Bayou Club) that Phillips-Goydan never shut up about that blocked the rest of the roadway. You could not convince Wharton that these food trucks did not breed allergies. Especially considering that the "farm-to-table" food came from Houston's new urban farms, where ex–Peace Corps volunteers taught indigenous hipsters the same skills they'd tried to impart to farmers in the third world who had been farming for thousands of years. At some point the drop in oil prices would stem the flow of these objectionable hordes to Houston, but to the city's old guard who had raised Houston up from nothing, a biblical pestilence would be faster and more welcome.

The Age of the Common Man, he realized in horror as he cut through a street of Philip Johnson–designed skyscrapers, had arrived on the backs of the invading Finks. When not all too busy snapping pictures of their food to post next to the description of the cultish workout that targeted their weak core, the rabble liked to boast that Houston was the nation's most diverse city as if this were an achievement. When they asked which school, they did not mean which private high school but which university one attended. Even the Mexicans appeared to be finally carving out an identity beyond Tex-Mex restaurants, the Hispanic males who had penetrated his office building growing bolder in their plucking of eyebrows and effeminate grooming of all hair.

Almost overnight, Houston had reinvented itself. Worse yet, no one had consulted Wharton about it. Lost in its current evolution was that Houston was better off being controlled by an oligarchy of good families, as it always had been, rather than storming their castles. Wharton took comfort that despite the fact that roaring Houston might temporarily be crowdfunding the American economy and fueling the long-held fairy tale of the wildcatting Bayou City being an oasis of social mobility, he had recently read that there was a growing equality gap in America of historic magnitude between the top one percent and all the others. The celebrity pastors at the famed megachurches of Houston might not say it to their menial masses, but God Bless the Top One Percent. Because when the dam breaks, room on the ark costs money.

In a world hyperconnected, where everyone linked-in feared burning a bridge to nowhere, as they told their whole biography upon being introduced to propagate their brand and expand their empty networks, Wharton still rejoiced as a declared misanthrope. Age of the Common Man or not, he would John Henry hammer Fink with the power of a real network. A little shock and awe. Terrorize the terrorists.

• • •

Wharton clutched K.K.'s bumpy hand under the table as he counted down to dessert, seasonal berries and cream. It would be strawberries, it always was, with the accompaniment of an odd blackberry. Wharton suspected they sent a wait staff member out to pick them when in season to dole out; he had seen the beady blackberries on the edge of the ill-conceived golf course being swallowed by the bayou each year. He recognized most of the faces in the River Oaks Country Club Main Dining Room, though he had made an effort to not make an appearance in the last year. But there was no avoiding the face of his father bearing down on Wharton across the table as his mother retold the story of an ostentatious wedding reception they had been to two years before at the old Petroleum Club.

A couple of minutes later, as he stabbed the last oozing strawberry on his plate, Wharton's mother came to the end of her affliction with the wedding table decorations. "When the bride's father is a plastic surgeon, maybe to be expected." Out of deference to tradition in the South, much in the way girls landed a frightful-sounding mother's maiden name as a first name, Wharton's father had been the best man at his wedding. "The tacky speeches, oh my, they would have made you blush," Wharton's mother said to K.K., who had not blushed the first time she heard her mother-in-law quote from the speeches years before. Wharton had never seen his mother blush, though he speculated a NED Talk might end her record. Her beautiful blond hair had finally turned gray and begun to curl after a minor stroke three years before. She refused to color it. No Christian he had ever known could hold a grudge in their face the way his mother could. She was a woman who tracked many anniversaries. "They lifted them up in chairs the way they do for that dance in their culture. You would never see that here at a reception." Wharton knew the married couple well and would have far preferred their dinner company, the groom a brilliant anthropology professor at Rice University who had allowed Wharton to take in a lecture of his once on the actor-network theory. Alas, Wharton had not taken notes. "Penelope Phillips stopped by our table here last week, Brock."

Wharton's mother had a talent for not letting a dessert be consumed without working some bitter herb down with it, even if the rest of the meal had managed to be relatively painless. Wharton looked over at his father, who leaned in his chair to get up to the gate. Like his son's hair, Dean Wharton's hair did not move. He had been coloring it a wild mink tint since Wharton was old enough to play organized football. Only after Wharton had left home to play at the University of Texas did Dean Wharton shave his trademark beard. He had not had a beard since. The beard might be gone, but the coaching leer was there as his father composed his inquest: "What is this about a new coworker who she says her son claims is the new star in your office?"

He had had many dinners in this room in which he had listened to his father's dislike of Pat Phillips-Goydan and for any other type of male that did not resemble Dean Wharton's image of himself. K.K.'s eczema-ridden hand squeezed his hand as she jumped in. "I don't know who they could be talking about. Brock assured me that he is CCG's star. Maybe lately with the pregnancy, he has concerned himself a little less with being the best at CCG for my benefit."

He knew his father knew better. K.K.'s defense of him would only reveal to his father that Fink was a more serious threat to his dominance. "*Since when?*" Dean Wharton sneered.

It was his father's eternal Socratic question for him: If being the best gives your life meaning, who are you then if you are not the best? *Since when?* Dean Wharton's signature inquiry put you on the defensive and made you measure drift. "CCG is not the good-ole-boy energy industry, Dad. Every year a young buck comes onto the scene and tries to establish himself by cutting down his coworkers." Wharton well knew, as he had been *that* guy every year. "This year the guy, Mike Fink, happens to be a more colorful agitator than in ordinary years. You wouldn't ever see him here at the club, if that is your worry." There was no one specific incident the way one was led to believe. But it would have been nice if Wharton could have marked a period in life by no longer concerning himself with what his father thought.

"Cut him down. Why are your mother and I hearing about this subversive at the country club with our last name attached to the story?" He wondered if Phillips-Goydan had told his bigmouthed mother about the Dr Pepper presentation, though he had not even been present for Wharton's abasement. "Unmask the masquerader." As part of his own masquerade of détente, Wharton thanked his parents for the painful experience of enduring another anniversary dinner with them and promised to drop off their gift over the weekend (which he would mail). He pushed in his chair and waited for his father to get in the last word from his repertoire of demeaning leadership quotes to close family dinners, usually from Winston Churchill, but this time supplied by Teddy Roosevelt: "'The credit belongs to the man who is actually in the arena, whose face is marred by dust and sweat and blood.' In the arena, Wharton."

After walking K.K. to her car under the giant oak trees in the club's expansive parking lot, Brock Wharton marveled for not the first time how he had ever had a chance in life with a total asshole for a father. His uber-competitive father had not even made the varsity squad his senior year. All his talks of courage in the arena to whitewash his five Vietnam War draft deferments. Whatever scars Fink had experienced in adolescence to justify the chip on his shoulder, he had not had to overcome living under the roof of Dean Wharton. Even years later, long after his father's Declaration-of-Independence order for him to not sign the prenuptial agreement had almost ended his engagement to K.K., Wharton accepted that it was easier to just lie than to allow his parents another emotional entry. Inside his own spotless car, away from the arena of his parents, Wharton checked his email before heading home. Just to thumb his nose at his conservative father whose ghostly presence he felt still brooding across from him, he turned the radio to NPR. Drone strike in Pakistan. Three terrorists suspected dead among the bodies. Was the increasing usage of the drone program for counterterrorism a policy of sanctioned assassination? the radio host asked, opening it up to listeners. Wharton dialed the phone number of his best friend rather than deliberate the issue further, the bloodless drones sparking his direct-action imagination. "Tricky Dick. Remember that friend of yours from HBS in the class below us who was in the Army and wrote a best-selling book?" He swerved his car to dodge a cyclist at San Felipe but caught the name from Richard. "No, the other one. The one who loved being a professional speaker after it came out."

• • •

It could be said of Wharton's best friend, Richard Muncher, that he also did not know the first thing about the military, let alone art. Richard would consider such a statement a compliment. Although he and his sales book were immune from the war as an investment banker, he had become a member of the exclusive Menil Collection art museum solely for the access to the money of old Houston society—of which he had married into the climbing sublevel just below, a level high enough to allow the wives to still pervert nouns like *summer* and *lunch* into verbs. "Portrait of a Douche" was how some Menil members referred to Richard behind his back, but that, as Wharton knew, was a reading that failed to capture the layers of his friend Tricky Dick. It was his idea that had brought Wharton to the annual Men of the Menil themed gala.

"Where's our war hero ringer?" Wharton asked Richard, after he introduced himself to the three other tuxedo-clad males in their thirties who sat around the table that Richard sponsored. He sat next to Richard. As planned, a reserved seat was on the other side of each.

"Promoting himself as usual like a good alpha dog." Richard motioned with his hand past the two fencing swords impaling the center of the decorated table for this year's "The Art of Fencing" theme. Across the room, an overly solemn, square-jawed figure from a military-recruiting poster appeared to reenact, almost as if it came naturally, a war story about losing one of his soldiers to a group of four CEOs with a combined net worth of over a billion dollars. "Random House just released his second book, *The Leader's Character: Honor, Integrity, The Code of Loyalty, Servitude, True Character, and Staying the Course in Life and Business*."

"Campaigne's got another book? Hasn't he bounced around a lot?"

"Fourth job in five years. His hometown of Dallas ran him out, so now he's in energy." Richard played with the screen on his phone. "This business book on staying the course in the workplace is about leadership life lessons from his thirty-six months in the Army, not business."

"Can our human drone hit its target?"

"What is a paid speaker but a *professional* actor? This is his book jacket bio from *New York Times* best-seller *One-Eyed Jack One: One Bullet Away from Truth*. 'After graduating in the top one-half percent from Princeton, Don Campaigne attended OCS, where he finished first in every category both officially and unofficially recognized. He served two exceptionally meritorious combat deployments in Iraq in the infantry and in Special Operations, later attending Harvard Business School, where he also finished number one in his class if the rank of valedictorian were awarded. He was chosen over the rest of his peers for an elite senior executive position at a Top 150 North American ink cartridge company.' Can he deliver, you ask? No veteran I have ever met can top that kind of calculated pedigree and decorated military record. He's just like us, but he determined that if he did a bit of military time it would separate his background even more in our circles. A better question would be when is he running for the Senate? He's organically a politico. You should have called me first before you paid a private investigator. What did he deliver?"

"He is supposed to deliver a report next week when . . ." Wharton said, trailing off at the sight of Fink entering in an evening tailcoat and white bow tie. He spoke with a man who Wharton presumed must be the gala chef: a loud, fat, bald guy in a white shirt with multicolored tattoos that began at the cutoff of his short-sleeved shirt and spilled over onto his hands that prepared Wharton's food. Thank bloody Christ that Phillips-Goydan was not here, as he probably knew who this clown was, doubtless some chef at a local, overpriced hipster restaurant who was treated like a pseudo-celebrity by this new unbearable foodie culture, tramping around like a guitar god instead of serving food as was his role in life. It had again become one of his greatest fears in life that he would suffer a fatal allergic reaction dining, but added to this anxiety was that it would occur during a mandatory business lunch at one of these unbearable chefs' establishments. Richard excused himself to go pitch the ex-mayor, now recycled as a director at an energy firm, but still the same short, crabby bald man with bad breath whose selfless public service was best remembered by his usage of mayoral influence to get his daughter off a DWI.

"We know commercial real estate development is the true economic engine that drives this city," one of the tuxedos said to the other two tuxedos at the table with Wharton. "They will Californize Houston if they get rid of the TIRZs." Wharton thought his least favorite type in Houston had to be developers. Take your most hated or favorite lobbying group in America and they had none of the disproportionate power that the unchecked commercial real estate developers in the City of No Zoning Laws had, a place where every scrub Houston city/county official nested in the back pocket of these developers who were the largest contributors to their campaigns. For the few conscientious developers, you had the hundreds of others who would pillage every nonconcrete square inch of the city for a quick buck. Fastest-growing city until there was no city left. Their answer to the increased Houston flooding that they brought on more than any other factor: *more* unbridled development. A great deal for the greedy developers, who got rich building whether it flooded or did not flood, but best in times of disaster when they bought up all the citizens' flooded homes on the cheap and made an even greater killing during reconstruction. Their tired argument was that no zoning kept rent down (while lowering the value of every neighborhood home when an eyesore high-rise popped up behind a home overnight), but the rent was the same or higher than the zoned Dallas. Wharton knew from business that a Tax Increment Reinvestment Zone (TIRZ) was the biggest racket of them all, handing the developers huge tax breaks to get richer developing while allowing them control of an unelected board with municipal powers for large areas of the city so they could bypass the already skimpy regulations on any flood-control measures. *Californize us!* thought Wharton, *or we won't have a city to develop after a few more of these floods.* Anything besides another blank check to an industry where a place could always be reserved for every talentless white rich kid to work for one of their friends' fathers, the younger commercial real estate property managers with their sunglasses tethered around their necks to mitigate the danger the queso posed at lunch.

Wharton was halfway through trying to put back together his "deconstructed appetizer" before Fink joined the table. "Don't laugh, but this was the only tux classy enough that I could scrounge up last minute. My ex-fiancée bought it for me," Fink said, as way of introduction to the table, exchanging handshakes. Wharton bit his tongue at the heaven-sent opportunity to make a snide comment about Fink's ex-fiancée so as not to jeopardize his subterfuge. "I love this place, and the collection of Surrealists is amazing." Fink nodded at his surroundings and sat in the seat next to Wharton. "This looks like a better-heeled crowd than I'm used to socializing with. I was hoping to have made more Houston buddies by now, but it is difficult when we're always on the road. No one ever tells you that leaving the military is like adjusting to society after years in a cult. Thanks for extending the invitation, amigo. A pleasant surprise. I guess I was wrong about us. What with our common passion for NED Talks! Does this constitute a new half-mentor, half-friend partnership?"

"You are the half protégé, half friend?"

Fink slapped him on the back. "I would prefer half horse, half alligator."

An uneasiness slithered up through the bristles of Wharton's nose to try to hook his brain with this potential arrival of Fink sincerity and unilateral disarmament, a separate peace. Cohabitation. Same peace term the Taliban threw around. The chinks in the armor of Mike Fink the folklore legend were easier for Wharton to spot than this real version of a human. Maybe the only thing worse than Fink as an enemy was him thinking he was your friend. Should Wharton trust the new Fink and halt the order to attack him? Too many pieces had been moved into place, and a momentum of its own demanded a strike. There was no room for gray in their history of absolutism. God, even Wharton's father felt affronted by Fink.

"I take it the fencing is after we eat?" Fink asked Wharton.

"They do it after the main course," Richard said. Fink's eyes darted over to Wharton's eyes and back to Richard Muncher as he sat down. "I believe we met once before—"

"Hi, everyone," Don Campaigne commenced, standing over the table. "I apologize I got carried away in a great conversation with some CEO friends of mine on the energy revolution's changing geopolitics. My wife says I'm fanatical about it because of my time overseas."

Even the time—within ten seconds of sitting—at which Campaigne's inevitable first question was clocked surprised Wharton. "What do you do?"

Wharton hesitated but knew that this natural phoniness of Campaigne's would unwittingly play into their plan of manipulating his vanity to destroy Fink's ego. After all, Wharton wanted only to encourage Campaigne's one-upper nature. "I'm a consultant at CCG. The drop in barrel prices only seems to be accelerating the changing oil landscape."

"That's so true."

"Hopefully the main course is not also some crazy concocted entrée."

"That's so true," Campaigne responded into Christ-knows-what mirror he observed himself in.

What was so true was that upon a close-quarters review Campaigne's face seemed less out of central casting and more like a politician's face that had elongated under the effort of constant self-promotion. Was not the one redeemable facet of military training, Wharton mused, its claim to remove the prima donnas from the ranks?

According to Richard, Campaigne always hit his marks onstage. It was a role he could not be challenged on, postwar. He had even attempted the part while still an undergraduate at Princeton to far less success. There he had tried to serve as the wise Christian mentor to people his own age who did not ask to be mentored and found him to be that annoying medal chaser who everyone's parents held up as the model neighborhood boy but who all his peers knew was a fraud. No idiot, Campaigne grabbed at the war like it was the last life jacket. He had been tragically lucky enough to have his soldiers' high casualty rate under his command give credibility to an identity that had always needed the right lines. Now both his affected self-questioning and false modesty never failed to align with his practiced voice, a voice that could on cue choke like an engine that had run its whole life on a kick. All dramatic techniques built to a finale onstage in which he would push out the tear or two he knew needed to be sacrificed to capture the civilian audience's heart. At his best, this method coincided with the tears profitably timed to piggyback on his preceding courageous confession that he wrote because he realized he had not put his soldiers in for medals while looking at his own medals one day in the mirror.

"And what do you do?"

"Very little," Fink admitted. "Mainly hot girls."

Wharton coughed some of his appetizer into his napkin at this non-HBS-mixer rejoinder. He had to concede that for a terrorist bent on the destruction of not only Wharton's life but also the whole Western way of doing things in both the real world and proper society, his psychotic enemy had his humorous moments. "Don Campaigne was in the military and he wrote a best-selling war book, *One-Eyed Jack One*, that you might have heard about." A sign of failing that had not escaped Wharton's consultant eye, Fink, in contrast to the impressive Campaigne, hesitated in discussing the details of his war record. Not that Fink, like Campaigne, didn't profit from his military experience by invoking it when it benefited him, he just did so in a vague way.

The shrill laughter fired from Fink wounded the entire Men of the Menil gala crowd, who reeled around to locate the assailant. Fink's face convulsed and he sucked for air as he writhed and laughed. Richard's rodent features scrunched and looked to Wharton for explanation.

"One . . . Eyed . . . Jack . . . One," Fink finally managed between laughs.

"That was my call sign in Iraq."

"I know, someone sent me the . . . thing," Fink said, pressing both of his hands to his chest to stop the laughing. "What the hell are the odds that I would meet the person behind it?"

"Actually, hardly a day goes by where I don't meet a fan of my war memoir."

"*Memoir?*" Fink erupted with laughter again, his ears a sunburn red. "Is that what you are labeling that corporate calling card? Hell, that's the one time I wished I had been a Nazi so I could have burned a book. Isn't a true memoir a literary quest, in search of some deeper meaning and dedicated to intellectual honesty? Not that shameless unreflective piece of slick catfish shit you're peddling to run for office. Try chewing on the memoirs of Robert Graves, George MacDonald Fraser, or James Salter; you might learn something about men and war." The hypocrisy underlying Fink's self-righteousness! Fink himself was an English literature major turned would-be thespian who had sold out to become a consultant when the money got tight. Wharton knew Fink's disparagement of Campaigne's presentation of his military service must be rooted in self-hatred, because Fink understood that in pandering to corporate tools like CCG and the NED crowd, he'd in part whored himself out just like Campaigne.

"I know a lot more about war than you. I fought in Iraq. In the infantry and in the—"

"I love the infantry as well. My first job was as an infantry groundpounder. Makes me damn curious what fellow infantryman Miguel de Cervantes, who lost the use of an arm at the Battle of Lepanto, and came home to a country he didn't recognize, would say about a narc like you. You know the author of *Don Quixote* would have had a name for a *writer* of your ilk, when just the dream of books and all that literature can show us was all he could cling to as a crippled POW. Fucking integrity. You have a better chance at reclaiming your virginity."

Ironically, Wharton could dispute this last claim, having once failed to do just that. He instead raced to pull up Campaigne's online social media CV profile on his phone. Fink's literary gibberish reminded Wharton again of Fink's English literature degree and the danger of allowing the contest to stay on literature, the one subject Fink might have greater pissing range in than their drone Campaigne. *Do not jump into the dusty, sweaty, bloody arena of art*, Wharton's inner consultant advised. This was about hammering Fink's integrity. Nobody at their table cared about literary truth, or the truth of Campaigne's overblown war stories; to deromanticize any military veteran's service from unthinking worship in the post-9/11 era was to expose the never-been-wider gulf between civilians and the irreproachable in uniform. It was also a violation of a gala's social norms and killed photo ops.

But Fink's voice rose so the surrounding tables could all hear, "How's this for a jaded MFA warrior-poet opening sentence: 'Dogs, lots of dogs, we shot—Operation Snoopy they called it—and I love dogs, even rabid wartime mongrels'? Or should I sell out more in a lowbrow vein, writing thrillers starring a Special Forces character named 'Mike Freedom'? Or what about writing a Quiet Professional 'kill memoir' with body count statistics like quarterback sacks in the appendix? Hollywood would lap up that hot garbage, especially if it were a reckless mission where we altered a few of the more unpleasant details for consumption. Maybe do a 'Patriot Speaking Tour' afterward in arenas, really bilk the paying patriots of this great land by telling a few war stories of all the terrorists we're not even sure we killed. Just bound paper to you, Campaigne, to be tallied so you can slip your total sales in softcore war pornography into the next dinner-party conversation. Not the kind of moral compass that can save your soul over there, or arm you with the belief that if enough readers experience it there might be fewer future wars."

Campaigne rose from his chair to best project his professional speaking voice. "I will not stand here and let you run down the war and my brothers-in-arms."

"Yet you exploitatively advance your career on the blood of your soldiers."

In contrast to the NED Talk, Wharton believed he could strike back from his seat. "Don, I didn't know that as a reservist you 'were handpicked by Special Operations Command' and that you 'created and started the Village Stability Operations plan for the war.'" Wharton held out his phone as proof of Campaigne's inarguable military merits.

Fink snatched Wharton's phone. A smile spread on his face that would have bridged the width of the river he claimed to be king of and led to yet another fit of laughter. "'Served eight years,' intentionally leaving ambiguous that less than half that time was active duty," Fink read aloud, mimicking with his raised right hand the quotations sign in the air. "'Special Ops,' cunningly writes the attached liaison reservist, who came closest to Special Ops by ensuring that the Special Forces operators' coffee was hot in the operations center. You're one of those fakes who lets people think he was actually in Special Forces, aren't you?" Wharton's phone was a prop, like Fink had stolen Scrooge's cane for character extension in the morality play he was starring in, directing, and producing. "Here's another diamond: 'designed strategic war plan,' suggesting that you crafted the winning war strategy, Captain America, as the morning PowerPoint briefer. Are you sure you ain't a fiction writer, Campaigne? Who needs fencing when you're around to poke holes in? Stand by for my call sign."

Employing a dramatic device that Campaigne himself might want to one day contemplate using onstage, Fink stood and turned to Wharton and Richard to deliver an aside: "Is this narc all you bullies could come up with for a fencing counterpart?" Fink melodramatically pulled out the erect sword from the center of the table as if pulling it from a stone and raised it high above before slashing Zorro-like to declare a resumption of hostilities. Pure Fink theater of the ignominious.

But no one clapped for Fink this time. Those in attendance just stared at the spectacle of the misbehaving child who had wandered into the grown-ups' conversation. The truth hadn't exposed Campaigne but *Fink* as not belonging. Fink was the fink. The mask had slipped. And slipping away with it: the victory Fink had thought was his. It was the first genuine moment in their relationship performed for Wharton. Fink's emotional acting had revealed his true disgust at a lack of integrity, his contempt even for his own ability to thrive in the bullshit part corporate America wanted him to embody as a veteran. The feelings of a human. Wharton had finally netted a victory by goading Fink into revealing his true feelings in a setting where no one had wanted to hear them. *Are we that different?* a triumphant Wharton caught himself wondering about his enemy, as Fink tucked tail and crawfished away to leave him to a night with best friend Richard Muncher, war hero Don Campaigne, and the three wise men developers who would build, build, build Houston until it had to be rebuilt.

6.
COUNTERINSURGENCY

"Your playing days are over."

"I had planned to cut out those overhead kettlebell swings from my workout."

"The good news is the rotator cuff tear seems slight for now. A degenerative tear. At your older age you are going to have to modify your behavior." The doctor listed with a certain amount of delight what he could no longer do in life. Wharton thought the list was long for a young person. He even coached Wharton on a few strengthening exercises. This was rich coming from the runt specialist whose own slack pear-shaped body tried to pull off the coup of having Charles de Gaulle hips and the illusion of greater stature. Wharton did not like that Dr. Clifford was Canadian, an identity subscribed to by a whole nation of people marooned by Great Britain and the United States. Or his big ears, which flopped out from his curly black hair, this atop his flaccid body, totaling a semierect penis look. Doctors: that irksome profession that made less than consultants but basked in an idea of nobleness. "Rest. Listen to your body. My advice is avoid any physical activity for the next two months." Wharton sold advice for a living. Fink had since revealed how much that was worth.

Unlike today's *Houston Chronicle* and its anniversary special section, "Houston: A City of Possibilities," which addressed the next fifty years in the city, life's possibilities seemed to be narrowing. And quickly. Within a few years, the paper predicted, autonomous vehicles would rule the car kingdom of Houston. All occupants as passengers in the self-driving vehicles. A future of virtual-reality workplaces. Consultants nonexistent, an automated link relegating them to the same pool of factory workers globalization left unemployed. Projections that the Inner Loop where he resided would double in population in the next decade. Buildings atop sinking buildings. Rising temperatures would bring historic flooding and new levels of killer hurricanes. Could innovation save the energy capital from the impending death of fossil fuels? Wharton tried to remember his hometown as it was, preserve some small history in amber while they still had trees. To kiss a girl as a teenager, actually be excited, before contracts were required.

As if it were not bad enough that the whole city was an agent of change, Dr. Clifford had bracketed Wharton on his screen chart under the category *Middle Age*. "Middle-aged" male, Brock Wharton? Fatherhood did approach. Now his body tried to quit. There was still the war with Fink, a young man's game. Not so long ago, in the days before Fink, Wharton had maintained his postfootball edge by pursuing extreme physical challenges. He had trained for and won the national Business School Best Athlete competition, which had earned a coveted bullet in the limited space he had for a one-page CV. During his first year in consulting he had used his vacation time to run, swim, and bike across the poorest state in Mexico for no apparent enjoyable reason and vaguely on behalf of America. To top that he had had to canoe a river in Oregon all the way to the sea the next year in a weekend race that did not allow him to sleep or contact the outside world. But while at no time happy when engaged in these activities, Wharton never tired of reliving his stories for other people, as nothing dominated a lunch more than absurd extreme challenges that could silence an audience. Though it was exhausting to be special, it had been worth it. Fink, of course, had made it all feel silly and forced, as Special Forces extremes were not by choice but out of duty, all while people were trying to kill you.

Wharton needed a victory. And such was life that an opportunity arose when he entered the Houston One Center building after his depressing visit to the doctor. He spotted his redhead architect forty feet in front of him on the escalator and began to pick up his pace on the metal steps. It was she who held the elevator door for him as he scrambled to pocket his wedding ring.

It sure was Fink's good fortune that men with the conventionally attractive looks of a Brock Wharton were out of the hunt. Would have been one thinned-out herd, thought Wharton, as he smiled at the architect. Horizontal black and white stripes covered her sleeveless sweater dress. As it was with the zebras of his African honeymoon, Wharton knew it was sensible that there were rules against petting the patterned hind hump. "I'm Brock." Wharton listened to his body. "I like your dress."

"My name's Amelia." Christ almighty, was she good-looking. Worse, she qualified as such by all the misogynistic standards Wharton was endeavoring to move past as he got older. He gnawed on a blank image so as not to fantasize about licking her golden legs that rose out of the cones of her heels. But her heart-shaped ass conflicted his virtue: its magical side-to-side beat carried him away to a world of black-and-white-film private investigators and sassy secretaries. Taking dictation and slinking around in a pencil skirt *but* with the spunk of a feminist. Up close, in Technicolor, her baby skin glowed. Without being creepy, he wanted to somehow steal it.

Wharton tried to remember how to do this. He hadn't made a move since college. Fortunately, he had plucked the gray hairs on his sides that morning with his wife's tweezers. Not much longer until ear hair attacked his flanks. "You're an architect, right?"

"One more certification exam to go."

For the sake of your eroding manhood, think of something charming to say. "Architecture. That's really cool." She blushed. That electric rush from contact. It appeared his playing days were far from over. The Art of Closing. "Architect. That's really hot." *What are you, a seventeen-year-old girl on that Instagram thing?* "I used to date a lot of girls who were majoring in architecture." At this lie, the inner strategic dating consultant in his head now screamed at the jailer to be released and staffed on a less futile engagement.

"Oh?" The bell sounded and the elevator stopped for her floor.

When she shifted he saw a flash of orange satin underneath her armpit. Orange? It seemed out of place, rebellious. A jail-suit-orange bra. He had reached the age where he knew he would think about it the rest of the day with sentimental longing.

"What's your number? We should connect and get a drink sometime."

"Maybe we shouldn't," Amelia said, tapping her empty left ring finger. "Your wife might not like that." His eyes traveled over to his left ring finger; a pale band of white wrapped around his sun-dried hide there. He could trust his skin to betray even a hypothetical shot at infidelity. Amelia exited the elevator with her familiar strut, which in no way she reserved for Wharton.

All day in his CCG cell, the shamed prisoner Wharton reviewed again the data of the dysfunctional supply chain from Phoenix Energy's Permian Basin operations. The seventh-largest oil and gas company in the United States, Phoenix held massive acreage in West Texas and should have been bathing in the blood of America's new reservoir of black gold from unconventional drilling. But Phoenix employed an average performance team of ten to twelve engineers per two rigs, versus the leaner independents whose companies operated with teams of six to eight engineers per five rigs. This was compounded by a tendency to heavily rely on the single-provider setup with the biggest oil field service company, thereby preventing quick decisions and an ability to pressure its vendors. In addition, Phoenix gold-plated everything, its roots in a mentality that incentivized safety rather than performance, while its leaner wildcatter competitors sourced most of the different services around the wellhead to contractors to drill aggressively for a higher IRR. The higher ROI for the independents was then used as capital to fuel more drilling. Phoenix, Wharton recognized from his study of counterinsurgency over the weekend, grappled with an insurgency from the faster-moving wildcatters.

The insurgency Phoenix battled was no different from any other industry-leading client of CCG's facing a disruptive technology. One had to be agile and adaptable to meet the perpetually morphing Finks in business. Peel the onion of the Janus-faced insurgency/counterinsurgency: insurgencies are cheap, counterinsurgencies are costly. Applying the traditional greater measure of blunt force like drone Don Campaigne was a conventional general's plan, Wharton had come to learn from reading, not altogether unlike the heavy-handed mistakes the American military had made overseas. To be a counterinsurgent, Phoenix had to be fluid and increase its appetite for risk, reinventing itself into a wildcatting insurgent. As Phoenix's reborn advisor, a new dawn had come for Mr. Houston, Brock Wharton, to rise up and embrace oil before it was all gone. Nothing less than an obliteration of his past.

When the private investigator called Wharton's office and pitched the idea that they switch their meeting to the new Chinatown in Bellaire rather than the closer old Chinatown east of downtown, Wharton, as the client for once, seized the chance to change it to a bar he had always wanted to explore. Wharton laughed to himself that only Houston, city of the perpetual new history, was capable of relocating the official Chinatown. That was the "Magnolia City" for you, no longer the Magnolia City after urban sprawl killed off all of Houston's magnolia groves and genteel Southern charm, the city renaming as either Baghdad on the Bayou or, for the more minimalist-minded, the Bayou City.

Lit only by candlelight, La Carafe was the city's oldest bar and one of the few Civil War–era houses standing in Houston. In downtown Market Square, the brick building was an orphan among the skyscrapers, its falling-over balcony creaking a dirge for the ghosts of the city's colorful boomtown history. Perez sat in the front corner of the empty bar by the entrance and windows that opened to the street, against a wall covered with old portrait paintings. The private investigator, who claimed to be half white and half Chinese under a Latin name, passed for one hundred percent Chinese. His tailored suit was all Italian and as nice as any Wharton owned. He handed over a folder to Wharton and ordered beers. Documents and pictures were labeled by section. Wharton searched for the section titled "Stolen Valor," that longed-for silver bullet that would explain away Fink's military career as one big lie and allow Wharton to pounce, ideally in the manner of one of those catch-a-predator type videos. Americans loved comeuppance on tape.

"During a belt-tightening economy I always see a spike in business like this from people's coworkers."

Wharton was not like everybody else. Even if the clocks got wound backward to 1986, it would not be the CCG 1-performers like Wharton but the 2-performers who would be the first to get cut. Today's darkening headlines were there to unnerve the little folks and second-place finishers: nearing 100,000 in energy layoffs, West Texas Intermediate crude falls below forty dollars per barrel, China growth slows, a historic glut in oil storage levels reaches perfect-storm proportions, and those fucking Saudis (advised by Fink) keep pumping out oil and terrorism.

"Why is there an asterisk by the mythology part in the summary?"

Perez gestured at the old portraits on the wall. "You know how it is with folk heroes. There's the myth and then the darker facts behind the myth."

Though Wharton could not substantiate it, he believed the portraits were not of folk heroes but of people who were just dead. "I told you it was my theory all along that Fink was not a descendant of a folk hero, as your family history tree shows and it says in your summary."

"Meant more as a note of caution. Because I bet your colleague is aware of Mike Fink's days as an elite Indian scout on the frontier before he assumed his throne as King of the Mississippi and Ohio Rivers. Paid for in blood. The history in there is about the Mike Fink keelboatman hero of American folklore. But it says something about your coworker that he modeled his identity on a man who massacred his way to the top. He knows his PsyOps."

Wharton wiggled his throbbing right arm. "You mean like murder?"

Perez laughed and tightened his red tie. "The least of it. Hacking off ears and noses. Disemboweling you and cutting your scalp off while you are still alive. Raping your wife and your sister in front of you."

"I don't have a sister. Indians or Fink?"

"Both. Stuffing your genitals in your mouth and dragging you behind a horse before they burned you to death. If you're lucky, they just cut your throat like these terrorist thugs."

Was that how business was done on the frontier during America's first Age of Terror? Wharton made a note to not support the new open-carry legislation so as not to bring back the wild frontier. Perez stoked a longing in Wharton for the simpler times of the mythical Fink, the ring-tailed roarer who could whip twice his weight in wildcats and leap the Mississippi, and was chock-full of fight to take on any man in a keelboat who challenged the long red feather in his hat. If he was going to wage a successful counterinsurgency, he would have to force insurgent Fink from out of the wilderness and onto a field where there were rules. Not a frontier war.

• • •

Finkelstein. Jewish. Mikhail Finkelstein immigrated from Poland in the 1830s aboard a packet ship destined for the Port of New Orleans and shortened the name to Fink not long after arriving. Mikhail Finkelstein, now Michael Fink, was a tailor of women's undergarments and passed the trade down to his son, whose own son eventually opened up a store, Fink's Fine Garments, in the Faubourg Marigny neighborhood outside the French Quarter.

The store was still family-owned in 1981 when the great-great-great-grandson Joseph Fink saw the birth of his only child, Michael James Fink. Not long afterward, Joseph Fink started to invest in commercial real estate properties around New Orleans. With the oil bust in 1986, Joseph Fink was forced to unload their family mansion in the Garden District and move to a modest home in the Riverbend section of the city that lay adjacent to the Mississippi River levee. In 1999, Joseph Fink closed the doors on Fink's Fine Garments. Michael—now calling himself "Mike"—Fink stayed in New Orleans to attend Tulane University. After 9/11, he applied for OCS, where he was known for finishing dead last as the "class goat" among the military cadets. He was the first member of his family to serve in the military. At the end of almost a decade in the military in both the infantry and the

Special Forces, he was engaged to a girl from a prominent WASP, old-money New Orleans family. Upon leaving the military, he worked in theater for six months, acting as Mark Twain in a solo show of the author's tall tales, and as working-class Jewish comedian Willy Sloman in a one-act parody of *Death of a Salesman* called *Death of a Comedian*. He gave up acting after his fiancée broke off the engagement for his lack of seriousness professionally and for his standoffish behavior socially. Not long after their breakup she got reengaged, and he applied to CCG.

*There are no records of blood lineage on either side to the fabled keelboatman Mike Fink, rumored to have been born around 1770 to Scots-Irish parents near the Fort Pitt area of the Pennsylvania frontier and to have worked both the Ohio and Mississippi Rivers.

Wharton smiled and placed the summary from Perez's report next to the dog-eared section "Information Operations" in his new favorite book, *FM 3-24: Counterinsurgency Field Manual*. He reread as well the email he had waited all week to push out (thereby limiting Fink's time to counterattack). It proved that Wharton, if needed, could Davy Crockett–like outshoot the tin cup off another's head in a contest of deflecting ricochets against Mike Fink. Even his right arm felt normal again. The title of the Friday afternoon email he sent to all in the CCG Houston office read: "Came across this interesting article . . ."

Below the link to the encyclopedia article on the legend of Mike Fink (that he had rewritten—using false credentials—on the open website to spotlight a birth in the northeast, Christian ancestry, and that speculated on Mike Fink's invention as a fictional character), Wharton pretended to have written a side note to Fink but with the intention of all seeing:

Very interesting article on your great-great-great-great-grandfather. The timeline seems a bit off, though, if he is your great-great-great-great-grandfather, right? Maybe the encyclopedia is wrong? Your family is also Jewish, which this article seems to contradict as well. Though my aunt from New Orleans, who was just visiting my wife and me, told us she remembers a Jewish Fink family who for generations made the finest women's underwear in the city. Any relation?

See you on the field tomorrow for the Consulting Bowl,
B.W.

Fink's insanity had never been clearer to Wharton: they were both driven by the same devil. This insight failed to connect Wharton to his competitor twin, no doubt separated by some clerical error in Hell's nursery. He perceived their showdown as an examination of counterinsurgency doctrine. Aside from its shaping-operations attack on Fink's integrity, Wharton's email baited Fink out onto turf in which he knew he possessed a lopsided, asymmetrical advantage over Fink in talent. On paper they would be on the same side and the opponent would be McKinsey in the Consulting Bowl, but their shared devil would never allow them to be on the same team. Sure, Wharton hated football even more than Fink did, but the Consulting Bowl was an organic challenge, fostered on competitive males by a business culture that largely rewarded bad-boy behavior if a trophy could be won. Afterward, Wharton would do the framing and write the history as he forever left the football field behind. An engagement thirty years in the making. Instead of holing up in his office after sending the email, Wharton headed to the kitchen area to get out among the populace and collect intelligence among the population he attempted to win over.

"Idea Man!"

"Interesting article," Piazza said, holding up his phone. "Somebody's been telling some tall tales. What's more interesting is that it took the new CEO at Dr Pepper all of a week on the job to reject Fink's branding strategy. Based on some type of warfare."

"Counterinsurgency."

"Counter-whatever, that account is now lost. An inopportune time for him with CCG's excess capacity."

"We're downsizing?" The 1-performer grinned at the thought of the numerous negative outliers that would clot Fink's annual review spider chart with Dr Pepper lost.

"There'll be streamlining this spring if oil doesn't correct. Big game tomorrow."

"A good reputation is everything in consulting," Wharton said, aglow. He had seized the high ground, and if he hadn't taken the high road, well, this was still war.

On the drive home, it began to come into focus why America struggled so hard in the wars. Instead of studying COIN (as Wharton called counterinsurgency when in the field), the troops spent all their time deployed dreaming up ways to film their families with a surprise coming home; this after a deployment of filming mock pop-music videos in uniform to post online. Not surprisingly, civilians loved the videos, connecting easily with the zany troops who showed that war could be fun and that you did not have to turn in your homework. If only they completed their first assignment on how to drain the swamp and flush the insurgents out into the open, then follow-up lessons on how to invest in infrastructure, provide security, co-opt and work with local leaders, and win the propaganda war at all costs. Hearts and minds. Special Ops raids alone don't work. Save the surgical strike for when you have the target sighted and no chance of collateral damage. Isolate Fink's reputation from the reputation of CCG and bring him down. T. E. Lawrence once likened counterinsurgency to "eating soup with a knife." Lawrence of Arabia he might have been, but waging war against insurgents did not have to be that hard, and Lawrence had not served as a strategic management consultant before the Great War.

Wharton walked in on K.K. commanding Inés in poor Spanish to sweep the baseboards, this time with some elbow grease. He rotated his wedding band around his finger and waited for K.K. to finish. Ever since the debacle with Amelia, he had arrived home before the housekeepers left in the early evening. To witness their exhausting labor was enough to make enduring Fink at CCG almost bearable. In a future of possibilities, a true case of ***hands*** would be to build diplomatic relations, for if they closed the borders, who would do this kind of work for the Whartons? Not Wharton, whose money-cutting hands were nearly as soft as K.K.'s.

K.K. tapped her watch. "I'm starting to worry about you coming home too early." Why, was she having an affair, his knocked-up ex-skank? "You're quitting earlier each week."

Her Dean Wharton critique agitated him. "I need some rest before the big game."

"I completely forgot, but I promised Kelly I would attend her baby shower."

"You've already been to three baby showers for her. The game starts at two."

"I'll try. But the shower starts at one."

"Babe, I need you there for the game."

"Toxic masculinity. You mean to say it's your fragile self-image that needs me there."

• • •

Enclosed on all sides by hedges and the great oak trees of Houston, the Rice University campus was a sleepy place on Saturdays. A few groups of students at the small elite university walked here and there, though none seemed to notice the return of Wharton to Rice as he strode in his football cleats toward Rice Stadium on the far south end of campus.

Built in 1950 to seat seventy thousand fans who never came, Rice Stadium had seen better days than Consulting Bowl X. Host of the 1974 Super Bowl VIII, the stadium had fallen into disrepair much like the Rice Owls football program. Once a powerhouse in college football, the football program came up for review about every ten years by the board of trustees. They debated whether it was in the best interests of the university to drop the program or continue getting sadistically ravaged by the University of Texas each year by seventy points, before inevitably concluding that such beatings were worth renewing for the sake of school spirit.

Most famously perhaps, Rice Stadium had been where President Kennedy informed the world: *We choose to go to the moon.* From the row of bleacher seats under the scoreboard, Wharton, no less presidentially, smiled down at the sight of the old field. Green grass had replaced the old Astroturf he remembered bitterly from his playing days against the

Rice Owls. The hardness and burn of the skin-peeling plastic sandpaper someone named Astroturf had been the only downside to his homecoming at Rice Stadium, where Wharton led the Longhorns to a slaughter of the Owls. The scoreboard read: Consulting Bowl X. His metal-tipped cleats ground a crunching of bone all the way down the concrete steps toward the field. Many of the fifty family fans gathered to watch the game squawked at the grating noise and rotated around in their seats to behold the quarterback. He half expected to see the return of his bearded father standing in the first row, arms menacingly crossed as he refused to sit down when the game clock ticked.

Adam Smith, the McKinsey consultant who had obtained use of the playing field through a backdoor arrangement with the athletics department, saluted Wharton with an upside-down Longhorn sign. The same age, Smith and Wharton had been in the same section together at Harvard Business School. Smith, a stocky prep school northerner with a chip on his shoulder the size of the football he was twirling in his hand, had started the first four games of one forgettable season at quarterback for Vanderbilt before being pulled after throwing more interceptions than touchdowns. Most memorably, according to a fellow HBS classmate of theirs who had been at Vanderbilt, one wag at the school newspaper coined the nickname that would forever trail Adam Smith in the world of consulting, thanks to Wharton: the Invisible Hand.

It was an ideal day, the blue sky devoid of any sagging rain clouds or the peppery smog that plagued Consulting Bowl IX. Last year's smog threat level of red had resulted in an automatic cough after every exertion. Wharton stretched and ran zigzag patterns to test his cutting ability over to the CCG table of jerseys and past the now-chanting huddle of McKinsey, the same assholes who had advised Enron all the way up until the checks began to bounce.

"Your lucky jersey, so no excuses," Katie said, tossing him a balled-up shirt. He smiled at her when he saw it was number one, his old playing number. She could not be expected to possibly know what was at stake for the male ego in this game, but he felt an emotion close to love for her effort to restore confidence in his leadership, one look at a time. He made a mental note to write a noncutting evaluation of her performance if she should ever return to consulting engagements, even if it portrayed her engagement showing as equal to his own. Perhaps the time had come to stop rooting against his closest friends. "Who do you keep looking around for? My friend Amelia?"

"K.K."

"You're the most insecure person I have ever met."

"I only flirted with Amelia to see if I still had it. It would seem that I don't. I wasn't aware she was your friend. I apologize for being a scumbag."

"You've never flirted with me. Get your head in the game."

He scanned again the crowd in the corner of the southern end zone, where Seymour drew plays on a dry-erase board. He did not want to ask. But he needed to know, as there had as yet been no response from him since Wharton's email had harpooned his aura. "Where's Fink?"

"Getting a pep talk from his girlfriend at the fifty-yard line behind you."

Before he would turn around, Wharton had to ask, "Leila Berger?"

"Our head cheerleader."

In the first row, Fink kissed a Dallas Cowboys cheerleader. "Good God, how?"

As if reading his thoughts, Katie answered, "She's not a real one. It's Carissa."

"Barnett?" He turned back to Katie, who laughed at his befuddled expression. This opened the way for his own probe. "Who are you dating, Katie?" Wharton remembered the local sports broadcast anchor, David Murphree Wallace, who had attended many CCG functions when they dated the year before. Despite giving off the impression he was sixty, Wallace was only in his thirties and had slipped into his stretched skin and balding head during his UT fraternity days when booing Wharton in his coach's polo shirt. Wallace was the sort of entitled Houston rich kid who normally either landed in private wealth management to suck the proverbial dicks of other wealthy friends or, in that other maverick element of trust-fund babies, went against the

grain to work for the family "business," the concept of self-respect as foreign as merit to a David Murphree Wallace.

"Hopefully a confident guy who knows who he is. Alas, if only they existed."

Wharton faced the other direction and jogged toward the huddle around Seymour.

"There he is," Seymour said as Wharton approached. The huddle of associates on a knee rotated around excitedly. Wharton felt a balloon of happiness rise up inside him until Fink shot it with an arrow and ran up next to Wharton, Fink breathing laboriously from a dead sprint as all eyes looked toward him for a comment.

"A case of beer to whoever scores first!" Fink gasped, rousing the cheering mass.

CCG won the coin toss and elected to receive. Smith's squib kick bounced the ball through the CCG players. The ball tumbled nose-end over nose-end in the air after each bounce off the turf sent it airborne. Wharton reached out with his left hand like he was fielding a baseball on a hop near the white sideline and cradled the ball in his hand as he felt the leather make contact, almost stepping out of bounds, before whirling around in a spin in the other direction like he was about to hurl a discus. He hugged the sideline for eight yards up field, his knees still low as his cleats felt the turf, and switched the ball to his right hand. One of the newer McKinsey faces was the first to arrive and cut off his path, crouching low as if about to hit him as he grabbed for his flag, Wharton slamming the flat of his left hand in the consultant's shoulder, guiding him down to the turf with the stiff-arm as he cut hard right. He ran around the backside of Ursula, who pushed back her smaller female counterpart to block for him as he crossed midfield. Ten yards ahead, Adam Smith pivoted to angle him toward the right sideline.

"Lateral," Wharton heard Fink call.

Fink sprinted five yards away, slightly behind Wharton along the right sideline. There was only the deep man Smith to beat.

"Lateral!"

Smith cut off the field to the left and came at an angle, his face locked in on Wharton's torso, his arms out wide to grab a flag or force a lateral. Wharton brought his left hand to the ball carried in his right and dropped his shoulder, lowering his hands for the lateral toss to Fink while watching for the lean by Smith of his upper body out over his lower body toward Fink. At the shift in balance by Smith on his fake, Wharton pulled the ball back into his right arm. He felt his legs push off the dense turf to the left and throw his body past a diving Smith, who lunged for the flapping flag and came down with only kicked-up turf as Wharton ran untouched for the thirty yards to the end zone.

"How's that for a deliverable?" Wharton asked Piazza as they regrouped to kick off to McKinsey. Cheers from the CCG fans in the stands drifted across the field.

"He's back!" Piazza yelled, holding Wharton's hand up like a crowned boxing champion. He high-fived Piazza, Katie, Connor, Nathan, and Ursula. Fink stretched his hamstring on the ground. K.K. was not visible in the stands.

"Make sure that case of beer is cold," Wharton said to Fink.

Nothing set the tone in football like returning the opening kickoff for a touchdown. After a defensive stop by CCG, Wharton took over as quarterback at CCG's own forty-yard line. Phillips-Goydan ran toward Wharton like he was trying to ride a broom onto the field to replace Nathan and bring the new play in from Seymour. "He says for you to fake pump a short pass to Piazza and then hit him long. Strike deep early while we have the momentum."

Wharton broke the huddle and set up in the shotgun position. The read was easy for him; an isolated Piazza on the left side in single-man coverage confirmed Seymour's play call. Piazza's legs hit the turf like pistons and seemed to stay in one place before the pump fake from Wharton, Piazza releasing the legs to blow past the defender on the fake as the wounded ball fluttered in the air and fell twenty yards short of Piazza. The pain in Wharton's right shoulder and arm throbbed enough that Wharton fell to a knee. The arm had tried to lock in place.

"Your arm acting up?" Piazza asked.

"I'm fine." Wharton wondered how he was going to be able to

throw the ball long, or even short, downfield. Without the pain he would not have believed his arm was attached.

"Requires a bit of M-A-N," Fink said, wandering back to the huddle.

Both Wharton and Fink now knew that Wharton was not coming out of the game on his own volition. A rollout run by Wharton for a few yards, and a short pass dropped by Phillips-Goydan that would have been a first down, forced CCG to punt. With great defense on both sides throughout two quarters of play, the score at halftime was 6–0. K.K. was still not in the stands.

"Progress review," Seymour said to the CCG team huddled in the locker room. "Broken down into buckets, dropped passes are killing us. Eleven dropped passes in the first half. Takeaway: catch the ball. Phillips-Goydan, you have to make that play when Brock hits you over the middle for twenty yards right in the numbers. Let's close the loop. I had the incoming Rice summer interns in the stands run the numbers, and our margins on run plays are not high enough. We need to increase our passing attack. Our defense was excellent, and we disrupted their passing game very well. We need someone to take charge this half and step up as a playmaker."

"All I've ever been called. I'm just the kind of playmaker you need for times like these."

"We know you are, Mike," Carissa added from behind the huddle.

"We'd have two more touchdowns than the one *I* scored if you hadn't dropped passes."

Knowing all eyes were on him for his response, Fink rolled up his sleeves to reveal a temporary tattoo on each upper arm that read DEATH BEFORE DISHONOR.

"Was it really necessary to tattoo that cliché twice?" Wharton asked, not moved by the ostentatious display of superficially inked manliness. He turned toward Carissa and motioned to the real tattoo of a yin-yang butterfly on her exposed lower backside. "What about yours, does it symbolize promiscuity among Taoist insects?" With a little more foresight, Wharton thought, she would have tattooed a cocoon, so ten years later, after several life miles and babies, it would spread above her ass into a beautiful butterfly.

Fink stepped toward him. "You take yourself too seriously to be this bad at football *and* consulting." Without doing a consulting double-click of the situation, his left hand a balled fist, Wharton jabbed and hit Fink in the face. It knocked Fink back a few inches. "It's just a game, Brock." He rubbed his face before his Apache war cry drowned out Wharton's cry of pain as Fink tackled him, Wharton's right shoulder hitting the rubber floor first as they fell down wrestling. The pain from the fall almost knocked Wharton unconscious. To take the pain, he bit down on Fink's forearm as a measure to deal with what felt like a Civil War amputation of his right arm. No holds barred, Fink bit into Wharton's left arm, which was locked around his neck in a choke hold.

Not until Piazza threw the iced water from the cooler on them did they stop. Both bled from the nose, their uniforms torn. They stood and stared at each other with fists still clenched like brothers who were not sure if the fight was over or who had won. Wharton replayed the sequence of events in his head and was encouraged by his own internal tally that he believed favored him.

"This isn't tackle football." Seymour attempted to make light of the situation. "If you must, please hit McKinsey."

A pain shot through Wharton's right side. Through the tear in his uniform, the skin above his armpit on his chest twitched and sank inward. The dimple-sized pit just as suddenly vanished. "Dammit, I can't feel my right arm." It hung like a wet noodle at his side.

Seymour threw his visor down and said, "If we lose this game because you two—"

"I didn't survive the war to lose to a bunch of fucking consultants."

"You *are* a consultant, asshole," Wharton said.

"C-C-G! C-C-G!" Carissa chanted, shaking pom-poms and her integrity.

"U-S-A!" Fink chimed in to mine the mindless patriotism that had brought him thus far.

"U-S-A! U-S-A!" cheered the CCG players.

Corporate America, Wharton thought bitterly as their chanting nationalism flagged. He needed to find a new career and maybe a new country. But that would be tantamount to conceding defeat, and the throne, to Fink. Wharton knew he could not work for another company if that would allow Fink to one day reach managing director of CCG. Wharton would be found complicit in this crime against humanity and betraying the Houston business community that lunched at the Coronado Club. His reputation would be as worthless as his noodle of an arm felt. For the moment, the two illegitimate brotherly halves each sized the other up, as well as what new terrain their physical altercation had thrust them into. Neither hugged but the thought lingered in the musty locker room air.

After a failed attempt at a surprise onside kick by CCG, the Invisible Hand, in a series worthy of his name, threw four incomplete passes to turn the ball over on downs to start the second half. Since no one else had volunteered to step in as quarterback with Wharton's arm incapacitated, Fink was given the role. Daring to enter into a shootout with the Invisible Hand, Fink rolled out and against his body threw an interception across the field on his first play.

Wharton batted down two passes with his one good arm covering McKinsey's speedy receiver on the next series to rescue CCG. As if to end the quarter the way he had begun it, Fink threw a Hail Mary while scrambling away from a blitz that resulted in his second interception.

"I believe in going deep," Fink offered up as explanation after each pass was intercepted. It was the same approach, Wharton noted, that transferred to Fink's destructive consulting style.

In the fourth quarter with three minutes left to play in the game, Fink accomplished a rare Consulting Bowl feat with his third thrown interception.

"In the name of Jesus Christ, would you stop airing it out long on every pass?" Wharton screamed at the Jewish Fink as they switched over onto defense. "Don't erase my victory."

"Well, if you have any play ideas, I could sure use the help, Brock. The fuckin' problem with you is you only want a war so badly because you've never had a war," Fink said, walking over to him at the safety position and leaving his receiver unguarded. "If you could feel—"

"Get back on your receiver—"

Wharton was cut off by the call to hike the ball, which sent the

McKinsey receiver running down the far sideline unguarded. Wharton sprinted at a diagonal for the corner of the end zone where Fink's receiver headed. He leapt to deflect the pass. Wharton collided with the waiting wide-open receiver but managed to tip the underthrown pass before falling to the turf. The receiver, not having had to sprint across half a field to cover another teammate's player, kept his feet and waited under the tip ball for the catch. With a minute left to play, it was a tied game.

"Don't think I don't know what you are up to, acting like we were playing zone defense."

"We call it team defense in the military."

Playing to win, McKinsey kicked a bouncy onside kick that CCG recovered after it slipped through the hands of a McKinsey player. The referee spotted the ball on the fifty-yard line and Seymour called a time-out. He looked at Wharton and asked, "Can you throw short?"

Wharton had always resented the persistent accusation that he had not played through injuries. He believed his wife would have admired his grit had she been there. And so in a game his father had had to force him to play, Wharton now refused to be stripped of the glory rightfully his. "Leaders lead."

After the first five-yard completion, he comprehended Dr. Clifford's point about his throwing days being behind him. His arm felt like one of those twisty children's toys, locking up in the middle of a movement because it had not been wound up enough. Two incomplete passes later, he ran around the blitz on fourth down and dove for a six-yard run that resulted in a first down and a stopping of the play clock. McKinsey blitzed again, grabbing his flag seven yards behind the line of scrimmage as he frantically motioned with his good left arm for a worthless Phillips-Goydan to move around. CCG called a last time-out to strategize for a final shot at a touchdown with six seconds left to play and almost fifty yards to the end zone.

"I don't think heaving a Hail Mary is going to help your injured arm any," Katie said, her hand on his left shoulder as he took a knee. They both knew what the expectations were. "Don't make your pride be on the line, Brock. K.K.'s not even here."

Seymour came over to them and turned to Wharton. "Can you throw long?"

"Has my strategy ever been to not win?"

Seymour drew four circles on the right side of the board and one on the left. "Phillips-Goydan, Katie, Connor, and Piazza on the right, and Fink alone on the left. Depending on how McKinsey comes out, Brock can call an audible and direct traffic as he sees fit before Ursula hikes it. Make sure you throw it up high for grabs so we at least get a shot."

At the line, Wharton made the easy read from the shotgun position: no audible. McKinsey had every man back but one female pass rusher for Ursula to delay by blocking and buy Wharton the necessary time to heave a bomb deep. Wharton shook his right arm out to get the blood flowing down to his hand again. During the time-out, it had been going numb and the skin above his wrist was a cool band of doughy white.

As Wharton called out the cadence, his left eye caught what appeared to be a receiver in motion doglegging wide behind Wharton to join the wide receivers on the other side, his defender covering him far back on the other side of the ball. Her head down, Ursula must have seen it too out of her peripheral vision as the Swiss center long-snapped the ball in the confusion. Long and wide and two beats early, the spiraling ball sailed off Wharton's fingers as he reached out his right hand to stop it. Hoping to scoop it off the turf before the McKinsey pass rusher had a chance to dive for the loose ball, he jerked around to see the ball bounce—bounce into the hands of Fink!

Wharton dove to tackle Fink—in what Fink would later describe as comparable to the crazed British POW colonel in *The Bridge on the River Kwai* who attempts to stop the British commandoes from blowing up the enemy's bridge that the British POWs had slaved to build—grabbing Fink's right foot and reaching for his flag. Fink broke away from dragging Wharton with a kick to the left side of his face, eluded the McKinsey pass rusher with a fake to his left, and rolled right to release a fluttery football high and deep in the air. A wide spongy mass in the end zone compressed tight as both sides went up for the ball, which tumbled down as a shot duck would fall to the earth. It missed the fingers of nine players but fell into the cradling belly of Phillips-Goydan and knocked him down, his elbows reflexively holding on to the object that had stunned him by its blow to his flabby stomach.

"Do you still believe?" Fink was yelling at the sky in the madness, as he rolled around on the turf to notarize, in the manner of Fink, his upset.

A gutted Wharton could not rise from the turf for Fink's coronation as the CCG Alpha Male. Except for a predilection for catching strange bacterial strains that infected and broke out his acne, the anemic dandy known as Pat Phillips-Goydan had never made a catch in his life. Would *never* make another catch in his life. The skin below Wharton's left eye was inflating like a tire from Fink's kick, though that still bequeathed him one good eye to witness the victory spectacle. Like an overthrown dictator, a part of him could not but respect the power grab.

"Do you believe in miracles?" Seymour repeatedly screamed, running around the field looking for someone to hug. Fink crushed Phillips-Goydan with a bear hug at midfield.

"Do you still believe?" someone in the CCG group of twenty fans who had swarmed the field shouted at Fink, who crossed an asymmetrical Star of David.

"I believe in going deep!" Fink announced as his consulting creed when his CCG teammates lifted him on their shoulders and carried him off the field holding the gold Cup of Arthur Little, founder of modern management consulting, from Consulting Bowl X.

PART THREE

7.
BLACK FRIDAY, BLACK FLAGS

"I didn't lose. We're on the same team."

"This video—'Idiot vs. Teammate'—shows otherwise!" K.K. snapped at Wharton.

The video, posted most likely by a McKinsey fan, had, as they say, gone viral. A crueler depiction of "Idiot vs. Teammate," complete with a soundtrack, captions, and slow-motion footage of his attempted tackle of Fink and kick to the face, was also generating a vast amount of attention on the Internet. In the last week, searches for "CCG," as seen unmistakably on Wharton's jersey, were trending. Wharton cursed his generation and their affinity for sensational clips that mocked human effort as K.K. played the video again at the kitchen table. You could play through remarkable pain, yet all they would do was rob you of your glory. Maybe what he sought was not in the realm of the sublime but of the ordinary, human experience that social media could not defile. Nothing in his own life had ever had any of the authenticity of K.K.'s pregnancy, whatever might be growing in the belly of the little viper. But he could not tell what would have hurt worse: that K.K. hadn't been at the game, or if she had been there to support him and watched the final play live. Neither K.K. nor Wharton had eaten half of their kale scones and eggs. The article on page six of the *Houston Chronicle* about the video's popularity and where ex–UT quarterback

Brock Wharton was now had not helped their morning appetites. As a football standout in high school, Wharton had made the cover of the same paper several times.

Most peculiarly in the stressful last week, K.K.'s topographic bumpy brown eczema on her hands had leveled and whitened. "This is so humiliating. On your birthday. Even if you don't have a black eye next week, we can't appear at the Polo Club Ball like this." Like *losers*, she didn't have to say. Good, thought the birthday boy; not attending would be a fine present. Horses were the most overrated animal, in the vernacular of Mike Fink, this side of the Mississippi. He would rather attend a coon-ass gala with Fink in honor of alligators (brother meat-eaters). And did this not mean her billionaire parents would have to travel elsewhere next weekend and actually pay for a hotel room? Fuck the Klays. Their very name, which rhymed with *sly*, as in *shyster*, had always grated on Wharton, exhausting him every time he had to correct people who thought it was obviously pronounced, as any non-billionaire would have it pronounced, like *clay*. It paired perfectly with his shrew mother-in-law's Christian name of Knoble, a name with all the silent first-letter class for a *noble* life of which Wharton no longer wanted any part. "Why were you ever confident you could battle a guy who's been in a war? Why?"

"Because I was cursed with a dick. Because Fink waltzed in acting like he'd earned the freedom to create the myth he wanted to—and would be damned if he wasn't going to have a fun time doing it at the expense of anyone who tried to stop him. Out on his victory lap with his ruler in hand. With all my achievements adding up to nothing by way of his measuring up. Because I haven't been to war. I'm hardly the first to overlook the unconventional aptitude of combat veterans. Classic failure in counterinsurgencies is to not have planned for contingencies, and my playbook had not accounted for my arm completely giving out on me." He looked at K.K. "I never even liked football. I was always just the best at it."

"Jealousy?"

Of Mike Fink? He smiled at the realization. "Admiration."

It was not an apology but thanks that Wharton owed Fink. How to explain to his own wife that Fink had stumbled on the golden breast of this land, where a selective tolerance nurtured remaking yourself into whoever you yearned to be if you had earned it. Even had the guts to try to earn it. Wharton attempted for a few minutes to convey this lesson without mansplaining. They both knew K.K. was the brighter of the two, her professional idleness in part a loving bone thrown to Wharton so he could shine brighter on life's stage. The analysis he needed was not the analysis he received (and deserved) in her recommendation that they postpone his birthday dinner two weeks. After she left the table, he tried to wash the yolk off their plates with cold water and placed the sticky plates in the dishwasher. Wharton stretched his right arm with the elastic band Dr. Clifford had recommended. He decided he would take the long route to his office along the bayou.

All of life was probably myth creation. Wharton recalled his father's merry Enron executive friends who had all divinely exited four months prior to the slide, selling their stock in the company before publicly wrecking it. They privately boasted about landing even better jobs elsewhere or starting their own companies with the money they had made off with. Half of them audaciously started their own namesake charities, the nonprofits around town all too happy to take their money, naming buildings and awards after the thieves-turned-philanthropists. The silver lining of the silver spoon was its own folklore in the constantly reinventing city of Houston. In the end, the scoundrels had been worthy of beginning anew for only one reason, for their faith had never been in Enron, nor in oil and gas, much less in consulting, nor in any other profession that did not understand the soul of the overheated city on the bayou: the energy of Houston was its true bequest, the exploration rights open to princes or paupers if they found the lost golden city, and had packed enough mosquito repellent to put down stakes.

His family's myth was certainly no different under magnification. Wharton need not even look as far as his wife's preposterous ranching family of frauds: they who would expertly lecture on the spiciness of barbecue sauce two feet away from their sweating galley slave who prepared for them his own family's sauce recipe passed down over hundreds of years of tenancy. Wharton's own proud father struck Wharton every passing day as more of a mythmaker: the hero who had saved his father-in-law's oil drill-bit company was really but a wastrel from a River Oaks family with a far smaller trust fund. Wharton's father had made the great sacrifice to leave his job as a waiter to marry Wharton's mother and into a highly profitable company with assets in excess of one hundred million dollars that desperately needed food service industry counsel to save it from bankruptcy. When he sold the company for a bit less than sixty million dollars forty years later, strangers who encountered him at a party could not have been faulted for thinking they were talking to one of the great turnaround artists of the last century as he spoke of the confidential business transactions of his late father-in-law's former company.

To Wharton's own credit, as accredited by Wharton, he had tried to prove himself in his in-laws' eyes, earning money of his own. Aside from their starter house, he had refused his in-laws' money. Well, there was the usual vacation money and free use of their six vacation homes, yes. And they had advanced Wharton and K.K. an endowed trust for their planned four children, yes. But the rest of the money he had accepted came from his side of the family.

The polluted water of the Buffalo Bayou, its depths unexplored, reflected nothing back at Wharton. He walked along the concrete banks of this rising half-ass river, where no king had ever held his court. He had parked blocks from the Houston One Center to visit Allen's Landing, a replica of Houston's birthplace, on the bayou. He ruminated on whether his black eye for the final presentation yesterday had been a factor in not landing a follow-on enablement project with Phoenix Energy. Screw Phoenix Energy. Karma was going to be harsh for the oil industry after years of plundering the earth. Already Houston had by far the most urban flooding deaths of any city over the last twenty years. Climate change had Houston in its target sights, and all the energy companies built to last should be focused on clean energy or carbon capture anyway if they wanted the energy capital to be above water in another fifty years. Even statisticians were bemused by how only Houston could suffer a five-hundred-year flood event every year.

The first indication that his thirty-fourth birthday would be known as the Black Friday of his business career came at lunch. The football-shaped chocolate cake—its buttercream icing soft enough for the tongue to separate the gritty sugar crystals—had cost Piazza some money, as it was clearly commissioned from a high-end bakery. The irregularly spaced hash marks of decorative white frosting, the presence of only one end zone goalpost, and the absence of candles on the cake told Wharton it had been a last-minute order. Nothing was worse than when Piazza was a concerned friend, as Piazza was always the first to know CCG news. The other indication of darkness on the horizon was that CCG made it a point not to celebrate birthdays.

"Thirty-four," Stanley Weinberg said to Wharton, the only other person left in the kitchen who had stuck around for a second slice of the cake. The Snail's bug eyes were on the cake atop the red plastic plate he held. No one had wanted to make eye contact. Wharton did not blame them; he had barely been able to look in the mirror during a hurried morning shave. "I would have guessed that was the price of oil before I would have guessed that was your age, Brock." Wharton wearily waited on the Snail to raise the guillotine blade (and his eyes) as the emissary pushed back his horn-rimmed glasses on the bridge of his nose. "Seymour needs to talk with you. A stop by his office in ten minutes after he finishes up with Fink should work perfectly." He lifted the plate of cake he held and finally looked at Wharton. "This football cake is the best."

Seymour's office had a great view on rare clear days. One could see out forty miles to the bayside of Galveston Island. The shipwrecked Spanish explorer Cabeza de Vaca had named it "Isle of Misfortune" before passing himself off as a shaman among a cannibalistic Native American tribe to survive. "What's with the dour look, Brock? It's your birthday, right?"

"Stanley tells me you have a gift for me. Is it for all the years of bringing you business?"

Seymour pushed a button on his desk that notified his secretary. "This isn't about downsizing or your annual review." Which now Wharton knew meant the summons was about both. Seymour leaned back in his chair behind his desk, an emoji of job security. "I don't doubt your ability to bring in future accounts, or more importantly, retain clients for us once your black eye goes away. But we're already at a crossroads and time is not on our side. This is about the future of CCG and who our clients will be. It is essential that a CCG partner be able to lead and mentor junior consultants. And this will be a great leadership challenge for you should you choose to accept." Seymour did not need to smile to make it apparent to CCG's fallen golden boy that he had waited for this moment. The Snail had served the news up with a similar gleam in the filament of his bug eyes as he dipped Wharton's birthday cake in schadenfreude. "You can't be a CCG partner without people management skills," Seymour said, looking at his watch. Wharton stared at the most senior partner without the aforementioned skill.

"I assume everyone else in the office has turned down this assignment?"

"Strangely, Phillips-Goydan volunteered, but he would only reinforce the white-shoe image problem CCG has in the field. Although I landed this project because of my relationship with Spencer Hill of our client Hill Corps, this unique assignment is not with Hill Corps. Spencer's staffing request specifically identified consultants with a certain type of profile." Wharton knew of the privately owned Hill Corps, though he had never worked on a project with the giant Atlanta-based construction firm. He thought he vaguely remembered an interview on a yacht in *Forbes* years ago with Spencer, or maybe it was his father. "The engagement is less than a month. Should be back by first week of March. Since K.K. is due in mid-April, talk it over with her first. I tell you, the business that could come out of this will explode—" Fink's knock and entrance cut off Seymour, who motioned for him to sit down next to Wharton.

"Where is it?"

"Kurdistan, partly."

"That's not a country. Iraq?"

"Iraq as well. The half not governed by ISIS."

Wharton expected Fink to be grinning down a grizzly bear with glee, but he stared out to the gulf. Seymour hastened to say, "Defense contracts. For management advising. And there is a clause for us to tie it to more work from public-private partnership after this initial engagement under the Task Force for Development and Stability Operations led by Spencer Hill. Defense is the real growth industry for consulting. Where the big money is with Iraq back on for business."

"With new wars popping up all the time," Fink said, still staring out the window and his foot tapping a faster rate than when he had interviewed in Wharton's office.

"War zone consulting."

"Why even have generals or an army?" Fink asked. "All we need are a few strategic management consultants and Blackwater."

"We could be a regional champion as part of the advising task force for business. And all the business to be had with all the private companies getting back into it over there. This is the lucrative soft underbelly of the military-industrial complex, our human capital carrying far lower overhead costs than armaments. The special initiatives we can lead with this mandate would be huge. We can do our part fighting terrorism by restoring an environment conducive to effectiveness and leading economic development."

"That's rich. You sure CCG didn't use this sales pitch to consult for Bush?"

The gaudiest wing of Harvard Business School had been remodeled and renamed after the Hill family when Wharton had been a student there, the memory of the golden wallpaper and curtains begging him to inquire about Hill's profit motive. "Hill left Hill Corps?"

"His dad is still CEO, but Spencer had to temporarily step aside as CFO when the secretary of defense asked him to lead this initiative."

"How patriotic of him. Even more if there are conflicts of interest," Fink added.

Seymour shook his head at Fink, who had saluted him. "If you ask me, he's gotten a raw deal for his sacrifice of spending half of each month away from his family and taking an astronomical pay cut to boot. Some of the criticism is his own doing because of his large personality, but he's received a lot of unfair press for failures that have nothing to do with him. Our involvement should ease those tensions and help him successfully execute his mission. Iraq was a mess long before Spencer Hill entered as the fixer." Seymour held out both hands apart to show the size of his catch. "McKinsey made over a hundred million dollars in the first three years of the Iraq War for procurement-related advice and assistance—and that was just with the British taxpayer! Getting back in again isn't going to be cheap for Obama."

Seymour could choose to ignore Fink, but Wharton could not. The horror in Fink's shaky voice told of a new revolt, one far more hostile than the campaign he directed at Wharton. Fink steadied himself with the arms of his chair. The trembling persisted. If Fink had ever had any fear, or wavering heart, if this was what it was, he had always been able to conceal it, yet now his unnerving began to unnerve Wharton. But why then would Fink have accepted the assignment? On a day that would mark his new age and, Wharton hoped, reinvention, in the moleskin journal he had bought himself earlier in the week, Seymour's present to him was humiliation. "What's the scope?"

"That's the beauty, Brock. The initial deliverable is to both assess the Iraqi Ministry of Oil's decision making and facilitate how best to unlock growth and development for large-scale private international investment. Joint ventures in the south and north of the country. But we can be pioneers over there and expand this to other parts of the economy once we get a foothold. I had a great discussion about this with Hill. For foreign investors, Iraq is one of the last 'ground floors' the world will ever know. Like China was thirty years ago when they opened it up. Iraq might have even more oil than Saudi. I expect you two as well to make contact and network among the private oil companies over there for additional possible contracts. Lay a pipeline of business back to this office while the U.S. is engaged again over there."

"Yeah, we don't want the war to end before we get a piece. Bad for business, and most un-American." Fink now sat motionless and with his arms flat atop the arms of the chair, his face blank and unreadable, his lines leaking out as if last words from the electric chair. "Apparently it is only the soldiers who aren't getting rich in our overseas escapades."

Wharton excused himself to go call K.K. He made it halfway down the hallway. Like Seymour, Wharton knew what K.K.'s answer would be regarding an engagement in Iraq. His bottom row of teeth pulled down on the soft coating of his upper lip skin trapped between his upper row. There was some truth that, as he told CCG applicants, he had not returned to investment banking after business school because consulting far topped banking in a daily tally of intellectual challenges. But there was something more to it than just intellectual ego. More that human factor that didn't want to be buried daily in spreadsheets, for at least at first he had not been immune to the desire to engage with other minds to solve the most difficult problems encountered by businesses. Wharton knew it was crazy to expect this feeling to be reborn in Iraq, whatever its strange pull was for Fink. The refugees from the region could not get out of there fast enough in rafts that would not make it across Wharton's pool. They didn't have the time for risk assessments. Wharton thought about his journal, what his father would disparage as a diary, and how of the three entries so far two had begun with, "You know what I hate . . ." He doubted it would count in Fink's book as doing his part, but assessing and assisting potential business development through his consulting experience would be a start to taking stock in his responsibility as an American citizen. He had no illusion of turning the humiliation of his current stature at CCG into heroics. But whatever Iraq was, it was something real. More real than anything he had experienced as an adult. This was not dinner with his father and a Winston Churchill cocktail quote about the cradle of civilization. So Iraq was presently a savage mess, Wharton judged, which meant about as civilized as Houston high society. Better to be lost in the cosmos than not aware of it. And over there, aside from his responsibilities as a consultant, there were no expectations of who he had to be. Even football was soccer.

"You know what I like . . ." Wharton began upon entering, as a silent Seymour and a smiling Fink listened to his outlining of the interesting aspects of the assignment he had just accepted.

• • •

From the steps of their transient quarters at Incirlik Air Base in Turkey, the roar from the fighter jets ripped open the fabric of sound on their way to bomb ISIS. Wharton observed soldiers in non-American camouflage uniforms strolling over to the chow hall without looking over to the airfield and the constant jet noise. Fig trees and greenery dotted the military base architecture lost in a 1950s time warp. More than the jets, the soreness in his left arm from all the vaccinations reminded him that they were not extras on a movie set.

"Goddamn, this place hasn't had this much zip since the Cold War."

"You think it's retaliation for burning the Jordanian pilot?"

"Daesh killed him weeks before. You can tell from a glance at the video they released how much time went into editing it to their marketing standards. But your hypothesis is probably spot-on." Wharton put his fingers in his ears as another fighter jet took off and Fink peered up at the streak of flame from the jet's tail. "You grow to be grateful for the loss of hearing that sound will cause when you have to call in the fast-movers for fire. Let's roll."

In the chow hall, the same faces from the chartered flight of contractors huddled together underneath the televisions tuned to the twenty-four-hour news stations. Fink led them to an empty table away from a group of contractors who Wharton had swapped movies with on the transatlantic flight (Wharton, who had mainly brought along a stack of Iraqi history books, realized quickly that those in the book-club crowd were in the minority), most of whom were field construction hands. With this gang, Wharton found himself wishing he still had his black eye for the sake of street cred. It was a shame that none of them could leave the base due to the heightened security over the spate of bombings across Turkey. Wharton and Fink had agreed on their flight across the Atlantic Ocean about going into town to talk with the refugees who had fled the chaos they headed toward. Wharton had largely assuaged K.K.'s misgivings about the assignment by assuring her that he would primarily be in the greater Turkey area—*practically Europe*. But it appeared the butcher's bill had come due for Turkey: a bloody vengeance at the hands of the radicalized foreigners whom Turkey had once allowed to intern under ISIS, and who now returned across the same borders with a brand-new plan. Before Wharton and Fink had finished their sandwiches, two DoD contractors sat down next to them with food stacked all over their trays as if they hadn't eaten in the three days since they departed from America.

Though they were dressed in the familiar tacti-*cool* pants (Velcro pockets for any size of ammunition or tobacco can) and multicam American flag hats with perched sunglasses to conceal their pale heads, nothing could hide the years of sloth their waistlines had been able to subcontract out to the legions of third-country nationals or indigenous Iraqi and Afghan contractors. Wharton was learning that there were just as many contractors behind desks in Iraq as there were of the more infamous hired guns providing security, though they all wore the same three-hundred-dollar boots from REI. Now, that company had discovered gold, Wharton thought, supplying these gold rushes of the past fifteen years. The more outgoing of the pink sponge representatives who had allowed the American military to privatize certain positions to adopt a leaner fighting force squinted at Wharton. "What outfit are y'all with?"

"CCG."

"Is that part of KBR?"

"Cambridge Consulting Group."

"The company handling the base's water purification?"

"We're strategic management consultants."

"What does it pay?"

Refreshing how this question was never socially taboo among his new salt-of-the-earth companions, Wharton mused. They certainly were a different breed from his Houston friends, a self-conscious lot of males who had all married up, usually guarding the degree to which until death. "Not enough but we do it for love of country," Fink chimed in.

"We do housing trailer maintenance. Doesn't pay what it did ten years ago during the contractor surge, but it's three times better than home and the first hundred grand they can't tax!"

Wharton tried not to gawk at the sheen of grease on the fried drumstick at the mouth of the bigger one, who grunted, "You two leaving this afternoon for All-you-dead?" Al-Udeid Air Base? Of course, an example of the famed barracks wit. Wharton mentally noted the rather forced pun for his war journal. The slick grease sheen reminded him of the clubby shine of a worn navy blazer at the elbows.

"Yes, we need to go pack for it, Brock."

Out on the sidewalk, Fink spit and said, "There's modern warfare for you. Whatever you do, don't mess up their shipment of ice cream. We have to put ten crackerjack contractors like those clowns on the dole for every boot on the ground. That's why we're losing. Goddamn corporate capitalism goes to war. We need to just insert a bunch of small-footprint Special Ops to advise . . ." A group of four younger civilian males walked toward them.

"*Fink*?"

"Whiskey. Tango. Foxtrot. Ginger Queen Tompkins?"

Fink embraced his old friend. Between his unshaven red hair and build, he was the spitting image of Wharton's freshman-year tight end roommate, the Loose Moose, who had aged poorly and limped to keep up among the promiscuous pretty young things of the medical sales world. Were these guys the snake-eaters of Special Forces legend? The other three males continued on into the chow hall. "Been since that first trip to Mosul, right? You still in, Swamp Rat?"

"I wish. Technically my last day of terminal leave was in June. Wouldn't you know it, right when 5th Group got the call to send three hundred and prevent the fall of Iraq."

"You're looking at the tip of the spear."

"Is that what you're doing here?" Fink laughed and fist-bumped him. "I should have known."

"Where you at now?"

"In Houston. I work for a company called Cambridge Consulting Group. Usually back behind a desk dodging papercuts like Mosul days when I had to support your ass outside the wire tearing it up on missions. This is my colleague, Brock."

"Nice to meet you, Brock. I'm Shane. Former Group guy, too?"

Fink cut in before Wharton could reply, "No, he's over here with me because we've got a project in Iraq to assess growth."

"Of the Islamic State? For State?"

"Commissioned through DoD. Believe it or not, so private foreign investment can come into Iraq. We're supposed to advise on how to make the Iraqi Ministry of Oil more efficient."

"I thought it wasn't about the oil." *Tell me about it*, thought the once-potential Mr. Houston. Wharton was going green after this engagement.

"Ironic how history fights its own war."

"You are going to have a helluva deployment if that's your mission. Hope you haven't forgotten how to sit through endless key leader engagements."

"That's all consulting is, one KLE after another. How's your mission?" Tompkins mad-dogged Wharton up and down and then looked back at Fink after his assessment of Wharton appeared to find Wharton wanting. He was silent until Fink said, "He's fine."

"Good and bad. The ratlines are set up and working. We can't really find a Syrian faction that puts up any fight. My buddies with the Kurds in Iraq say they are pretty good and they're getting into it some without making the news."

"Man, it's good to see you. I know you need to get going to more important things. If you see any of the guys, pass on to them my best and to hit me up if they need anything. I'm filled with envy at what you're doing. Civilian life pays better and you can have fun in a normal city, but you're miserable and there's no sense of purpose. You guys are making a difference."

"Thanks. Doesn't feel like it."

They all shook hands and parted, though Fink stopped after a few steps and turned back around. Whatever he had planned to say to Tompkins he didn't, just watched him silently as he walked into the chow hall to rejoin his teammates. Wharton bent down and pretended to tie his shoes to give Fink a moment. When Wharton came back up, Fink had a pair of orange foam earplugs in his outstretched hand. "Take these. You're going to wish you had them for any military aircraft we fly on. Your hearing is one more thing you can lose in Iraq." Fink showed him how to roll a foam earplug between his fingers to make it skinny and properly emplace it after he had used the other hand to pull the opposite ear up like a Dickens-era schoolmaster would with a mischievous child's ear. Before Wharton could thank him for this unforeseen kindness, Fink clarified the rationale behind the cease-fire. "I've got enough to worry about without you undermining me in Iraq. And you ain't got a chance without me and a shared sense of purpose."

Wharton and Fink passed most of the time until their flight in a secluded corner of the Internet-less passenger terminal reading about Iraq. Fink would put down his book every couple of minutes to look up a word in his Arabic dictionary.

"What did your friend mean by ratlines?"

"Ratlines are how we supply MWE—men, weapons, and equipment—to the resistance fighters. The terrorists have their own ratlines as well. In the eighties, America ran ratlines through Pakistan to the mujahedeen to beat the Soviets."

"The same mujahedeen who now fight us in Afghanistan."

"We never learn. You can control what goes down the ratline but not always what blows back up the ratline."

"Swamp Rat, huh?" This intelligence had failed to make it into Perez's report. The insider worlds within Special Operations must be as byzantine as those of any royal family.

"You can see why I prefer 'King of the Mississippi.' He gave me that nickname in SERE, a school for survival, evasion, resistance, escape. Our SERE team sure regretted picking the city boy to be the procurer of food during the evasion phase. My foray managed to bring back only one prickly pear cactus. All my knowledge of river tall tales hadn't made me aware either of how to properly clean it before eating. The almost-invisible thorns lodged in our throats for a week kind of exposed my soft rich-kid upbringing."

"So why did you join?"

"The Great Question," Fink said, putting down his book on the making of the modern Middle East. "I used to think I did it to serve, do my part during wartime. Accepting this engagement and the itch to get back over here is making me question that romantic view. Now I think I'm as addicted as the misguided jihadists who only know themselves when at war. Originally, maybe there was some psychological bullshit to joining the military, like as an awkward kid I had to prove myself by taking the greatest risks. Or define myself beyond the label of Jewish. A lifetime of watching my castrated father get owned by my domineering mother didn't help either. Never won a single fight in his life. This on top of his job selling lingerie, the Panty King of New Orleans." Fink rolled his eyes. "The banality of postwar life can be more traumatic than combat. It's a fight to remember the feeling of my premilitary life, how after 9/11 all my buddies bailed one by one on our idea to jump into the fight."

Thank your lucky stars for a weak father, grumbled Wharton to himself. "A domineering father is not kind on the psyche either. You spend your life trapped in someone else's skin."

"Fathers and sons. Rejoice that you're having a girl. But as millennials would caution: don't assign gender roles. Of course as the Harvard study this past week shows, our generation is all gung ho for sending troops to fight the new evil Islamic State but not for serving. Effectively meaning the eternal bum-rush of thank-you-for-your-service handshakes will remain the lucky prize for the few." A mocking Fink fondled Wharton's hand in a two-handed handshake to jerk it up and down while he queued grateful tears at the corners of his eyes to thank him for Wharton's service as a soldier stand-in. "Back home among people with money, I'm like an exotic animal in a zoo for having served. One day we'll be even more idealized, like World War II's 'Greatest Generation,' another sentimental label given to a mostly drafted generation by another generation of males who felt so guilty for dodging service in Vietnam that they later had to mythologize their disappointed dads and 'The Good War.'"

Wharton was in no danger of mythologizing Dean Wharton. But could Wharton be a worse dad than his own father? He wondered how scared his father had been in the months before his birth. "You're making me nervous about being a father."

"And you're making me nostalgic for the military, which means I am losing it. Normally, I reflect on what was I ever thinking volunteering for the military. I'm expecting that to hit me hard once we land in the desert in Qatar."

The chartered flight for contractors to Al-Udeid Air Base arrived an hour after dark. They passed through Qatari customs and registered with the American contractors at the air terminal. A Bengali subcontractor drove them over on a bus to the other side of the base, where trailers housed thousands of U.S. Air Force personnel. They had to carry their personal bags and the big tan bag that contained their individual body armor and helmets all the way across a field of rocks to the last row of trailers. Talk about a place that could use some VIP services; Wharton had never experienced so much time mismanaged. Lights glowed orange in the near-dark desert and beyond that nothing. After a twenty-minute march at the front of a dispersed gaggle of passengers from the contractor flight, Wharton and Fink arrived at a transient bay filled with thirty mattresses on the ground. The open showers overtaken by black mold ended Wharton's hope for a purifying cleanse.

"How much cash did you take out in Turkey?"

"Five hundred, why?"

"I reckon I'm going to need it to expedite our departure for Iraq."

"We have to pay to go to war?"

"You want to stay here for a week on that list they put us on? Hell, I'd rather consult."

Wharton handed over his cash. The desolation of this place could make a consultant beg to stay in Manhattan, Kansas. They lugged their bags back outside a few trailers away from the other contractors to stage them for a discreet getaway should Fink's bribe land them on the flight departing at one in the morning for Baghdad. The darkness made it impossible to make out anything on what might as well have been the moon's surface. After an hour, Wharton had counted the arrival of four U.S. Air Force cargo jets on the distant runway. The logistics, the weapons, the risk assessment, the costs, the strategic value, the necessary manpower could be the case study of an era. Here was one of the ends of empire.

When Fink returned he arrived in the back of a white Toyota Hilux pickup truck. They threw their bags in the back and Fink passed Wharton a surgical mask to put over his nose and mouth as Fink gave the thumbs-up sign for the Filipino contractor to race for the air terminal. Fink had to yell to be heard over the howl of the desert wind: "A decade and a half into the War on Terror and money still talks! We're a couple of strap-hangers on a C-130."

Wharton, a CCG principal, was still the nominal head on an assignment in which it had become clear he would need Fink more than Fink would need him. Fink's dark assurance all week had been that Wharton at least had someone to leave his money to from the special war zone death insurance CCG had made them sign. Now clamped on Fink's left wrist was a silver band that came together like the letter C on the backside of his wrist. The metal had had writing inscribed on it before it had been worn out. But the letters KIA could still be made out. Wharton pulled his mask off to shout, "I will notify our DoD contact once we get to the terminal that we are arriving ahead of schedule." The dust that had coated the rest of his face caused a sneezing fit.

"The Middle East isn't the best for allergies. I hope you have a solid agenda for coming."

An agenda? "What?"

"Don't tell me you're the first Westerner ever to head to Iraq without an agenda."

Wharton was still not tracking. He let his worry slip. "What's yours?"

"Certainly not to make CCG or any other American company more profits in this war."

• • •

Wharton tried again to move his feet in the dark. But his right leg was locked between the legs of the asleep soldier across from him. How could anyone in thirty pounds of body armor and a Kevlar helmet sleep when every breath of the fuel fumes was an effort to not puke? Fink had again displayed his experience, for he sat himself diagonal to Wharton against the "skin" of the cargo plane. Wharton was seated on a canvas seat in the middle of the plane. There was no back to the seat, just a red nylon net and a metal bar in the middle of it with another soldier on the other side to bump against. Fink had joked they were lucky they weren't parachuting out of it; Wharton wasn't so sure that would hold true, as the ride had had more sudden drops than a roller coaster. Nor had any of the crew been able to answer why this flying metal cow of a plane still depended on propellers. Wharton tugged again at the chin strap of his green helmet, which was far more uncomfortable and complex than his football helmet had ever been. Were it not for the earplugs, Wharton's eardrums would have aged a good twenty years.

Fink's response prior to their flight had not really answered the more pressing question of Wharton's regarding Fink's agenda. It unsettled Wharton that this was not the first flight he had spent decoding the mystique Fink liked to introduce, though the first where the destination was a war zone. Wharton had surprised himself by seizing a shot at Iraq, agreeing to the assignment rather than be laid off and start anew. Part of his own variation of reinvention, he now reflected, consulting a nation on the brink, picking up the shattered glass pieces for a mirror test of self-identity. But Fink's disclosure stirred within Wharton an old fear, a fear of being duped again in life by a partner. On their honeymoon, K.K. had insisted on Africa for the peacefulness of its scenery, when in fact she had arranged the formal consummation to coincide with the carnage of the migrating wildebeest across the crocodile-infested rivers. If Wharton had no true conscious agenda, no Fink testing of integrity in the overseas crucible, he did wish to not come home reeling like a mind-fucked bitch at the hands of a companion.

The red lights inside the plane went out and the nose of the plane dropped straight down. Wharton's testicles claimed his abdomen like a homeless hermit crab happening upon a discarded shell. Streaks of fire lit up the darkness outside the window. "Flares to counter surface-to-air missiles!" the now-awake soldier across from Wharton shouted at him, which had the countereffect of not easing his concerns about the plane's dive. The plane tactically swayed like Death's own metronome in its inferno maneuvers.

"Of course."

The plane landed with a crash. When the plane's back ramp dropped they were rushed out of its hostile womb by the type of airport personnel no different from ones in the States. Inside a wing at Baghdad International Airport, Wharton and Fink were ordered to watch a briefing with the other six contractors from the flight.

"No one goes anywhere until they sit through this briefing. I'm retired Army, twenty-two years as a master sergeant in logistics. Shut up and pay attention if you want to know what to do over here," a woman in her late forties with dreadlocks barked.

Onscreen were PowerPoint slides below even Fink's standards. Stranger still coming from an expert in logistics, but there it was: a muddled slide on suicide bombers followed a slide on venomous snakes and spiders. "Isn't it standard tactics, techniques, and procedures for the terrorists to follow up with a second or third suicide bomber? Your slide instructs to take cover and remain until forces arrive."

"You do whatever you want there, killer. Be the star of your own action movie."

Wharton did not ask any more questions of his fellow logistician, waiting until the presentation was over to call the number of their DoD contact. "Is Spencer Hill there? This is Brock Wharton with Cambridge Consulting Group and we are here in Baghdad at the airport."

"Did he say if we had a military escort?" Fink asked when Wharton joined him outside.

"I didn't ask, but he said he would arrive with a convoy in a few hours."

"Great, the sun will already be up and people out after first prayer. The last time I was in Baghdad there were no lights like this. The effect transported you back to the eighth century. It was one of those magic tricks aided by the electrical grid having been blown up."

The lights of the ancient capital, city of Wharton's childhood dreams from his nanny's reading to him of *One Thousand and One Nights*, were a hazy glow in the dusty distance. Wharton rued not having brought the old leather copy that he had kept with him in college and would read after losses. He started to share this anecdote with Fink but thought better of supplying him with any ammunition in a war zone. Years after his nanny Annabelle had passed away from cancer, Wharton had read a three-volume biography of his dad's hero

Winston Churchill, and how he too had been closer to his nanny than to his distant mother. But what struck Wharton the most from the only book ever passed to him by Dean Wharton was that much like Churchill, his own father had also abruptly terminated Wharton's nanny when he was a teenager and away from home one weekend. Wharton never saw her again.

Their convoy to the Green Zone did not arrive until almost ten in the morning. Although Spencer Hill and his swarm of armed cargo-pants contractors had already bypassed the Iraqi airport police and security inside the airport as if they worked there, Hill alone removed his sunglasses and stopped halfway across the lobby for a sovereign wave. It appeared to be directed, in part, at Wharton and Fink. If it could be said America had no exit strategy, it sure as hell still knew how to make an entrance. Had Hill been an applicant at CCG, Wharton would have scrambled fighter jets to dismantle any gate in his way. Wharton nodded as he walked past the Iraqi security, who in their crisp uniforms stared at a scene replayed daily for them over the last twelve years.

Every article mentioned his hair. The Swoop. Like that of any good Southern white college boy with the means to go to a high-end salon, the brown hair retained its indulgence to fall over the beginnings of wrinkles on the forty-three-year-old forehead of Spencer Hill. In person, Wharton thought it subtler. Had to be the best hair in all of Iraq. It was fifteen years easy of turning-back-the-clock hair, youth preserved in all the ways that skin never could. Not surprisingly, such perfect carefree hair reportedly drove Spencer Hill Sr. crazy flopping around inside the hallways at Hill Corps headquarters.

But Hill's hair was overshadowed by his monarch-among-his-legion uniform: navy blazer with gold buttons and khaki pants tucked into desert boots. More, he was all too aware he cut quite a figure in an ensemble that gave Hill the air of a proconsul with a mandate from America. Even Hill's oxford shirt was pressed, with *S. Hill* monogrammed in red above the breast pocket. Though the shirt was blue, the collar and cuffs were white in the vintage banker's I-go-out-of-my-way-to-be-an-asshole style. And yet Hill pulled it off, the starched collar and cuffs paired with his soft skin, of an almost-tasteful orange hue that had so far gotten the better of tanning salons and seemed to balance a strategic reserve of gentleness with a dominant personality. He might have quit lacrosse after his first year at Washington and Lee University, but Hill had clearly not quit steroids, as his small childlike hand managed to own Wharton's in their handshake. "Gentlemen, welcome to Iraq. We've got my own little private army to escort us back to base. I know you're tired, so bear with us as we need to make our way to the waiting convoy. Once we reach the Green Zone, you guys can catch some shut-eye before our first meeting. I apologize for the heavy-handed security posture, but these restrictions come from Washington, never a quick study in counterinsurgency. If it were up to me, we would take a ferry on the Tigris with some Iraqi businessmen and pick their brains about development. Not cocooned like occupiers with body armor." Hill had Wharton and Fink strap on their body armor and helmets.

They followed Hill and carried their own bags as the security contractors collapsed in from their fanned-out perimeter to hustle them to the waiting convoy. The contractors held their slung rifles at an angle that cut across their bodies diagonally like they were an almost-living coat of arms. A burly guy in his forties with a long beard and a Dallas Cowboys hat on next to Wharton never looked at him but answered a voice in his headset several times with "Roger."

"Easy there, Hollywood," Fink said to a security contractor in a skull-and-crossbones hat who had put his hand on Fink's back to direct him into the blackened suburban. Fink had stopped at the truck door to turn around. "You might want to flick your M4 back onto Safe so you don't shoot me in my femoral artery playing hopscotch. Brock, please note how difficult it is to see when one's selector switch catches on body armor in high-speed sunglasses indoors. Where operator discipline comes in." Hill put on only a helmet, his helmet spray-painted desert tan over its original coat of Kevlar green, before he climbed into the vehicle. Wharton followed and hauled shut, after two failed attempts, the heavy armored door that must also have doubled as a bank vault door.

The big highways had green signs with white Arabic and English letters, and palm trees on the sides of the roads as they got off the highways. Wharton and Fink were with Hill in the middle of the three full-size SUVs, with a pickup truck in both front and back of the SUVs. Wharton thought the older highways looked very much American-made. Some construction company had benefited from Saddam's infrastructure initiative in the totalitarian decades prior to the latest wars. Wharton's father had been friends with one Houston oilman who had gone to prison for funneling millions of dollars illegally to Saddam's regime for oil in spite of international sanctions after the Gulf War; his fabulous party-throwing wife had been allowed to maintain her socialite status without penalty, Iraqis having a more torturous memory than Houstonians for profiting off large-scale murder under a dictator.

"CCG in Iraq, turning around companies and countries." Hill himself turned around in his seat to face them and touched his cocked helmet, the chin strap of which dangled undone like he was a war-weary John Wayne. Yet Hill looked almost like the war was aging him in reverse and he had never had such a golden experience. "When the secretary of defense handpicks you for a mission, you trade your hard hat in for a Kevlar helmet. America came here for WMDs, stayed to build a democracy, but we're back for capitalism, gents. Over time it is the most effective weapon in our arsenal against this new evil breed of terrorism." Hill turned toward the window to look at Iraq for a second before returning to the subject of himself. "Not like I don't have better things to do than be in Iraq. I won't go into it, but if you only knew how much money I lose every day I'm here leading our Task Force for Development and Stability Operations." Hill removed the helmet from his head, a smile now appearing with the weight of modesty lifted. "America is finally calling for the best after a decade-plus of pussyfooting about over here. Not everyone is talented enough to wrestle with history, tackle the ultimate challenge of restoring an old civilization through change. These people have never won. They're not used to a winner. They don't even know what it would be like to win."

Not until after Hill finished his speech about how he personally could make Iraq great again did Wharton think of Fink, who acted as if he'd been pulled into the other world flying past outside his window, like not a word of the rallying cry had registered with him. Mosques and minarets towered over the road. Fruit cart vendors littered side streets, a carpet shop next to a cell phone store. Men and women and children in all sorts of Arabic and Western dress. In the backseat, they faced Hill, who had turned back around from his seat in the middle row. "The Department of Defense will fill a void if it sees it in war. There is no question we have the finest military the world has ever seen. My point is we need to allow them to win. Because we're not winning wars anymore. Let me tell you something: the men and women in uniform I meet over here every day that make up our all-volunteer force want to be here. But is it fundamentally fair to send them into a combat zone where there is no real path to economic development? That's why the DoD is using economic revitalization as an instrument of war. The Task Force for Development and Stability Operations is augmenting that missing piece of our foreign policy. This country needs a businessman." Hill held up three fingers. "Jobs, jobs, jobs." He hit each finger and then raised three fingers again; the fingers had Fink's full attention. "Kurds, Shias, Sunnis. Jobs are all the Iraqis want. No offense, but I don't have the luxury of being a middleman consultant. I'm a dealmaker, I close deals. I take ownership, and I intend to put the Iraqis back in business by owning a portion of their war." Like a top consultant, Hill had his speech down pat, pitching when he was presenting, selling himself first to sell himself. A true believer. In terms of sales, even Wharton was taking notes. *Do I sound* this *sincere when describing how talented I am?* wondered Wharton. Hill's war stories would be good for years of business lunches if not a lifetime of free drinks with his fraternity brothers in the golf course clubhouse.

"Isn't this the State Department's lane?" Fink asked.

"USAID and State Department can't provide the tactical business expertise. Not during a war. That's actually a myth." Wharton nodded for him to continue, as this carpool group was well versed in myths. "In pragmatic terms, only the military has the ability to marshal the resources to travel across the country and play a strong hand engaging the different actors to facilitate deals and prep the no-man's-land of a war zone with large-scale private investment. What is the DoD but the world's largest corporation many times over? We have this task force because people in the DoD understand how to run a business efficiently."

"*Efficiently*. You just answered my question whether you'd ever served in the military."

"Regrettably, no. I thought a lot about serving in the military." Wharton was always unsure why thinking about serving counted as credit. If one lacked the mindfulness to not voice this around an actual veteran, shouldn't it count more negatively than Wharton's lack of participation in the armed services? "After college, I went straight to HBS. With that kind of advanced knowledge, I knew before I even got there that I would better assist my country in growing industry—knowing that being the heir to a construction fortune comes with the responsibility to keep building." It had taken Wharton, no slacker in self-assurance, until almost graduation at HBS to obtain the knowledge of what he wanted to build, none of which had survived Fink. "The one thing I missed out on in my meteoric rise at Hill Corps, and it is what I now tell students when I'm asked to speak at top business schools, 'Graduate and go put a shovel in the ground for a year at a construction site, get your hands dirty, learn about teamwork, add a brick to your wall—no different than being in the military.'" Such jumbled building metaphors must be part of the inheritance left to construction fortune heirs, as Osama bin Laden had also instructed his acolytes, in one of the terrorism pamphlets Wharton had read in translation, with similar advice. "The hardship of undertaking this project and having to constantly fly back and forth on my jet has attuned me to the sacrifices our military makes. Still, the military needs to work on its sales pitch to us Ivy Leaguers, or Wall Streeters. You know, there is a new initiative from a think tank in Washington gaining traction about how to attract the best and brightest to the military. Our government needs to look proactively at ways to address this problem in our time before we have a second-rate military." Wharton prayed that if they were destined to roll over a roadside bomb that it would wait at least a few more seconds to trigger, just so this would not be the last conversation he ever had in life.

"It's not too late for a healthy guy like you to join. They always need bodies. Put you on the fast track."

Wharton knew that Spencer Hill all too well understood how the absence of a half decade or a decade of civilian work experience on one's CV because of serving in the military stacked up against one's fast-tracked peers. Better to get Hill back in pitch mode than linger on his phony regrets of not having tested himself in the military, and so Wharton asked, "Is almost all the foreign investment here in oil joint ventures?" Aboard the C-130 flight into country, Fink had advised that they run everyone they meet in Iraq like a source. Assess, develop, and collect actionable intelligence.

"As of now, yes, though repairing the port down in Basra has become a project with a lot of buzz. In the north, the Kurds are embracing a free market—at times a bit too eagerly and leaving an emergent democracy centralized in Baghdad struggling to keep pace, if you listen to the prattle out of Foggy Bottom. For the next few weeks you two will be concentrating on advising the Ministry of Oil, but we would like to take that model and expand it to assessments of idle Iraqi factories throughout the country and make it look more like Kurdistan. The whole western part of Iraq is very economically depressed."

Fink snapped his fingers by his head like he had just had an idea pop off. "I think that's why Daesh must be consulting there. The Daesh brand has a talent for moving into depressed areas to develop economies with a beheading visible hand ethos."

Sarcasm failed to pierce the Swoop's force field, as Hill replied as if addressing the matter for the hundredth time at a briefing, "As the Islamic State has done up north, tragically. And in the west. However, not in the south. It would help if the region had a modern Marshall Plan, but in Washington now there is no courage for it. Unfortunately, the more effective our task force is in Iraq, the more sensational the violence and more spectacular the barbaric attacks by the most extreme of the terrorists to scare people away. Very similar to what happened during a period in Vietnam when we were winning there."

Although he did not have Fink's operational background, Wharton believed he saw an angle to handle Hill. "How are the investors you're assisting with access responding?"

"If you're an investor, the window to pull the trigger remains open a little longer when there is terrorism. If you get in during that time to invest, you can do very well. Not only oil wealth. I told a major Silicon Valley entrepreneur I flew around the country in a Black Hawk last week, 'Iraq is the last ground floor.' In a few months that ground floor won't be open, as I foresee an acceleration of investment in the next quarter that will reach a critical mass and make Iraq one of the most prosperous countries in the world. Notice how you aren't seeing any Islamic State black flags in Baghdad. An individual can write a multigenerational legacy in Iraq."

Motivated by ego, Wharton reflected. He could run this type. Already conversant in the "last of the ground floors" mythos, Wharton asked, "Then why did you request us?"

The convoy stopped. The driver rolled down his window to show the Iraqi policeman his diplomatic badge. The policeman motioned up ahead and addressed him in Arabic as the other security contractor asked someone in the lead convoy vehicle what the issue was in his headset.

"There's a strange bomb a klick ahead," Fink said.

"How do you know?" asked the security contractor in the front passenger seat.

"Because anything designed to kill a person is inherently strange. Knowing the language can be your best weapon. Say, how much is DynCorp bamboozling the taxpayer for your mercenary 'skill sets'?"

The security contractor in the passenger seat stepped out of the vehicle and pointed his gun at cars stalled in the other lanes of the traffic jam. Ten minutes of this style of communication later, the convoy exited the main road and cut down a series of streets through a residential neighborhood. Like a dense spiderweb, hundreds of metal wires attached to power lines hung a few feet above the roofs of their SUVs. Fink had instructed Wharton to scan the rooftops for suspicious men or weapons. "One RPG or well-placed IED will still tear through this up-armored SUV," Fink warned as his fingers rubbed back and forth over the top of the silver band on his left wrist. "Good sign that there's kids out. I bet these cowboys' SOP is to fire first." Fink handed Wharton a pair of ballistic sunglasses. "Might stop some of the glass from a bomb."

At a bend in the road, children stopped kicking a soccer ball to run over and wave at them. The adults that did not turn away made sure to scowl, and at least one of them was aware of American hand gestures of the obscene variety. Corrugated metal doors clanged as they were locked by shopkeepers. A group of teenagers in tracksuits pelted the convoy with rocks as they turned past a small park and back onto a major road. "This won't aid my case with K.K. that victory's in sight."

The major road turned into a series of roadblocks in front of huge concrete T-walls the color of dust. "The Emerald City at last," Hill said at the sight of the tops of the tan Green Zone government buildings where, in this new land for pilgrim Brock Wharton, the Yellow Brick Road ended in a snaking briar patch of concertina wire. "To answer your question, I requested you because we're going to analyze and correct this mess of a country exactly like we would a company that has begun to flag but that we refuse to let fail." As if Dean Wharton had come along to ape Winston Churchill, Hill held up the V for Victory sign with his left hand. "And I spelled out for your boss in no uncertain terms that I needed his two consultants most obsessed with winning."

8.

ADVISE AND ASSIST

Wharton was grateful for the three hours of sleep as he leaned into the exhausting heat well over a hundred and twenty degrees on his walk to the old chow hall. Alongside him, Fink wagered that an audit would uncover that Swanberry meals had gone uneaten on this base as they walked past a Chernobyl-like part of the old American camp that had been abandoned in a hurry in 2011. The old chow hall was in fact the office of the four-month-old Task Force for Development and Stability Operations. Next door to the new chow hall, the old chow hall had only recently been reopened to serve as an office after a suicide bomber had closed it down ten years before. From the outside, it appeared to be a leaning tan metal circus tent, though it was unclear if the lean was a result of the bomber. Inside the giant air-conditioned structure, in the center of an otherwise empty and brightly lit room was an oval table very much like the one in the CCG conference room. Although the chairs were a mishmash of different styles, an identical laptop computer was in front of each chair. At the head of the table, in the highest chair, sat Hill, one hand lost in the Swoop. Behind him was a screen the size of a king bed with his stateside travel itinerary for the next two months displayed on it. There were ten other people focused on their computer screens so as not to lose Iraq by erring in their spreadsheet columns. Hill hollered something upon seeing them enter, though it was impossible to hear him over the loud generator hum that permeated the drafty room.

"I'd say we've scaled back our ambition since I was last here," Fink said to Wharton as they walked over to greet Hill. Wharton could not believe that this passed for a war room.

"We call it the Treasury," Hill's female assistant said, gesturing at the room for them with the sort of manufactured enthusiasm that did little to push the bastard variation of war confidence bonds Hill's office was basically charged with selling to private investors. The spartan furnishings of the Treasury were embraced by Hill and his team in much the same way Wharton had seen ultrarich hunters shell out extra money to rough it, always a guide somewhere behind the scenes sweating his ass off to simulate their self-made expedition. There was a pride in this shabby room that weighed heavier than the air. Wharton knew it was that pride that comes from the concentration of power, the same pride seen in warlords who affected regions beyond their own base.

"Let's begin our daily battle update with some introductions," Hill said, after pointing out to them the corner where several cases of bottled water were stacked. With his indulgent hair and his far bigger active upper body dwarfing his smaller dormant lower half, Hill looked like an overgrown baby stuffed into a high chair. "I'm pleased to welcome Brock and Mike to our squad for the next several weeks. As you know, they will be helping us assess how to better streamline operations at the Ministry of Oil and business development in Iraq. I ordered CCG to send its two best and it gave us an ex–UT starting quarterback and HBS winner in Brock. And tell them why you used to call Iraq home, Mike."

"Hi, I'm Mike Fink. I used to serve in the Army."

"He was a Green Beret. It's in his file if you don't think he looks the part. I don't know that I believe it either, but Fink can prove it to us at the base gym!" The rest of the table joined Hill in his laughter, including Wharton, who had always had his doubts about Fink's ability to astound in a gym, whatever his credentials on paper might be. "Okay, we've got some new faces and others who have been traveling throughout the country, so let's go around the table." Hill turned quickly and glared down at Wharton, ready to torch his allies who had just laughed with him. "I've had to fire four of the original ten people from this task force already. You can't be afraid to fire if you're playing to win. This is the mistake Bush made with Rumsfeld, who should have been fired three years earlier."

The female assistant took that as her cue to again pledge her fealty. "Let me just say, it is the greatest privilege I have ever known to be serving under you, Director Hill." *Director* Hill? Was Hill head of the Iraqi FBI as well? "We are embarking on a great pursuit here with you as our leader . . ."

At this point the power was lost, and the lights thankfully went out on what even Wharton, no stranger himself to lapping up recognition and pomp, thought was a servile scene. The whole country was a sea of oil and gas and they could not get the electricity to work. Before Wharton could utter this joke aloud, the next person on the task force began his pledge of allegiance to Director Hill in the dark. Wharton turned to Fink but in the darkness could not see his reaction. Hill, who was normally all about his own monologues and had not been quiet since Wharton met him, listened to the praise without interruption.

Not to be outdone by their colleagues who preceded them, the unctuous vows went on for some time before it came back around to Hill. From his chair in the dark, Director Hill began to answer the burning questions with a pathologically narcissistic twist on Socratic questioning that would have made Wharton's father redden: "Why is Spencer Hill here? Is it because the secretary of defense is a longtime family friend and asked Hill to do this? Is it because Hill is one of the youngest CFOs at one of the biggest private companies in America and is known for having snatched victory from the jaws of defeat on several past projects? Am I here to be a hero or a zero, as my dad always asks?" Wharton began to rub his week-old itchy beard. "The Kurds get it, so how do we get the other eighty percent to be like them and buy in? Since when does a talent like Hill—"

Aware that Hill exhibited enough grandiosity to go on for hours, Wharton jumped in. "Have you leaned on the Kurdistan Regional

Government though to streamline its deals more through the central government in Baghdad? KRG prime minister Faruq Hawrami undercuts the Ministry of Oil and democratic foundation when he cuts side deals with Western oil companies, which we should address in a meeting with him. Your mention of talent made me think that there has to be deficient levels of talent here in Iraq with the refugee crisis, and that is worth examining." Wharton considered for a second and then dismissed the idea of having Fink add a stat about the refugee effect, as he remembered that Fink's time on the Iraqi Refugee Project Now had primarily been logged in Leila Berger's pants. "Any kind of temporary economic injection that facilitates a path to sustainability to maintain balance in this wrecked country—such as shoring up state-owned enterprises even if that runs contrary to our mission of stoking private foreign investment—should be considered to reduce unemployment and drive other development." Wharton could almost hear his father and the other country club counterinsurgents decry such a tactic as socialism. "We don't need to run a regression analysis to determine that there is a statistically significant tie between higher unemployment and a higher number of insurgents."

"The only reason the Task Force for Development and Stability Operations is in this space is to provide meaningful economic development," Hill said, standing up as half the lights had come back on and his hair swept across his forehead. "I've steered over a hundred million dollars in U.S. contracts to Iraqi businesses so far. We hope to see that trickle down to all Iraqis."

"Nothing in Iraq trickles down," Fink said. "Nor is hope a course of action, as we used to say in the Army over here. The tactics have to align with the strategic course you set."

"That's why we have you guys and your CCG matrix expertise to help us advise and assist the Iraqis. Iraq needs a regime change of the mind. If ISIS can obliterate the past here, so can we with traditionally poor economic policies." Hill started to pace around the table with his head down and fists clenched, arms locked at his sides. He pushed for the first time that wheelbarrow, which he had only watched others push before on construction sites, invisibly uphill. "We have slides and spreadsheets on every big idea we've examined and thrown money at for the last four months. This place has been in the news since the Bible and yet until this task force came along capitalism had never left its mark. One would think the articles being written about my efforts would portray me as a savior and not another Paul Bremer. A winner. You know me, I'm first and foremost a competitor." Wharton did not know him, and he was not sure if anyone knew him. Hill sounded more like the boxer who had just lost his title fight but already pleaded for another shot. "I'm going to change this place but I will be damned if I go down known as a Stalinist who pumped money into state-owned businesses. This power broker needs all the leverage points identified."

Wharton did know how much a Hill wanted to win, and because winning aligned with the interests of the Iraqis, he believed in the task force's mission. Nor did he and Fink have a leg to stand on between the two of them in faulting another for this one-track desire. Yet Wharton could not shake the thought that with Hill being a prideful CFO and fast-tracker who had never started a business, his trickle-down strategy overlooked the role of small businesses and entrepreneurship in Iraq. More worrisome was that the insurgents did not appear to have overlooked the entrepreneurial spirit in Iraq, historically a hotbed of innovation. "What role is the Task Force for Development and Stability Operations playing in the growth of entrepreneurship and small businesses?"

Hill pivoted back to his seat. "That's a good question. We're going to have to assess if there's a place for that within the task force's directives. Since we have the power back on, let's for a moment all look at recent coverage we have received in the media and what needs to be addressed to make this situation a fair portrait." A media slide came up on the giant screen behind Hill listing news articles for the past week on the Task Force for Development and Stability Operations and a photo of him from the *Washington Post* shouting at a person not in the frame. Wharton could not tell if the photo was a task force inside joke or a photo from an article this week, neither option comforting. "Did anyone read the *Times* article and not want to assault the reporter? We must combat this growing false storyline of me as unqualified to lead this task force in the media. I wouldn't have been appointed to this job if that were the case. The thanks I get for serving my country is to damage my business reputation permanently. I'm so tired of leakers. Why, I fired two of my staff last week . . ."

Four hours and dozens of slides and a full psychoanalysis session later, Wharton and Fink escaped for dinner at the new chow hall. Fink beat Wharton to the punch as soon as they stepped outside the task force office. "At least we know who the enemy is now."

"His leadership style is a bit much." Wharton had never seen anything like it in business: it was like an oversensitive, spoiled prince had been handed the keys to the kingdom by default. There was a moment or two during the meeting when a tantrum-throwing Hill seemed more like a royal from the Kingdom of Saudi Arabia, or even the ruling family of North Korea, than an executive from America. "I'm sure we've handled more difficult clients. And if he gets half as much done as he promises, that will be great for Iraq."

"That's what they said in 1930s Germany about another egomaniac director." Fink patted Wharton on the back. "Little did I know that all this time I was battling the premature-brother, junior-varsity version of Hill."

A part of Wharton, perhaps the inner majority, wanted to take issue with this monetary notion of success: Hill had been afforded far more advantages and connections growing up than even Wharton as the successional heir to the vastly wealthier Hill Corps fortune. But he let it go to inquire, "Was . . . *am* I that bad?" Some reward, this increased awareness. One was left to hump more cosmic responsibility, Wharton had thought, summing up his first encounters in-country.

Ever the actor when prompted, Fink paused for effect to mull Wharton in relation to Hill. "Your small business development idea isn't half bad," Fink complimented, apparently somehow mindful that how to best trump Wharton, unlike an eager Hill, was to weaponize praise.

• • •

It was a week before they had a meeting with an Iraqi. Each day Wharton had brought up to Hill the need to conduct workshops to engage

Iraqis across different class levels for feedback and buy-in regarding the task force's strategy and small business development. Fink had started putting cans of Dr Pepper in front of Wharton's computer screen and urging him on by the moniker "The Last Populist" the more he insisted at the daily battlefield update on the importance of connecting with everyday Iraqis in regular settings. Their first meeting was in a palace.

The palace was one of Saddam's small palaces. Almost a decade after his hanging, an American flag dangled from a pole outside the palace used by the U.S. military as its command and control center. In the far western wing of the palace, Wharton sat in the middle of a U-shaped table that could accommodate a United Nations assembly. Both he and Fink accepted the forty-year-old Iraqi page boy's offer of another sugary chai tea.

"*Inshallah.*"

"*Inshallah,*" echoed the dozens of Iraqi political representatives seated around the table. Aside from Spencer Hill, who directed a campaign of emails from his BlackBerry on the other side of Fink, Wharton was the only other American present. The room's proportions had a macabre fun-house element: Iraqis were dwarfed by their oversized thronelike chairs adjacent to the three Americans in small fold-up chairs, all under a dome ceiling a hundred feet high with an unrepaired hole in one section that on occasion leaked a handful of dust.

"If God wills," said Hassan, their interpreter, into Wharton's ear. Under Hill's directive, Hassan translated for them only the discussions he deemed necessary. Of course the *one* part Wharton had understood was about if God wills. Oh, how he understood that after six months with Fink.

Annoyed that Saddam or the terrorists or America had destroyed all the normal chairs in the country, Wharton tucked one leg under his bottom to elevate himself closer to Hassan. "What was the representative from Ramadi yelling about before God willed you to translate?"

"He says that black flags have begun popping up in the city, that the wolves of Daesh come into his city each night to talk to the elder tribesmen about turning their back on the corrupt Iranian Shiite government in Baghdad. He warns that if the *majlis* does not come together and allocate money from oil revenues to defense forces this session, then Ramadi will be eaten like Sunni cities Fallujah and Mosul. And these bloody hands will knock on Shiite and Kurdish doors next." Did he mean *hand of death*? And wolves, both the normally well-adjusted apex predators and the radicalized talking wolves, had paws. Wharton let it be.

"Which is exactly what Daesh wants as it redraws the lines of the Middle East by inciting sectarian violence and creating its own black-market economy," Fink said, tapping a paper map on the table before them. Most of the Iraq-Turkey pipeline was shaded in red. "Bulldozing and blowing up ancient ruins is only one way they intend to rewrite history. Hassan, what was the representative from Irbil saying in Kurdish to the deputy minister of oil before that?"

"KRG prime minister Faruq Hawrami complains that the ministry and Hakim al-Amiri are withholding funds that the Kurdistan Regional Government needs to pay foreign oil companies and to finance the Peshmerga's defense of its area against Daesh."

The Swoop moved. Hill put down his BlackBerry to pick up the Iraqi draft of the foreign investment regulation he had obtained and said, "After this meeting we need to meet with those two to hammer out some acceptable terms between the KRG and Ministry of Oil and push through a plan that would actually enable joint ventures. No more stopgap measures."

Based on the risk calculation of the area, the terms of the translated draft seemed fair to Wharton. Hill, however, had made it clear that the current terms the Iraqis planned to propose were too niggardly for large-scale foreign investment in an unstable country by the private sector. And in light of the aid and defense America and its coalition partners had provided Iraq in the fight against terrorism, Hill claimed the business terms bordered on disrespectful. Thousands of Americans had lost their lives.

A scream. The huge front doors of the room spread open like wings. A man in black pajama-like clothes shouts and heads toward them. Wharton drops below the table, sure his moment of death has come with this suicide bomber. But no explosion, only cries before the protester is subdued. Wharton rises again and asks in embarrassment at life's second chance for a strategy: "Who's this man?"

"A Christian man like you. He lived in Qaraqosh until Daesh crucified his brothers and eldest son and enslaved his two daughters. They killed his wife like an animal, cutting her throat." Wharton had no desire to ask Hassan for more details, not out of lack of curiosity, or even to respect the privacy of the Iraqi Christian's suffering, but because Hassan was so used to translating these horrors that his face became animated with the enjoyment of his own ability to share them in another language. The disturbing aspect for Wharton when Hassan leaned in like this was that the register in his voice dropped as it tried to admit no vibrations while he scanned the room to see if the walls had ears. It took all Wharton had to not stiff-arm him.

The meeting went on. And on. Not until Wharton had consumed eight small tulip glasses of the sugary tea to sustain his attention throughout the constant bickering between representatives of more ethnic groups than he thought existed in the whole world did the meeting adjourn. Goddamn the colonial powers and America for drawing the lines of the modern Middle East at their Western peace conferences. Who had they consulted? He doubted the forefathers of the parliament members before him had ever been engaged, though partly because the conferences would never have ended. Hill had come back into the room after a three-hour absence. He picked up the copy of the draft regulations. "Follow me. Time to talk to Faruq Hawrami and Hakim al-Amiri."

Faruq Hawrami jumped up from a chair in the chamber room and hugged Wharton like a friendly older cousin who knew but did not care what the other relatives said about him. His gray one-piece jumpsuit was divided by a traditional Kurdish cummerbund of gray to pair with his tribal red-and-white headdress, coiled and stacked as tightly as excess line on a royal yacht. Though shy of fifty, Hawrami had a gray goatee against a dyed black mustache, a look that, in all honesty, Wharton had never encountered. Perhaps there was a greater likelihood that Fink had, should he have attended any theatrical auditions to play one of those two-faced comic book characters. "Welcome, my friend. I am Kurdish and we are friends of America since I was young man and Ba'athists attack us and gas us." Wharton tried to not wince from this greeting, his small bit to bridge the clash-of-civilizations etiquette. The past was never dead in Iraq. Not when World War I–era chemical weapons executed thousands, gases burning their skin off in blisters, the chemical cocktail purging their insides forever from bodies in a green bile of vomit, the hysterical others laughing madly before death dropped them to the ground. Springs in the mountains that would poison the survivors and their descendants for generations. The gases etching red lines in the sand for a new generation next door in Syria. Even laughter could bring death.

Wharton walked over to where Hakim al-Amiri sat. Only then did the deputy minister of oil in all black stand up. The volume of his grand black cape could have enshrouded a prized Klay Ranch black Angus bull, or an obese superhero. A block of a black turban perched on the back of his head, his gray beard groomed short as an extension of the turban. Al-Amiri was always in the news, his solemn imam eyes a favorite of photographers. Wharton knew he had a PhD from the London School of Economics and had spent six years sheltered in Iran after his cleric father had been arrested by Saddam's Mukhabarat and disappeared. "*As-salaam alaykum.*"

"Peace be upon you too. Speak in English and, as is your custom, frankly, about what you think of the terms the Ministry of Oil proposes."

"You cannot expect terms like this to jump-start foreign private investment."

"I know what you think, Spencer. I am asking *sayyid* Wharton here to speak his thoughts."

Thoughts: *That what was left of your bloodied country is up for sale, but your own concern is negotiating the best deal for your own interests. A perfect environment for a moneymaking consulting engagement. And add* easy oil, *so every company is a winner. Surely the only thing left that a rich American could not acquire was what the veterans had found in their service here, which at best was high risk and a nonmonetary return long term if you*

and your soul survived in one piece. It might be less egregious to just parrot the delegations of visiting American congressmen (who would not even engage each other at a D.C. funeral) and publicly lash the Iraqi politicians on their failures to reach political agreements. Those congressmen, though, had not had their brother kidnapped off the street and tortured for two months before his body with holes drilled into it was found in a canal being eaten by a dog. Whatever his engagement parameters might be as defined by CCG, Wharton would not assist in the final carve-up of Iraq. He would be a true partner in transformation. For the first time in his consulting career, he could see how an engagement was an opportunity to transform not just the client's mind-set but his own. Enduring impact. A partnership beyond self-interest. "If I were an Iraqi—not a wealthy businessman or a minister, but an average Iraqi—I would worry less about terms for private foreign investment than settling the differences between the central government and KRG over how to share and allocate revenues from oil sales to fund economic development. A focus on compromise rather than getting caught up in one side winning. The deal you struck in December to allow KRG to export oil in return for cash from Baghdad has to be the start of the process for the Iraqi people." Wharton turned to Hawrami. "KRG knows firsthand the fallout of failure in this process after many of the towns outside Irbil were captured." Wharton could not get the familyless man in the black clothes from earlier out of his head.

"The Kurds live off this division too."

Hawrami snorted and dismissed al-Amiri with a wave and words in Kurdish, which Hassan translated as: "We have oil. Now we have more oil because Iraqi forces abandon Kirkuk. We are happy to make our own deals with American companies. Independence."

Hill nodded at this when a loud sound thundered against the walls and rattled the glasses. A second explosion a minute later shuddered the city with greater force. Wharton found himself following Hill and the others to a section of the roof adjacent to the main room of the palace. Two large grayish black smoke trails in different sections of the city filled the dusk sky. From a distance, it sucked them in like a spectator sport. Hill had his phone out to snap pictures and record himself to feed his Twitter obsession. "The color of the smoke is what you look for as it twists up. Large blasts back to back. Has to be suicide truck bombers."

"The bazaar," Hassan said, and Hakim al-Amiri nodded and bowed his head.

Hill stepped back and snapped a picture of a surprised Wharton. Fink faced off in the other direction. Hill walked over with his phone out to show Wharton. "That's a good pic, caught you with the explosion smoke in the background." In the foreground of the picture, Wharton's mouth lay open, catching the small trail of filmy clear mucus that had run down from his nose into his beard. "Those are two of the largest tremors I've felt from a distance. Did I show you the pictures from two months ago when a suicide bomber hit the factory next door to a building where we were in a meeting? Word had leaked of my design to expand the factory's output with new machinery and more skills training for its workers. Killed sixteen Iraqis and the blast waves left me and two of my staff with concussive-like injuries and some scratches." A picture of Hill and two assistants covered in dust and smiles as they held up the torso of a mannequin with a shiny fireman-red leather jacket blown over from the factory. "Won a Purple Heart for it. Called the Defense of Freedom Medal when it goes to civilians. All in a day's work here at Iraq Inc. We flew thirty-two investors that month over to Iraq."

"How many invested?" Wharton asked, turning back to the burning city.

"No one yet. Once they do we can put ISIS out of business by giving suicide bombers jobs."

It went without saying, Wharton thought, that it would have to be one hell of a job offer to counter ISIS's martyrdom sales pitch to hopeless males of seventy-two virgin maidens and front-row seating in the afterlife. In the meantime, Spencer Hill could swing away at targeting potential female suicide bombers with the unequal compensation angle once the factory was rebuilt. If the private foreign investment ever came. Wharton's eyes, like Fink's, were back on the two smoke trails, his thoughts on a management fix not solely contingent on hoped-for private foreign investment that had never arrived, and yet more years of Americans and other foreigners with big ideas coming to Iraq, during peace and war, for business and politics, leaving with plans of action destroyed. If there was a solution, they were going to have to adapt on the fly, as soldiers, diplomats, civilians, and terrorists had done to mixed results and a stalemate. This engagement was midproject by over a decade going on a thousand years, and there was no risk matrix invented that advised any engagement that pulled you toward those black smoke beards of destruction. Which made it the ultimate consulting coup.

"My father is eighty-three years old," Hill said, reading the smoke signals as well. "He still hunts, sails, skis, and runs one of the largest construction companies in the world. Friends with every president still alive and any world leader who matters. Survivor of five marriages. But the only explosion he's ever heard was a controlled detonation on a construction site." Hill shook his head and then smiled boyishly. "Gentlemen, this is a call to action for us leaders at the top to manage a future course for Iraq."

Wharton saw another lesson of influence in those twin towers of rising smoke. And any change in that dynamic would have to come from the bottom up and interaction with the populace. Fink had humped that risk before and learned it from the bottom a day at a time. He had left with the power to connect with people only to return to Iraq. Wharton was going to need Fink. They were going to have to act like consultants.

• • •

Fink typed at the small table inside the aluminum pod CHU that he and Wharton shared with an air-conditioning mechanic named Bo from a Halliburton subsidiary. For the last eleven days the cramped and windowless CHU, short for Containerized Housing Unit (Wharton believed the military had even more acronyms than consulting), had been home for the two CCG consultants when not in meetings at the old chow hall or in the new chow hall in the Green Zone. Along with body armor and helmet, Green Zone living required a pair of decent earplugs to shield against Bo's deafening snoring. All three civilians were in the CHU when the air-raid siren went off an hour before dark and a female recorded voice repeated, "Incoming."

Wharton was knocked aside by Bo, who had jumped off the top bunk in just his no-longer-so-white skivvies he had been resting in to grab his body armor and helmet. Fink picked up his laptop to allow Bo to crawl under his table as Fink moved past Wharton to sit on the bed and work. Wharton heard the rapid Gatling gun bursts from the base's Phalanx anti-rocket gun for the first time, only understanding the noise when one enemy mortar or rocket slipped through the defense system and the ground shook their CHU from the explosion. Had he just been baptized by fire? He waited on an epiphany to come.

It was a minute or two after the siren had stopped before Bo emerged. He put on his boots and Wharton's shorts and mumbled that he was off to the fortified bunkers of concrete and sandbags. Shirtless but armored, he crashed into the CHU door as he tripped over his untied bootlaces.

Combat advising. It was not for everyone. Next to Wharton, on Fink's computer screen, graphics cascaded in another barrage. Fink added arrows to contrast with the colors of the squares in this slide so their message about cooperation would be more poignant in the final presentation. With a retooled framework for a more streamlined KRG/central government alliance, Fink stressed, it would be possible to move forward on whatever terms Iraqis negotiated with foreign private investment. Bottom line up front, the disconnect is an internal problem that, if fixed, can provide a solution to the external problem of bringing in development. Disregard your mutually exclusive, collectively exhaustive framework, Fink argued. They're linked at the hip.

Or as any classic irregular warfare tree diagram graphically represented the problem. Yes, Wharton had come to understand the branches of this tree well, his face having hit each one on his fall. As a result, his epidermis could now pass for rawhide. Fink turned the computer screen toward Wharton. "I'm not sold on this slide's color scheme."

"So now you want to be a consultant. How come you quit acting?"

"Do you call it consulting? I spent too many years over here to not want to see Iraq survive. Forget about that ponce's dream of remaking the region into a cradle of capitalism for the legacy of his own ego. Hill's combat tourism will land him deals, he need not worry. Yet more trophies to put up on his Hill Corps office shelves." Fink handed his laptop to Wharton.

Wharton used the touchpad to navigate their presentation, an image of an oil rig on the first slide with revenue figures and costs in boxes below it. He changed the color of the graphics and enlarged the spacing on a slide about the costs of a loss of Iraqi human capital in the growing migration of refugees and deaths through violence. "Give Hill credit for being open to our unconventional small business development advisor idea."

"That's only because he's not aware of the risk. Let's see if the generals go for it. Unlike civilians that drool at the mention of anything commando, the generals well know the limitations of Special Forces. Hell, in my war we never saw anything like a front line over here." Wharton handed Fink back his laptop and he saved their presentation. "Your tolerance is actually worse than your bilious superiority. Go shave that stupid-looking beard off before we meet Hill for dinner."

"It's for rapport building."

"In Iraq, it's only the religious fanatics who wear beards. You just took fire, so you just checked the biggest box—so go shave your foreign jihadist beard off before you offend a local."

On the other end of the Green Zone, Fink led a clean-shaven Wharton to a small kebab shack that backed up against huge blast walls. They sat in plastic chairs at a circle table next to the restaurant's outdoor grill. The smell and smoke of roasted lamb over burning charcoal engulfed them like the best kind of djinn. The only other people occupying a table outside were a group of loud war journalists, high as yuppie junkies on the risks they dabbled in. The lone female reporter, who had the ponytail of her hair tucked into a keffiyeh she wore around her neck and was dressed in cargo pants with a black tank top with Arabic writing on it, tilted her head back to look down her long nose at Wharton. He felt that had he only been a soldier he would have been permitted by the rules of engagement under hostile intent to fire back.

"Dispatches? Anya only does gonzo long-form journalism starring herself in 'terrorist-controlled villages,'" a British male in an Iraqi-flag-colored headband explained to the other male journalist from New York, who styled his perm and dress after Jesus to overcome his innate nerdy Jewishness. "Telling the story of women weaving a rug for a donkey saddlebag for two years can't be told on deadline, jackass! You can help fund her travels by making a donation on her website."

The female journalist shot the Brit a smile for all of a second to show she was not humorless before her seriousness took back the key terrain. "I do it to capture the people here who aren't on anyone's Google map so when consumers go buy that carpet in Manhattan they know what culture it was appropriated from, what world tied those asymmetrical knots of sorrow," Anya hissed loudly, affecting such preeminence that her Russian accent seemed distorted by some speaker box hidden in her keffiyeh. Wharton would have picked this coldblooded cobra in a fight any day over her male counterparts in a careerist competition.

"And you do it to try to capture the MacArthur Genius Grant."

Wharton turned his attention back to their own table, where the waiter set down some chai for them. "Her shirt says *Texas*, if that's what you were staring at," Fink said. "Not that she can read it." Wharton overheard the white American male correspondent drop a variation of the *New York Times* five times in a quick barrage, lamenting that his love of Africa enabled "the dark part of his heart" to indulge in on-the-job extramarital affairs.

After another forty minutes of waiting for Hill, they decided to order. The Iraqi restaurant owner, Omar, came and sat with them for a while and asked about their families, following the ritual of all Arabs, even if the country burned in front of them. It was who they were and anything else was a betrayal of that. Just as somewhere else in the city, in a covered courtyard to hide from drones, an Iraqi refilled his guest's chai glass, exchanging these same inquiries before they walked down into the basement to torture and murder an infidel for their own beliefs in a god that gave them meaning. Omar had lost one brother in the Iran-Iraq War and another in the U.S.-encouraged Shia uprising after the first Gulf War, a war that from Omar's story had lasted longer than the American drive-by shooting. His cousin had lasted a week in a Shiite retaliatory death squad before al-Qaeda in Iraq killed him first. Wharton mopped up the eggplant sludge and slimy okra stew appetizers from bowls with bread, and Fink dipped in and out of Arabic and English as he conversed with Omar, and the current of all this pushed on. They were not far from the Tigris River, a river that had once run black with the ink of all the library books thrown in the water by the Mongol invaders but now ran red from all the floating headless corpses. Why, Wharton now found himself asking, would anyone even want to be king or caliph of such a river? Life was enough of a slog battling it out each day to know who you were, all in an uncaring world while still trying to get laid occasionally.

Wharton abandoned his examination of the existential problem of pussy when the waiter set down a big plate of rice with grilled tomato slices on the edges and more Frisbee-sized circles of bread. He laid the kebabs of lamb still on the metal skewers on top of the communal rice plate for them to feast as equals. If it was a ritual not to speak during a great main course, then Wharton and Fink obeyed this Middle Eastern custom until they had wiped their plates clean with the last of the bread. Wharton was dipping his baklava in his tea when he heard the clapping behind him.

Hill stood clapping above the table of seated journalists. "Here they are, journalism's finest. Not covering the real stories going on in this country. How I've steered over a hundred million dollars to Iraqis. You don't like to write about that in your stories. All you want to talk about is the twenty-page memo of lies from two jaded ex-employees submitted to the DoD's inspector general accusing me of sexual harassment and wasting taxpayer dollars. You can try to make me the bad guy, the face of other mismanagement over here, but there is no smoke at the Spencer Hill–led Task Force for Development and Stability Operations."

Hill walked over to sit down at Wharton's table, smiling victoriously like a prep school bully as the journalists got up and left. "I apologize for being late and if you had to spend any time with those muckrakers and their fake news. They say we have inflated our numbers. They're our real problem over here."

Wharton was sure there were other real problems in Iraq after a decade of civil war that called for greater attention and so ordered more caffeinated tea for the table. "Did you have a chance to review our presentation and suggestions?"

"I did. Looks marvelous," Hill said, tapping on one of his phones. A round-the-clock IED bombmaker had fewer phones to play with than Hill. "Why I hired you guys."

Wharton looked over at Fink. This was Iraq, so Wharton said to clarify, "All good to go regarding our suggested approach with Kurdish leadership? And no issues with the proposed small business development idea of embedding civilians in small teams closer to the front like we outlined in there?" If they successfully peddled a trial of the forward business advisor engagement to the military command tomorrow, they didn't just risk failure of a pillar in their strategy. They risked getting killed. All in order to engage. The true mission behind all consulting projects, which was all fine as consulting dogma until you titrated this quixotic tenet with a drop of war and a couple of hearts-and-minds underdogs who additionally believed in going deep.

Fink put down his sticky baklava and leaned back. "You comprehend the possible second-order effects, third-order effects of pushing out small development teams? The risks not just to the forward American advisors but also to the Iraqis you're asking to stand up for democracy by planting the capitalistic flag in terrain that is gray? Not a lot of second chances for an Iraqi entrepreneur if Daesh cuts off his head in retaliation."

Hill put his phone down and confidently clapped his hands together. "Locked and loaded. In it to win it."

As if Hill had initiated a bomb blast, Fink sprang forward in his seat. "There's no winning over here. If you declare a war against cancer, do all forms of cancer ever get beaten or officially surrender? This is an eternal war that can't be won, Hill. Only studied, preparation taken, and treated after much analysis. If you preemptively enter, you lose; if you reactively enter, you lose. If you voluntarily withdraw, you lose. And you can lose year after year by staying to not lose. *Winning?* Our countrymen talk this way because of our Molotov cocktail of wounded ego and fear, and only dead Iraqis ever believed in or gave a shit about this American myth. All the winners died when we started a war here for false terrorism links and then remained to wage a war for *humanitarian* reasons and now we're here again to battle a group of terrorists—who we created with our intervention—not on behalf of preventing a genocide but on behalf of preserving capitalism. Losing any notion you have of winning is your first victory. The only half-ass winning to be had is in the war to not lose your humanity."

Hill was silent. Wharton empathized as he too felt struck by a rattled Fink and his sudden explosion. No one had prepared Wharton or Hill for the past year. That life could take a turn like this. In their sporting culture growing up, either people succeeded or they didn't, and that was a mark on them. Here in Iraq it was less easy to escape with a winning identity intact, the surviving myth of oneself scaled down if one had the courage to eschew all the other tall tales in a war where fact and fiction had merged since its insemination from both warrior and pencil dicks like theirs. Probably like all wars. And they were the foreigners, for God knows neither HBS nor CCG had taught Wharton a matrix to understand the innocent Iraqis victimized by decades of violence. He knew not what trauma Fink had buried in myths. Fink shucked the PTSD label by claiming every combat veteran had a little PTSD, adding the artful dodge that he had been crazy before he joined the military. His own healthy tonic to that was finding a sense of purpose in a war-torn place like Iraq. Wharton put his right hand on Fink's left shoulder and tried again. "Then it's like you told me, Mike. All we can do is do our part to stop it from getting worse. Maybe even make it a little better while mindful of possible unintended consequences, and be lucky enough to return from it with a little awareness to give out."

Hill studied them before he sipped from his tea and then spoke. "I don't have your wealth of experience in war to draw from, Mike. From the bottom of my heart I can say I wish I had, and I am thankful you are speaking so candidly with me as my advisor. I came over here to win, and it has been a disaster. They didn't tell me I would spend half my time in turf fights with the State Department or fighting to not have the task force get rolled up under USAID. Not what I signed up for, would have stayed stateside." Hill's bunker mentality at every real and perceived slight had been an educational wake-up call for Wharton that he had work to do when he got back to Houston, the first step to not be such an asshole. "I'm about helping the little guy. Even though my father had always warned me to stay out of politics, I had entertained the notion of running for office as just a construction everyman. I don't know if that is possible after the hatchet job the yellow journalists have done on my character over here." Say what you want about Hill's political future, Wharton thought, he had the natural politician's talent to turn his self-inflicted wounds into the tale of a victim. The everyman's plutocrat. If he wore his bottomless hurt on his sleeve, it was because he only wanted to be liked. "I want you guys to walk into military command tomorrow with this same piss and vinegar and sell the general on this new tiered strategy. I won't be there—"

A flushed Wharton almost fell out of his chair. "You won't be at the *presentation*?"

"Unfortunately, I need to be in Kurdistan for a KRG meeting regarding the critical necessity of new infrastructure projects." Hill looked at his watch and stood up. "I'm glad we got to go over the new strategy some more. I have to head over to the embassy as I am supposed to be in a meeting in ten minutes with a Chevron senior executive. Good luck tomorrow."

They both watched him walk away. With all the bad press lately, a savvy Hill knew it would be better to not have a possible rejection of the task force's new strategy by the military command laid at his feet. Who better than Cambridge Consulting Group to come in and give you an out whichever way the military command decided. Wharton knew Hill had made the wise business decision.

"Too bad the journalists missed that performance," Wharton said.

Fink snorted and shook his head. "Everyone comes to Iraq to find an image of themselves here. Yet you came to be yourself." He laughed and put a few more dollars on the table as a tip. "Be careful what you wish for, Brock Wharton. This place will give you an immense amount of responsibility and not a lot of oversight, so you better know who you really are. I wanted to be tested until I was. It was then that I learned all the combat had been the easy test. Maybe I'll tell you that war story one easy workday in Houston when we're on the beach, if I can't succeed in contravening CCG's real development objectives over here. When we're not at war."

"With our own company." In a situation less fucked, Wharton doubted they would have had a shared sense of purpose. Funny how Wharton also no longer cared in the slightest about CCG's objectives of using Iraq to land further business and development projects. It might prove to be Wharton's last CCG assignment, but the change agent had found a cause bigger than himself. Social impact (though without the plus of babe Leila Berger to witness such noblesse oblige). Winning alone wasn't transformative. The most effective way to create enduring value for a client was to become the client's partner. That was the challenge in their consultant role to the Iraqis, as identified by them in their assessment, whether Hill wanted to risk it or not. That was the test Wharton sought.

"With ourselves."

"It's bad enough collaborating with you without you presiding as the wise mentor. Let's go practice this presentation. Show me this influence."

• • •

"Again."

"Recipient of three Bronze Stars and won a Purple Heart in Panama."

"*Awarded.* You don't win a Purple Heart. This isn't a contest, or a medal you want to receive. The more you know this stuff, the better prepared you are to target these alphas and their world when they are sniping at you. They make business decisions with lives. I've never met Dyke but he's a legend in the military." Fink paced back and forth in their CHU in front of Wharton. The CHU was still cool as the sun had not yet risen to end their sleepless night.

Wharton took a deep breath and continued their last chance for targeting preparation of friendly forces. To sell the military command on their strategy would come down to one shot, one kill. "Awarded a Purple Heart. Received a scholarship to Yale. Only member of his Yale class to be selected as a Rhodes Scholar, studying twentieth-century British literature at Oxford. Served first in the 1st Infantry Division and 75th Ranger Regiment, then commanded a Special Forces A-team and saw combat in Operation Just Cause in Panama."

"Yeah, you could say he saw combat. Legend has it that he pointed his sidearm at the Air Force pilot's head when he refused to drop down under fire to five hundred feet for his team's parachute insertion. Then when they landed under fire, Dyke commandeered a construction site cement mixer so his guys could advance forward under cover."

"Fluent in Arabic. Earned another master's from U.S. Army War College, his thesis on the failures of counterinsurgency techniques at the village level, which he later applied to the Sunni Awakening, known as the Sons of Iraq, of which he was the architect during his second Iraqi tour in 2006 and 2007 as a CJSOTF commander. He was awarded his third star in 2014 to take command of Operation Inherent Resolve. This is his fifth tour in Iraq. He has four sons, each named after a member of the rock band The Who."

"Nice, it's like you believe in the presentation. Your forward advisor plan would be a big shift, but it gives the Iraqis a shot. I think you're as battle-ready as you could be for this presentation, considering. Remember, be confident, but have the balls to admit you don't know something. We must earn their trust and build rapport. Special Forces 101 here. If you stumble, don't worry, ole' Mike Fink will be there to help you quicker than hell can scorch a feather."

A company of weaponless American soldiers in workout uniforms and neon plastic belts performed PT in the early morning of the Green Zone, singing a politically correct warfighting cadence about diversity as if it were another day at their stateside military station. Wharton had nothing to compare the current iteration of the Iraq War to and relied on Fink's daily headshaking at Green Zone absurdity for clues. In slightly wrinkled business casual, Wharton and Fink passed through an American palace checkpoint and a Ugandan soldier scanned their laptop. An aide to the commanding general waited for them and led them to the briefing room. Sandbags covered the windows on the walls of the large room. The front of the room was a wall of television screens with aerial footage of Iraq. At the end of a long rectangular table in the middle of the room, a huge monitor screen was set up for PowerPoint briefings and VTCs.

"On your feet!"

At the shout, Lieutenant General Bryan Dyke entered the room at the head of his staff, a long train of men in different service uniforms trailing behind him. Some aide somewhere in the shadows pushed the play button to pipe in the Rolling Stones song "Gimme Shelter." A tall man with longish gray hair for a senior officer, Lt. General Dyke seemed like a retired college professor called up from the reserves and forced back into a hellish classroom. If it weren't for the Special Forces long tab on his left shoulder. Above the shorter Airborne and Ranger patches sat this longer Special Forces tab at the top of the tower of power, with four more achievement patches sewn on the upper chest area of his brown Army uniform, which Wharton thought could pass as the most testosterone-infused Boy Scout uniform EVER. In the old Hollywood version of this long war without a theme, an earnest Jimmy Stewart would have been cast for the humble commander part to soften the American aimlessness motif. But that would have rung false to those who knew the general, as there was an artist swagger that said *Don't take me seriously unless I'm trying to kill you*. The general came around the table to introduce himself to Wharton and Fink. Many articles had been written about Dyke's pacification results in Anbar Province, when he had been the lone jewel in the war effort against the terror reign of al-Zarqawi. Whereas most of his contemporaries had preached counterinsurgency doctrine then with all the conviction of every ticket-punching field-grade officer who had become a COIN expert five years into the war, Dyke had ignored the theater commander's battlefield objectives, dropping out of the race and sailing off on his own course of pacification. When he was thrust back into the spotlight of the never-ending war in his new command appointment because of his pacification success, journalists and senators hounded the mystic of war about when the battle for Mosul would begin.

Lt. General Dyke played a few notes on air guitar, then snapped his fingers and the plug was pulled on the Rolling Stones. "Where's Small Hands? Can someone explain to a slow-talking country boy like me how he will deliver Iraq from evil if he's always in Kurdistan doing development for Hill Corps? Meet the new boss, same as the old boss." The only Rhodes Scholar in the room pretended to be baffled at his staff before he sat down and asked Wharton and Fink, "CCG, maybe you can provide an enduring solution to the most pressing issue of this client's unique reality: If we're 'not at war' over here, how do we win the war?" Dyke held a dying hand out and took on a hoarse voice: "The irony! . . . The irony!"

In a first, Fink began the client presentation. Wharton's unwanted protégé not only had gathered most of the material onsite but had also contributed most of the slides to the presentation. The strange grab-ass wonders of the Levant, for Wharton had crossed an invisible threshold and was as much customer as salesman of the product they were hawking with Fink's assumption of co–project leader for the presentation.

It was an hour before Fink fielded an interruption, and it was more a political statement than an objection to any of the presentation's details. "And less refugees flooding into America," guffawed an aide when Fink listed the possible results of pushing accelerated development in the hardest-hit areas of Iraq. While the tinge of an adopted Southern good-ole-boy accent masked his Midwestern origins, little else hid the aide's political leanings. Although it went without questioning that he and Wharton would be voting for whichever white older male the Republicans would ritually trot out for president, it did astonish Wharton that this all-volunteer military, dominated so by its Southern white working-class culture, voted overwhelmingly in lockstep with the elites of Wharton's world who hadn't known of the other demographic's existence since the Industrial Age. Strange bedfellows indeed in these culture wars.

Fink hadn't come back to Iraq to whitewash the situation. "The refugee crisis is a threat to both Iraq's stability and development, and therefore a threat to any American advisors here because of it," Fink said, addressing the aide. "Brock, will you skip ahead for a second to slide fourteen." Fink's suddenly wide posture and command gestures guided Wharton to follow him on what was clearly not Fink's first rodeo briefing an operation. "Since we uprooted the region in 2003, approximately 1.5 million Iraqis have been displaced. As you can see on this slide, one casualty of the brain drain from the refugee crisis has been medical doctors, with half of all registered doctors fleeing the country—and this is prior to the resurgence of the Islamic State from 2014 until now. This affects the health of the entire country, increasing rates of illness and disease. Combine this with the fact that seventy percent of Iraqis lack access to clean water and eighty percent lack access to sanitation, and how those two factors spiked the recent increase in cholera. I point this out because the figures my colleague will go over about potential revenue streams out of the Kurdistan region are largely valueless to regular Iraqis if they cannot address these instability problems."

"My dilemma is that the mission we have been tasked with is not to provide stability but to advise and assist against the Islamic State," Lt. General Dyke interjected. "The catch is that stability is the key. I want to buy it by funding economic development and investing in those tipping points where you think an investment in a system or process can fertilize the economy and security simultaneously. The leverage points." There were few in uniform or out of uniform who knew more, Wharton thought, about leverage than Fink, who never negotiated with a BATNA. "Humor me like I'm one of these brilliant-but-fired celebrity four-stars who civilians love to venerate on the speaker circuit. Pretend I'm not Hill, that it is my duty to stick around here for the rest of the year without a golden parachute. Enlighten me as to which leverage points you've identified in our illogical position."

The luster of Fink's blue eyes flashed at the surface. Wharton knew that Fink was positioned to catch any illogic thrown at him and introduce a little illogic of his own to play catch with. "Since the start of the war, per capita income in Iraq is twenty-eight percent less than what it might have been had we never started a war here. The next slide identifies such a leverage point that we hope to assess further in the Kurdistan region this week."

For the next two hours Fink, and then his consulting partner Wharton, took turns up in front of the room breaking down the differing perspectives and terms the Kurds and the central government advocated for foreign private investment regulations. Using the CCG matrix, Wharton outlined the projected growth for KRG with the cooperation of the Ministry of Oil while also showing the potential pitfalls of instability that were a part of any expansion. "Then there are the geopolitics, sir, which ISIS has only made more complex with its black-market oil through the region, often ratlined through Turkey." Fink grunted with approval to Wharton's left. "Companies in Britain and Europe are all too happy to undercut the federal system and sovereignty of the central government in Baghdad to have a non-Russian supplier of oil and gas to Europe. And now the KRG has a huge deficit and cannot pay its civil servants because the central government cut off the KRG when it cut Baghdad out of the loop."

"So no one is winning," Fink said as he stood up and joined Wharton at the front, as rehearsed.

"Which is what we hope to stress to the Kurds this week. Iraqis have to learn to play on the same team first before they can battle others." Wharton paused to use the clicker to bring the presentation to their last slide, RECOMMENDATIONS. Before the presentation, Wharton had checked *just* to make sure the file had not been saved in the last four hours.

"So how can the Task Force for Development and Stability Operations incentivize, or attempt to inspire, Iraqis whose communities have been ravaged by this war?"

Fink had thrown this same question at Wharton ten different ways last night as they pulled an all-nighter. Fink now stepped forward to lean his upper body over the table to address Lt. General Dyke's question. "We've talked a lot about strategy in this presentation. Yet it is really only at the tactical business level that the Task Force for Development and Stability Operations will succeed in its advise-and-assist role in the fight against terrorism. That means embedding military and DoD civilian advisors throughout the country in what you might call industries and businesses of identified leverage-point capacity to work *by, with, and through* Iraqis in developing local economies in the hardest-hit regions of the country. Which will entail taking on more risk initially, pushing some advisors out closer to the front lines where Special Forces are engaged. No different in some ways than what you forged in Anbar with the Sunni Awakening by tailoring your efforts to each sheik rather than trying to force the school-lunch approach."

"Not the Special Forces method-to-everything approach again. How cool can Special Forces even be if they let me wear the patch? I'm never going to be able to rebrand myself if I adopt this as part of an economic weapons mix strategy," Lt. General Dyke exclaimed, rolling his eyes. "Have you identified a place to test this?"

"No, but the towns along the Green Line up north—"

"Makhmur," Fink said, cutting Wharton off. Makhmur? They hadn't talked about Makhmur.

Lt. General Dyke put his left hand to his chin. "What do the Iraqis prove?" Here, Fink came up from the table and took a step back as if considering for the first time what could be proved beyond his own ego being tested by the risk.

But it was Wharton who delivered the unconventional answer to this unplanned-for challenge. "That the Iraqi people now know themselves and their enemy better than the Islamic State understands them and Iraq." It occurred to him that, of all people, his father Dean Wharton might have passed down this lesson to him, for that was the great takeaway from the duel between Churchill and the madman Hitler: that Churchill understood Hitler better than Hitler understood Churchill. Before the newly enlightened quester Brock Wharton could bask in this epiphany, it struck him that lessons of Western history were not always the most applicable road map on an Iraqi track. Easy to put forth until you had finicky skin in the game and had to engage. "It's a chance, though maybe a Hail Mary, for Iraqis to reinvent their country by rediscovering themselves before time runs out on the clock."

"And Spencer Hill will be with you for this trial run in enemy-contested terrain?" Lt. General Dyke inquired.

"Naturally, he's the leader of the Task Force for Development and Stability Operations and we're the ones advocating this route."

Lt. General Dyke turned to his most senior aide and asked, "There aren't any *Rolling Stone* reporters in the room, are there? Though if there are, I just want to say on the record that the best thing that ever happened to the morale of this man's army was when they repealed the discriminatory 'Don't Ask, Don't Tell,' and the jokes about my last name ended." The senior aide shook his head that there weren't any reporters present. "I would hate to take a risk in war where Hill would be in danger. There would go any chance at a fourth star." The senior aide smiled at Lt. General Dyke, who turned to Wharton and Fink. "Approved."

By the time Lt. General Dyke and his entourage had exited to "Sympathy for the Devil," and Fink had finished shaking his hand, the only thought an exhausted and parched Brock Wharton had was of the unlimited supply of Dr Pepper that awaited him in the chow hall.

9.

DE OPPRESSO LIBER

Faruq Hawrami was so used to American businessmen in his Wild West boomtown that he opened the plastic Pelican case full of money right in front of them. In place of the gold-bars glow was that impressive evenness to the bills, the way only America could cut its paper currency, a precise percentage of crisp linen melded with dyed-green imported cotton to stack between the inner black foam lining the long skinny case designed to transport guns, each row of bills resting on the same level, with self-made Benjamin Franklin's resigned stare on top. The quick tribute to capitalism seemed to satisfy Hawrami, who whistled for one of his assistants to pick the suitcase off the less-than-knee-high coffee table before Wharton and roll away the case, its two wheels on one end for convenient transportation of guns or loot. The tan case had ridden over with Wharton and Fink in Hawrami's Range Rover from the new Irbil International Airport that afternoon as Hawrami's assistant exchanged two departing American oilmen for the two arriving consultants.

KRG prime minister Faruq Hawrami's penthouse, on the twenty-ninth floor of Irbil's one true glass skyscraper, was his official KRG office. A mammoth tile mosaic mural of the red, white, and green Kurdish flag with its blazing yellow sun in the middle provided a backdrop behind his desk. Rocky foothills climbed up toward mountains outside his floor-to-ceiling windows. Behind the sofa where Hawrami reclined hung a portrait of his father, the KRG president, in tribal dress. A secretary in a red dress without a hijab and with a heavy amount of mascara set down three Coca-Cola bottles with Kurdish labels and a plate of assorted nuts on the table where the money had been. Dressed in a black suit with a gold tie, newscaster hair, a newly clean-shaven face, and all down-home Kurdish mannerisms eschewed, Faruq Hawrami struck Wharton as a total stranger from the man he had met in the Green Zone meeting who had recited an elegy for the generations of Kurdish victims. Hawrami picked out the largest Brazil nut and asked, "Is this your first time in Kurdistan?"

"Mike has been here before, but this is all part of my first trip to Iraq."

Hawrami outstretched his hands. "This is not Iraq."

"Funny, our assessment is that the Kurds could make more money as part of Iraq."

"This speech worked better on my uncles and grandparents. Now we own our country. Money is not such a problem now; our GDP is seven times what it was ten years ago."

"KRG's debt also increased by several billion dollars over the last eighteen months, Prime Minister Hawrami," Fink said. "You're behind and starting to default on payments to oil companies who are pulling out. Do you want the Islamic State as your permanent neighbor? They're already twenty-eight miles from here and launching attacks against your front line. What about when Baghdad succeeds in halting your deals because they pressure the White House to squeeze American companies to uphold the sovereignty of the central government?"

"There are always other Western oil companies. The British love us and don't give us rules. It was during my first week at Penn State for my MBA that I was taught that the best business ethics are in making the best deal." Hawrami evidently had not missed the orientation week class on power broker dress either. Or Fink's guest lecture on the value of shape-shifting. "My family donated money to build the Joe Paterno statue because he was the greatest leader. An icon of winning. But now they have torn the statue down."

Wharton could not recall anything from the MBA lectures on ethics he had received at HBS but wanted to believe they would have at least frowned on the management style, or ethics, of a winning pederast protector. He grabbed three cashews from the bowl. "Each whole nut is a hundred thousand barrels of oil." He placed one of the greasy cashews on the table. "This is what Kurdistan pumps out in this region a day currently." He added the other two cashews alongside the first one. "This is how many barrels a day Kurdistan is capable of." He used his fingernail to pry open the third nut in two and separated one half with each full cashew. "And this is what Kurdistan can still produce even if it splits the profits with the central government as much as fifty-fifty—which is on the high end of estimated percent sharing! A great victory for all Kurds to share in the wealth of their homeland and be kings of their future." The cashew speech, with that elusive common touch, elucidated his point, but it was his ending plea that made Wharton wonder if he was, in spite of himself, becoming a true man of the people?

His budding populism had not yet begun to flower when Hawrami picked up the cashews and crunched them in his mouth. "Nuts," he snickered after he swallowed the cashews if not the lesson. Hawrami offered in his increasingly improving English to drive them to their hotel. What wasn't lost in translation was how even Fink seemed overmatched by Hawrami's acting chops. Both consultants were operating on foreign turf. "You can talk with Spencer Hill about the discussion we had yesterday. He likes the café at my hotel a lot and goes every evening he is here. It's not far from the American Special Operations headquarters here in Irbil. My hotel is a very fun place that all Westerners love. Russian girls and drink. Spencer and I went over your presentation there."

Throughout the ride over to the hotel, it dawned on Wharton that they had perhaps underestimated Hill's capability for duplicity beneath his bombast. Hawrami spoke as if Hill had already resigned from the Task Force for Development and Stability Operations. Of course, Wharton and Fink were no innocents when it came to duplicity. It was their agenda that would drag them all southwest toward the fight and the conflict zone of the sectarian-divided Makhmur area. Consultants were supposed to not be afraid of ushering in unwanted change. The driving goal: implement a strategy to be the best. Not sign off on the status quo that Hawrami and Hill found acceptable. The forward business advisor plan was an unconventional strategy, but it was Wharton's strategy. And as Wharton shifted in his seat, he recalled all too well from Dr Pepper that it was best to be the engine driver and not the passenger on such an unconventional journey.

The Hawrami Hotel was past downtown and on a hill by itself off the main highway. It was half the height of the glass skyscraper and modern. During the drive Hawrami had pointed out any building owned by a member of his family to Wharton in the passenger seat. His finger had come within inches of Wharton's face so often that Wharton wanted to pare back his white-capped cuticles. If Irbil still qualified as a third-world city, it at least had second-world security and felt more like a Middle East tourist city, something you might pass through in eastern Turkey, unlike Baghdad, where the wrong turn could end in an Al Jazeera segment of you kneeling in an orange jumpsuit in your last lead role. The many apartment buildings they passed were occupied and devoid of any blast marks. People walked around in parks and held hands. Cafés were bars, and they were open.

The Dream Baby Dream Café was on the first floor of their hotel and owned by Faruq Hawrami's cousin, who had been granted one of the few KRG-authorized liquor licenses for his bar by his cousin. Spencer Hill raised his beer glass to Wharton and Fink on their approach. "Welcome to Kurdistan. You guys made it to the Dream Baby Dream Café. Too bad you missed Faruq's cousin selling me on why we need to invest in Dream Baby Dream Bowling Alleys."

"Then the Western businessmen will have a place to take the Russian prostitutes on a second date," Fink said. "The Task Force for Development and Stability Operations should spearhead that. Essential in a kleptocracy."

"Easy there. You're criticizing the only Iraqis embracing capitalism. It is a good thing that I'm married, though, as you should see some of these girls. The complete package."

"I bet they make double for American clients as salaried Russian intelligence agents. I wonder how long Kurdistan would have lasted had we not intervened to bomb Daesh. Look around, Brock, this is how it starts. We support a few corrupt strongmen who get greedier until the growing have-nots become radicalized and rebel against the racket for a new battleground."

"Someone should be permitted to achieve something over here," Hill said fatalistically at the ceiling, the Swoop tumbling down over his brow. "Our Kurd allies are the most like us."

And only twenty percent of the Iraqi population, thought Wharton, even if they were the largest ethnic group in the world without their own country. They probably deserved a better ally than America, which had at times left them stranded in places like Syria and turned a blind eye to let the Turks crack down on them. Wharton was fortunate that he was with the DoD and under the capitalist banner and for the moment need not trouble his conscience with the only thing that united the countries over here: denying Kurdish independence. His path to success was connecting through business, the sacrosanct transaction of money between seller and buyer, which would constitutionally rip off a Kurd or an Arab for a profit. "Why did you have us meet with an unreceptive Hawrami if you had already given him the presentation?" Wharton asked.

"So Hill could check the box with the CCG brand on the American taxpayer's dime. Business as usual, but better because it's wartime. This whole hustle has been a rubber stamp."

"A feather in both of your business caps too."

Wharton had not come to Iraq to be stage-managed in his career. "Did you line up the helicopter flight to the camp outside Makhmur?"

"Helos are a problem. Even the JSOC guys can't get enough to run raids. And the Special Forces camp outside Makhmur is as close as it gets to the front lines."

"The theater commander signed off on our proposal," Wharton reminded Hill.

With his nonclenched hand, Fink patted his mentor on the back. "Brock, what do you think the *Wall Street Journal* would make of an insider's account of Spencer Hill's task force leadership?"

Hill got up from his stool. "CCG would terminate you for defaming its client."

Wharton thought it best not to allow his mentee to direct this insurgency. Hill was a prisoner of his own male ego, which Wharton understood—and, as dictated by the needs of the mission, should be massaged. "Or it could be great press for you. Bring the press along to Makhmur. Part of your legacy."

"Why would I need to go?"

Wharton wanted to tackle Hill but stood up in front of him to block his exit instead. He knew how to lead this charge by, with, and through others. "Because you're the leader of this task force and you're asking all Arab Iraqis and Kurd Iraqis to put their lives on the line to embrace capitalism." Wharton thought of Makhmur, a town pulled two ways. "Now, *there's* a high-risk, high-reward possibility."

• • •

Wharton tightened his strap again. With the turn, the side gunner in the Chinook leaned forward and his hands fingered the butterfly trigger of the machine gun that stuck out of the helicopter and swept potential targets on the ground. The gunner on Wharton's side wore an olive-green scarf and gloves, the glove end of both his thumb and right index finger cut off on the side where one would take a fingerprint. Wharton swiped again with his sleeve at the nose drip from the wind that swirled inside the helicopter. The crew chief sat on the open back ramp, the checkered tan and green pattern of northern Iraq fields thousands of feet below visible whenever the helicopter hit a bump and dipped. *Whop-whop-whop.* The thump of the blades whooped louder as they descended in altitude. Four helicopters for four passengers. "A ratio indicative of where we are at in the war," Fink had scoffed during the preflight briefing. The fourth passenger was the *New York Times* journalist Geoffrey, who Wharton recognized as the wannabe Jesus yogi from the Green Zone café. The two Apache helicopters and one Black Hawk Medevac helicopter with PJs inside flanked their Chinook helicopter in the sky and bobbed like lethal baby crib ornaments because the week before the resupply helicopters had taken small-arms fire from ISIS on the way to the same FOB. Below the helicopter Wharton rode in swung a giant net of cargo, which they were prepared to cut sling load on should they take ground fire.

The crew chief stood up and walked over to them. Behind him an intercom cord dragged like a tail and he held up two fingers in front of the sun visor attached to his space helmet that hid his face. "Two minutes!"

Long before a minute and a half had passed—another yell: "Thirty seconds!"

Wharton looked out the back ramp as the ground rose up to swallow the dropping helicopter. But before they touched down the helicopter stopped to hover as the crew chief directed the pilots and they detached the cargo, afterward landing well in front of it on a dirt patch. The three other helicopters circled above as the crew chief rushed Wharton, Fink, Geoffrey, and Hill off the back ramp. Wharton followed a hunched Fink as he ran off the ramp straight out a hundred feet to a gaggle of people waving at them. The helicopter off the ground again, a wall of dust came at Wharton and crashed over him as he turned to look behind him at the ascending helicopter.

The first thing he heard was laughter when the noise of the helicopter faded. He dropped his hands from his eyes and through what was left of the grainy helicopter sandstorm saw a sand-colored dune buggy, though this was occupied not by beachcombers but by four bearded armed descendants of the pirate Blackbeard. The dune buggy itself had machine guns and grenade launchers mounted on all sides. Fink and Hill were throwing their bags in the back of the dune buggy. One of the long-haired men pushed one of the machine guns away on its metal swing arm mount and stepped out. He wore desert camouflage pants and a T-shirt with a pistol holstered on his belt. A checkered Arab keffiyeh was draped around his neck. "You look like we caught you wanking."

"You're English?"

"Don't tell anyone," the Englishman said and laughed. Wharton stared at his sandals. "Standard-issue flip-flops. 'No boots on the ground' here in Iraq." He grabbed Wharton's bag, which dragged down by his hip because of his bulky body armor, and threw it in the back, where Geoffrey, Fink, and Hill stood ready for the short ride up the hill to the base behind the helicopter landing zone. Wharton joined them and held on to the roll bar as they drove over to the small Special Forces FOB, where a soldier with a Kurdish flag on the upper right arm of his blue camouflage uniform pulled back a coil of concertina wire and opened a metal gate for them.

The nucleus of the base was three pockmarked one-story houses, the one in the middle with a satellite antenna on the roof and a wooden ladder to a crow's nest of sandbags; all of this within a wall of dirt-filled Hesco containers with more concertina wire on top of the wall. They stopped at the far building next to a group of Hilux pickup trucks and armored vehicles. They left their bags in the back of the dune buggy and followed the Brits through a wooden plywood door. The smell of grilled steaks and cheap boiled crab hit them as they entered.

"A-merica is here!"

A tall black guy in tight-fitting MultiCam pants and a Rolling Stones lapping tongue T-shirt hopped up from the long wooden dining table and moved toward them at the front of the line.

"Yes we are. I'm Spencer Hill, director of Task Force for Development and Stability Operations."

The man walked right past Hill's outstretched hand and embraced Fink until one of the Brits nudged them aside to stop blocking the line of metal trays containing the food. Or what was left of the food, as the loud American had portions of crabmeat tangled up in his scraggly beard. "You couldn't leave us one percent of the one percent behind for the civilian one-percenters? Or did the only 'Jewish' Green Beret ever come back to save the last seven Iraqi Jews exposed by WikiLeaks?"

"Someone has to win these never-ending wars. I'm surprised an anti-Semite African American team leader like you, young Luke, can appreciate the rich ancient history of Iraqi Jews. Top one percent of the military, my ass. Could it be just a coincidence that as soon as the King of the Mississippi gets out of 5th Group, we have to get back in over here?"

"Does he still give himself nicknames?" Luke asked Wharton. "I was hoping a self-proclaimed Special Operations legend like you would be able to tell me what the mission is."

"To defend a few Kurds, maybe a Yazidi or two, and lest we forget defending corporate greed. *De Oppresso Liber.* You can't even get off your lazy ass to come greet me at the HLZ? You and your low-intensity Special Operations conflicts. I thought we were brothers."

"VTCs, man. Meetings about meetings might as well be what the command considers the mission over here. General Dyke sending you guys here is like a welcome respite to the monotony of being shackled. At least we'll get outside the wire this week."

"Luke, this is my teammate Brock Wharton, who is at Cambridge Consulting Group with me. He was a college quarterback like you, though someone must have advised him to pass on the golden opportunity to run the wishbone for the Black Knights of West Point." *Teammate:* that inferred a special kind of bond over here, right? Considering they were in Iraq, Wharton thought it better to save the conversation of which schools had once recruited Luke to play a game for another occasion. "This is Spencer Hill, who is the director of the DoD's Task Force for Development and Stability Operations."

Luke turned toward Geoffrey, who was dressed head to toe in designer safari garb he had spent all night scuffing up. But Luke's eyes were on Geoffrey's impressive jawline. His chin integrity was such that it fit the profile of a television journalist rather than a newspaperman, adding up to more of a Brian Williams–like strong jowl. "Who's Kenny G here?"

"Geoffrey Betman, correspondent for the *New York Times.*" For the sake of Geoffrey's perfect chin, Wharton was thankful he omitted "author of *Love, An Affair with Africa: A Memoir of Surviving War and Love at the End of the Horn.*" Not even any of Geoffrey's many writer friends or colleagues could nominate the tell-all for the book prizes they juried that year, awards at least initially conceived to be based on a semblance of literary merit.

"Welcome, gents. Grab a plate of food and I will give you guys a brief over in the OPCEN. Our camp is your camp for the next two days. We do surf and turf once a week for American food and have a great Yazidi cook named Nuri who can make anything, even a version of fish and chips for our SAS brothers. You lucked out and missed the first part of the tour eating MREs, Fink. Only one jambalaya MRE per box put us Creoles on an unwanted diet."

The operations center was shared by the U.S. Army Special Forces A-team and the British Special Air Service troop. Giant maps from floor to ceiling lined the walls. The room had three rows of desks and five computers. It seemed to Wharton devoid of any of Hollywood's Vietnam War baby boomer personality: neither peace signs alongside born-to-kill slogans, cold beer, hazy marijuana smoke, nor R&R whores. One of the sacrifices or casualties of war in a Muslim country. Or a sign that though their era was the craziest since cities burned across America during the sixties, Wharton's generation had not yet undergone a similar seismic cultural revolution, as why else would any youth of sound hearing champion indie music? Only by the coffee machine was there one naked headless pinup girl the Brits had hung up in defiance; with a cutout of ISIS caliph Abu Bakr al-Baghdadi's passionate face for the pubic bush, it could have resided in the Surrealists wing of the Menil Collection. Fink himself had decried in Baghdad, in contrast to the lifer generals, that a draftless military meant a less diverse force, and that even between the volunteers pre-9/11 and post-9/11 there were stark differences in mentality best exemplified by their reasons for joining. In the front of the room was a white bedsheet that the team projected pre-mission briefs on. Instead of presenting them with the VIP PowerPoint briefing, the team leader Luke used the terrain map, which showed the current front line on the northern front of Iraq. He used a red laser to show the towns ISIS had controlled in June 2014 on the map. For twenty minutes he jumped around with the red laser to highlight the different towns they had conducted partnered operations in. "Actually, our one unilateral mission was our first mission here in August. On Sinjar Mountain to assess how catastrophic the refugee situation was from the Islamic State's push. The Yazidis had put up some resistance with AK-47s but were quickly overwhelmed by ISIS's advance guard of foreign jihadists and weaponry. The entire northern divisions of the Iraqi Army had all but dissolved, aside from a few Iraqi Special Operations Forces battalions."

"Have you run into any of the old ISOF guys?" Fink asked.

"No. I was hoping for that in the beginning. Our two intelligence sources said most got killed from the fighting, or were rounded up after they dissolved back into the population within greater Mosul. ISIS went door-to-door with execution squads."

They were five klicks from the center of Makhmur. The Peshmerga now held it. But ISIS fighters were positioned only a klick and a half farther south of the center. They hung out at the high school that was visible from the town factory's roof. Often walking around on the school's soccer field right out in the open. The team had flown a few Switchblade missiles into them when they got out onto the roads in a convoy or when they mortared the FOB. Luke walked over to a computer and pulled up a slide that showed where they had dropped on ISIS. "They're not idiots and know we usually can't get permission to leave the wire to engage them directly. God, if they only knew our CONOP process and what it took to obtain approval for operations. They would have overrun the whole country while we sat inside the wire with our thumbs up our asses and our S-3 altered the font size again on our PowerPoint slides, only to kick it back to correct the graphics before approval."

"Sounds worse than consulting."

The size of the enemy element was usually thirty to fifty armed males, though Wharton made a mental note that the intelligence analysis indicated that they had the ability to amass a hundred men from the greater area. PKMs, RPGs, heavy and light mortars. Possible crude chemical weapons. According to their intelligence, most of the fighters were Iraqis and Syrians with a few European jihadists, but for the sake of fascist diversity the ISIS area leaders were an Egyptian named Abu Misri and an Algerian named Muhammad who came up through the proving grounds of the Algerian Civil War. The team's intelligence cell even followed the two social-media-friendly jihadists on Facebook. "You should see the pictures we 'like' of these idiotic glory hounds," said the team's intelligence sergeant. "They're exactly like us with their long hair and cool-guy photos posing with guns to try to impress the girls back home who they never could get while in high school."

The team's primary partner force to advise and assist was the Dizha Tiror, the Kurds' elite counterterrorism force. Even a few Yazidis and Christians were sprinkled within the unit. The team had also formed the Makhmur Strike Force, composed of some Iraqi Army infantry units and police special mission units. They would try to roll with some of them for the KLE in Makhmur, and the Brits if they got cleared to go out. Luke went back over to the wall and pointed to a spot on the map, "There is a small factory on the outskirts of town you guys might want to visit—"

"Who are the officials we are meeting with?" Hill asked.

"The mayor and chief of police of Makhmur."

"What's the factory?" Fink asked.

"It was a factory that made shoes, largely sandals—the popular leather-strap kind that Iraqis love. Air Jesus sandal. I'm not sure how much revenue the factory generated, but it employed over seventy people from the area before ISIS overran the town and operations there shut down. If we go there, I would almost guarantee we would be engaged by ISIS."

"Absolutely, let's go there. If we could help consult on how to get the factory back up and running, that would win some hearts and minds in the area."

Hill shook his head. "A small factory of seventy employees does not move the needle enough to qualify as strategic. Even the officials hardly warrant our time here. Are we doing any pre-mission briefings tonight?"

Wharton walked over to the map to get a closer look at the factory's location and said, "We sold the revised vision of the task force as providing tactical business expertise in accordance with Lt. General Dyke's overall strategy. To advise in areas closer to the front."

"We're still putting together the slide deck, but we'll hold a briefing tomorrow four hours before we launch. You guys can shower now, or if you have more questions I am happy to hang around and answer whatever you want. There should be four cots out for you in the barn."

The wink from Fink unnerved Wharton as much as it was supposed to comfort him. Hill and Geoffrey left to go shower, but

Wharton pretended to also have questions for Luke after Fink's secret communication. Fink suggested they take their conversation to the roof and the sandbag tower.

"Look at this sunset," Fink said, sitting on one edge of the crow's nest. The usual reds, oranges, and pinks against the dark blue sky in the distance of a sunset in Aspen. Though not mountains but hills. Though not life but death in the gritty air. There were good reasons why Richard Muncher opted for Aspen. "I would give my right testicle to be part of the Battle of Mosul whenever they go in to take it back from Daesh. There are parts of that city where I wouldn't even need a map. Was it just chaos on Sinjar Mountain?"

"The whole mountain was so covered that it moved. When we landed we were mobbed. Had to almost shoot people to get the helicopters back off the ground. We gathered intel and assessed how desperate it was and it was bleak. But we determined a practical solution where we could create a passageway to safety with aerial bombing and airdrops of food along the way. Buy everyone time. They were doing bombing runs on one side to keep ISIS back and we sent the CCT and the Echo to laser targets to drop on. Like always, the kids were the worst. The violence—much of it more horrible than usual because ISIS wanted it to be felt over the Internet—had been witnessed by many of the kids. A good many of their sisters had been pulled away from them and taken as sex slaves."

"All Yazidis?"

"Yazidis and every other group you could name. What was left of the living walked out of their towns for weeks and only had what they could carry. It was Exodus. With all the shit details they left out in Bible school. Why did you get me up here, Fink? You don't have to juke me with your feigned romanticism in sunsets. Not getting along with your 'task force' boss? You don't know how much pleasure it brings me to see a tool like that finally reining you in. I interjected with that bit about showers to run interference and find out what's going on."

"Brock here is the reigning boss. Hill, who has leeched his whole life off Daddy's fortune, is our client if you don't count the people of Iraq he is supposed to be helping as the real client. Maybe he's not as bad as I make out. If you can look past his boorishness. It's a bit tense because in order for us to come this far forward we sort of extorted him in Irbil so there would actually be a chance to remake—"

"*We?*" stammered Wharton, who if anything felt a confused compassion for the self-deluding Hill rather than Fink's natural inclination for hostility toward anyone with a shinier silver spoon.

"*We* are going to that factory."

"Commanding your superiors, good to see nothing has changed, Fink. This must come as a surprise to you," Luke said, smiling at Wharton, "but Fink didn't win many popularity contests in Special Forces by always speaking his mind. Hell, I assumed you wanted to go there because I mentioned that we would probably be engaged by the enemy."

"Of course that's why I want to go. Life ain't worth anything if it can be managed. Can't quantify its value either with metrics any more than you can art. But it—"

Was this the agenda? "Is this why? Are you crazy?"

"I think we know we all are. You don't have to go on this engagement. This is nonbillable soul development. I'm being straight with you since we're now teammates and you're going to be vulnerable out there. I know you love your wife, why else would you have signed a prenuptial agreement—"

"How . . . do . . . *you* . . . know about my prenup?" Wharton sputtered.

"You think you're the only one who knows how to gather intelligence? Forgive me, but I thought my mentor might be crazy enough to try to get me fired."

"I *was* trying to get you fired! That's why I hired a private investigator to snoop on him," Wharton said to a bewildered Luke, whose eyes darted back and forth between the CCG mentor and protégé.

"I respect your honesty," Fink said. "Nothing worse than a teammate who tries to cover up something when confronted. Trust me, I know all about that. The cowardice and lack of integrity that comes with a war crime are bad enough, but it's the betrayal that stings and lingers. To have been manipulated on behalf of covering up evil." Fink held out both his hands to beseech the serious consultant. "But time is too short in life to not do the hard right over the easy wrong, huh?

At the end of the day, isn't CCG actually paying us the big bucks to be assessing ourselves?"

Wharton would stake his salary that this was not what CCG was paying them the "big bucks" for. Little point, Wharton supposed, in now bludgeoning Fink with reason. They were already in a war, together. They, no differently than Fink's half-ass philosophy, were connected like one of those piggybacking scorpion-and-the-frog aberrations in nature at this point. "To make an impact. That's what *I* came over here to accomplish," Wharton answered, less sure of what all Fink was seeking. "Lasting change—"

"But the factory being close to the action is really," Fink said, having resumed with his analysis, "only an added bonus in this case. All I ever wanted when I was in the military was to get out, and now all I ever want is to be back in the military. Going to that factory is within our mission set. We were sent over here to engage, and undertaking that kind of responsibility is not without danger. This is still a war. We don't need much runway on this. Is it time for the old KLE-to-contact, Luke?"

"We've done that once. Twice if you count when we set up a training range with the Peshmerga close enough to ISIS, knowing that they would group and start firing at us. Was by no means the worst combat I have ever seen. But we still killed twelve of their fighters. Isn't Makhmur where you lost your teammate?" Luke asked, gesturing to Fink's silver bracelet. Fink had lost a teammate in this area? The acid in Wharton's stomach crashed on one wall and bounced back in a wave in the other direction. Wharton began to wonder if he was being manipulated more than he wanted to be by Fink. After all, it had been Wharton's idea to shuck the safety of the bases, a risk that no doubt matched the criteria of soul development.

"OIF V. Shot in the head breaching."

"I was an infantry PL in Mosul then. Being here at the Alamo isn't enough for you?"

Fink laughed. "Don't say that. The Alamo is where Brock's hero, Congressman Crockett, made his last stand. If you're not in the fight, you're out of the fight."

Wharton countered. "How did the King of the Mississippi die?"

"That's the comical part. Not even on the water, as the steamboats had run his beloved boatmen off the river and he had lit out for the West as a pathfinder. The King of the River was shot by his own teammate after Mike Fink had killed another one of his fur-trapping team by missing the tin cup on his head by a few inches in a shooting contest in the mountains."

Wharton, needless to say, failed to find the comedy in this tale of modernization and murderous teammates ahead of their coming mission. Advise and assist, Wharton recited to himself, as Fink told how legend had it that Mike Fink never really died but returned to the river disguised as a giant catfish to whip up storms by stirring the river with its tail.

• • •

"QRF will be the Brits in Trucks Five and Six. Any last questions, gripes, concerns?"

Wharton twisted his head around in circles again to correct the crook in his neck he had woken up with. "The Barn" had proven to be less than comfortable for humans. He tried to study the aerial shot of downtown Makhmur up on the bedsheet screen in the OPCEN.

"What are the odds that we might take the alternative way up Route Virginia coming back from the KLE?" asked the senior 18Delta. Wharton could not remember his name, as they all sort of looked alike with their beards connected to their dip cups by tobacco juice saliva, but knew he was the medic who would try to save him if shot. He had given Wharton an antibiotic pill packet to take if he got wounded and they got separated. Each person on the twelve-man team had a specialty, and they all trained each other in the specialties. If this team was indicative of the talent of other Special Forces teams, Special Forces could smoke any consulting dream team in concentration of talent. Of the two communications sergeants on the team, the senior radio operator had been an investment banker in New York at Goldman Sachs until volunteering for service after the 9/11 attacks, and his no-neck junior, a half-Hispanic weightlifting beast of a man with fluency in three languages, had attended Harvard as an undergraduate on scholarship, graduating in just three years with honors.

Team leader Luke, the 18Alpha, looked around the OPCEN and asked, "Is operator Hill outside on the satellite phone still?" Fink flashed Luke a thumbs-up in answer. "Between us, I'd say about a hundred percent because I have a feeling I will have to call up that we have received intelligence that the enemy is setting up an ambush on our primary return route." The team chuckled at this. Route Virginia took them by the shoe factory. "For our two SF babies out of the Q Course who joined us in country last month and are hungry to get some, be ready to get your gun on. We all accepted there would be risks when we signed up. Our mission is to influence our battlespace through combat advising. Sometimes we have to get creative to make that happen. Be cognizant of civilians on the battlefield if we get attacked. We know what ISIS's MO is when it pertains to civilians. As always, don't do anything that would disgrace the regiment."

With the increased risk of casualties, the command dictated that they take the RG-33s. Wharton did not understand why the armored vehicle with submarine portals and monster truck wheels weighing a couple hundred pounds apiece was not classified as a tank. In the front, there were two seats for the driver and TC. The tactical commander of the truck Wharton, Fink, Geoffrey, and Hill were assigned to was Luke. Behind them was a special seat for the gunner, who operated a .50 caliber machine gun on top of the RG-33 from a remote-controlled screen and joystick within the cabin of the vehicle. Small, thick, bulletproof glass windows lined the back part of the RG-33 cabin, which seated five others. Fink claimed the driver had the hardest job on an operation like this; the major design trade-off for the vehicle's capacity to deflect an IED blast better than a Humvee was control of the unstable top-heavy RG-33 while driving. Metal ammo boxes filled with .50 caliber rounds, loose 40mm rounds, and extra magazines of 5.56mm rounds were all tied down inside the cabin with green cord. A portable handheld mortar tube, two AT-4s, and a Gustav rocket launcher were strapped against the sides with bungee cords by the back-exit door. On compartments on the outside of the RG-33, more mortar rounds and

Gustav rounds. Enough firepower to lay siege to a small city, remarked the junior weapons sergeant from Waco, who definitely had a different notion of what was required packing for an enablement project trip.

They did their test-fires at a range adjacent to the firebase as the sun came up. Hill took off his body armor and helmet but kept his keffiyeh around his neck and walked down the line of trucks to send some emails on his BlackBerry. Geoffrey stayed inside the RG-33 and fooled with the camera he had rigged to his helmet, which Wharton assumed would require a bit more than the usual tinkering because of the potential obstruction of Geoffrey's prominent chin. Since they were infilling during daytime, the element of surprise would be lost as soon as they left the wire. When the Special Forces guys dismounted to fire their small-arms weapons, Wharton tried again to call K.K. on the satellite phone within the cabin, pressing the last digit of the phone number to connect when there seemed to be a lull in the shooting. Though he did not feel guilty that he had only talked to her twice since his arrival in Iraq, he now wished he had made more of an effort, if just to hear K.K.'s voice more. Wharton attempted a third time to call when the back door of the cabin opened slowly to its hydraulic sigh and Fink was standing there next to the outside toggle rear door switch with an assault rifle. "Stop trying to call your wife, you're only going to make her nervous. Time for some on-the-job training," Fink said, as Wharton climbed down. "Give me that satellite phone before you or Hill drain any more of its battery."

"Are we allowed to shoot as noncombatants?"

"Not technically, unless it comes down to you and a promotional video on ISIS's website. Then you might have wished you had test-fired one."

"Same thing as an AR-15?" Wharton had fired a few of them at K.K.'s ranches.

"Look at you, Mr. NRA. Except these M4s are fully automatic." Fink pointed it downrange and held it out for Wharton. The Special Forces gun accessories on all the rails' sides appeared sleeker but the whole rifle felt heavier and a lot deadlier than he remembered from his ranch shooting range experiences with K.K.'s family. "You ever been shot at?"

"Every consulting assignment I've been on with you." Wharton steadied himself and fired two magazines of thirty 5.56mm rounds apiece downrange, barely a kick into his shoulder and a tap of a kiss on the cheek, the clucking pops of the rounds reverberating through his earplugs, before they loaded back up in the vehicles. They momentarily paused to radio up kickoff to the command in Baghdad. The distance to the village as the crow flies was just over five kilometers. But because of blown-up roads and varying up their route pattern for safety, they took a circuitous route to the village. The convoy was primarily Peshmerga pickup trucks and armored vehicles, with the three RG-33s of Americans interspaced in the middle. On the deserted dusty roads, the speeds fluctuated every five minutes: follow the leader in a race, lose the truck in front in the dust brownout, the truck behind almost rams into the halted truck in front of it once it catches up, for an erratic caravan that Wharton felt moved like amphetamines working their way through a caterpillar. In his body armor and helmet, he began to feel nostalgic for the C-130 ride and his baptism in military transportation.

The white Hilux in front of Wharton's RG-33 had halted. Emerging from out of the pickup's brownout, his RG-33 again braked hard to avoid crashing by a few feet. The truck bed full of Peshmerga soldiers howled at this, as unlike Wharton, they had wisely gotten stoned for their pre-mission nerves. Each one was dressed in a different old uniform and style of body armor, a mishmash of cast-off American gear. "Truck Two, this is Truck One. Be advised that the terp says that Major Piran warns there is another suspicious dirt mound in front before the culvert again."

"Roger, we will send up EOD again to check it out. Could be a fake to divert us over to the other side of a rigged culvert or pressure plate." Ian, a tall surfer from California and the Explosive Ordnance Disposal technician attached to the team, dismounted from the back of their truck with gear clearly stolen from UFO chasers. A woozy Wharton leaned forward to gasp fresh air before the door closed and Fink threw the lever to blast-lock their armored crypt. Wharton wondered if they were ever going to reach the town if each dirt mound required a halt.

The whole country was dirt mounds or suspicious trash or animal carcasses, and even America had culverts.

Thirty minutes later, Ian returned to their truck with his unexploded countercharge. “Damn, I thought I was going to BIP something today.” He fiddled with what looked like a small laser attached to the side of his gun.

“All, this is Truck One, we have movement on rooftops of town’s edge. Four MAMs.” Wharton searched out the small portal window for four MAMs (Who? What?).

The convoy drove straight down the center road of Makhmur to the police station. The new police station was in an abandoned mud-brick home that had overlapping corrugated tin sheets as a roof. Across the street was a burned-out building, the old police station ISIS had used until an American airstrike “recaptured” it. The only thing claiming it now was a pack of mangy dogs in its courtyard. The walls of the roofless building next to it had the same bad case of pockmarked bullet hole acne as the rest of the half-standing concrete walls in the town. Six months later and less than a quarter of the residents had returned, the chief of police told them. He was a tired old Arab who had returned after a week in the mountains on the run from ISIS because he had nowhere to go in Kurdistan. Even his groomed mustache was a gray boomerang. His black beret puffed out like a spotless mushroom top. He offered them tea and apologized for no sugar and the mayor’s cancellation. They were seated on the dirt floor. Fink asked the chief something in Arabic and he answered while he poured tea into wet glasses for Luke, his interpreter, Hill, a note-taking Geoffrey, Wharton, and Fink. The other Green Berets, Ian, and the Air Force Special Operations Combat Controller had stayed with the trucks to pull security down the alleyways and monitor every military-aged male (MAM) spotted.

“What did you ask him?” Luke asked Fink. “My language was Dari.”

“About the sandal factory south. He said the workers have not come back and it’s closed as you said, but that the *sahib* is there and living in the back part of it.”

"Give it a rest," Hill said. "On-site assessments are for core economic revitalization."

The KLE lasted another six hours. At times, Wharton had to pinch his own leg to stay awake as Fink asked every consulting question relevant and Luke gathered atmospherics. But all the discussion seemed to really achieve was to underscore the now-nonexistent society that they had previously intended to impact. Hill groaned when Fink asked Wharton to grab a case of water and Gatorade from the truck as a parting gift to the chief, though it was a relief for Wharton to get up and stretch. He heard Luke tell Geoffrey that he would be switching trucks to swap his seat with the Air Force CCT for the ride back.

A couple minutes later back in the truck after they had posed for a picture with the police chief, Luke called up over SATCOM to the command, "This is Alpha, sending in the blind. We are taking alternative route back. Break. We have received intelligence here on the ground from the chief of police's office that ISIS is rumored to be setting up an ambush on primary route."

"What intel are you talking about?" Hill asked Luke, who just held up a finger back to him as he talked on the radio to the other trucks. "Why Alt Route? Where's the satellite phone?"

Fink pulled out his binoculars from his small assault pack under the seat as the truck began to move. "For birdwatching."

"Because I'm the battlefield commander, Hill. But you can do your job at the factory."

Wharton looked over at Fink. Instead of handing him their CCG pink slips, Fink fired Wharton his best Chairman Mao grin for what was going to be a great leap forward into God-knows-what. With the town behind them, they halted at the factory twenty minutes later and set up security in a crescent moon facing southward. Fink stood up and, bent over at the waist, moved to the rear door with his bag. "And they thought the Islamic State has a close relationship with business!"

With the black radio headset still up against one ear, Luke yelled back to the cabin, "Fink, y'all have ten or fifteen minutes for the factory while Ian and the Charlies check the small bridge in front of us and the CCT and I hit the roof to scan ahead."

Hill motioned for Wharton to follow Fink. "Be my guest to advise however you see fit in there, as you two are both relieved from consulting any longer for Task Force for Development and Stability Operations. Enjoy your hijinks until CCG hears about it. Please do let me know when you find the team's satellite phone."

Wharton would have shut down the factory without a second thought—had recommended the shutdown of far larger factories now all rusting throughout America. The facts were there in the little pieces of curled rubber and charred leather laid scattered on the long tables. The inside of the factory had been torched from the middle with gasoline. A few remaining legs of the burned worktables in the center rested next to mounds of ash. The main press in the center of the factory might be in salvageable shape, as some lower minion from ISIS had failed to properly carry out his destruction orders of ensuring the direction of the flames. But there was a hole large enough for a human to walk through in the eastern wall where an RPG had probably hit. Could Fink still see a different bottom line? Even in good times, there must be nary an excess factory worker here to lay off for a cost-cutting initiative. With a CCG coloring in their lives below the spreadsheet columns for human costs, private equity would terminate the place with the extreme prejudice the PE whiz kids had shown every plant they had had to burn in America in order to save.

Luke and the interpreter found the *sahib* in the back, in a room beneath the stairs to the factory roof. The room's glass window had been blown out and the owner had left the glass in a neat pile. The Kurdish owner would not give his name, because his family was in hiding in a town outside Kirkuk. Daesh still mortared the factory every week and took shots at him when he walked the grounds outside his vacant factory. He chose Luke, the man with the rifle and pistol on his waist, to ask when they were going to destroy Daesh.

"Tell him, 'Americans are helping advise the Iraqi Army and Peshmerga to destroy ISIS,'" Luke told the interpreter, "'but that the Iraqis are in the lead and make the big decisions.'"

"Inshallah."

"How many shoes were made here a day before Daesh attacked?" Fink asked. Wharton was flummoxed by how Fink thought there was anything here to consult for. "Nothing to manage, no strategy, no consult" was the policy of every strategic management consultant since the serpent sold Eve the apple.

The interpreter began to translate when they all heard the rapid clacking sound in the distance. Even Wharton understood it was the sound only a machine gun makes. A familiar sound had echoed earlier on the range during test-fires but without affecting the primal equilibrium deep in the marrow of Wharton's bones. It was answered by a much louder eruption of machine-gun fire from the closer trucks.

"PKM fire from the southeast and armed males on motorcycles maneuvering from the southwest." Luke repeated what he was hearing over his 3M Peltor ComTac headset. He had shown the headset to Wharton earlier, the latest communications solution to overcoming the many noise issues on the battlefield. "I'm going up on the roof to join the CCT and get eyes on. Get Brock back to the trucks, Fink."

The first enemy mortar to hit must have been a larger round, or hit close enough to the factory, as the press shuddered in the middle of the floor even after they felt its impact on the ground. Fink stopped running alongside Wharton and asked, "You remember where the truck is?" Wharton stopped and nodded. "Get there. Go out the back way. I'm going back to see if Luke needs a hand. I will get the old man out before we exfil. We won't leave anyone else behind over here."

Before Wharton could take it back he had already said to Fink, "I'll get the owner." They would rally again at the trucks. Wharton ran back across the factory to the owner's back room. The old man stood just inside the door as if waiting for Wharton. His immovable face was lost in its creases, indentured like the rings of a tree trunk. He couldn't have weighed much more than a hundred pounds. Wharton considered picking him up when he spoke in Kurdish and didn't heed Wharton's motions to follow him. But to do so felt sacrilegious, and it did not help that the old man appeared to the white male foreigner Wharton more like an ancient Sitting Bull than a CEO. He reached out nervously for the old man's hand. Different-sized enemy mortars were now taking turns shaking the ground.

Wharton had not led the factory CEO more than ten steps out the back office onto the factory floor when the old man refused to continue on with this plan. Wharton turned back around and frantically tried to sign in universal Consultingese how problematic this new strategy was, what with their lives being engaged by enemy fire. The burning platform was that they were on a burning platform. The old man only shook his head. Wharton was trying again to convince the stubborn old man of the unsustainable nature of his leadership stance when the owner's right hand made a circle motion to encompass the factory space. It was not some thirty-thousand-foot answer as to why manhole covers were round or that the factory was aware of profit maximization. But to say, if just from one man of a passing generation to another man: this was all. Shut it down by terrorism or consulting and there was nothing. Left were ashes from a man-made vanished way of life. Death by different means. An argument against extreme efficiency and automation for everything everywhere, especially if the no-longer-required essential workers swelled the ranks of disenfranchised terrorist groups long term. No longer so cocksure that he knew what was best in a civilization thousands of years older than his own country, Wharton nodded at the old man and shed his role as an advisor.

Wharton had almost reached the back door of the factory when he heard the scream. It stopped him at the door. He was so scared that he mustered the courage to move again. He stopped again upon sight of what lay beyond the door.

"Come help me!" cried Hill, who lay on the ground ten feet away. "My leg."

A petrified Hill, his keffiyeh sprawled out on the ground, dust on his face, with the perfect Swoop in every direction. The stink. A man who had soiled himself, his arrogance traded for shame, and caked by mud, who squirmed on the ground shaken by mortar barrages, machine guns talking back and forth in the air, yells of back-blast areas being clear and then thunderous explosions. Seized by war. All, and no blood. Just a smelly leg? The electricity of Wharton's awareness, from buzzing head down to his own dirty hands and feet, assessed again. "Where've you been hit?" He had patted the whole of Hill's left leg after inadvertently sliding into it in his rescue sprint over.

"Help me up, you idiot. I tore something twisting my leg in this slit trench." What? Trying to locate them, Wharton found out later, because Hill had discovered that Fink had stowed the satellite phone in his bag. Then the bullets had begun to fly, and rather than crack and run back to the truck for safety, Hill ran to notify them, which was when he tore his ACL in the open-air restroom that the *sahib* must have constructed since ISIS had briefly managed that public utility. Both sewage projects undertaken without any consultants.

The only combat carry Wharton knew was to grab Hill's left arm and drape it over his shoulders, the bad leg against Wharton's right leg, and hobble him quickly to the truck in his armor gear like a hurt football player off a field. It might not qualify as "Cajun creativity" by Fink's standards, but it was Wharton's best idea with the hourglass turned. He got Hill up and stopped at the end of the wall. Their truck was about a hundred feet away, the .50 cal swinging around and firing away, controlled by invisible hands. Both top rear hatches were open. In one hatch, a helmet barely poked out and was recognizable by the camera attached to it. In the other open hatch, Ian, the top of his frame exposed, fired the grenade launcher: a pop, and then a small explosion hundreds of meters away. Metallic pings. Bullets were hitting the armored trucks. There was a strong case to be made for a crown of losing, Wharton realized with a certainty a consultant could never know, if it did not get you into maniacal battles. He leaned forward to run but froze. Hill was *not* a little guy and in his body armor was too heavy to make a dash with. Wharton hoped this was not how it ended. But the thought of Fink speaking at his funeral ("No, I'm here to tell you he did sign a prenuptial agreement, out of love—and what would he have done with all her family's horses anyway in a divorce?") pumped new fight into him as he dropped down in a squat to hoist Hill up.

Before Wharton could run across uncovered in the open, Ian spotted them and had the driver back up the armored vehicle to the end of the wall. The decision might have saved their lives. Overhead a minute later, two helicopters swooped in low and tried to make a gun run at the enemy who, having assessed that their time was up, fled back into the no-fire zone of the high school. All of it was relived so much by the group later in the delirium back at the base that the tales cast doubt in Wharton's sobered mind if only he could recall the closing of the rear door and the roar from Fink's snapping jaws of "Jump in!" If it had occurred, it was a command for Fink alone, as the American and Iraqi soldiers on the other trucks had not waited on the mad consultant to declare the firefight over as per the rules of engagement.

EPILOGUE

Brock Wharton returned to the front page of the *Houston Chronicle*, helmet camera footage of him carrying a feces-covered Spencer Hill off the battlefield having gone viral after Geoffrey posted it. The *Cambridge Consulting Group Consultants in Iraq Firefight* headlines made them heroes upon their return to the CCG office. In classic male face-saving, Hill had had to commend their actions from his hospital bed while pledging to donate some of his family's wealth to the rehabilitation of Makhmur. Unusually for the era, their actions didn't even attract the ire of the self-righteous, antibullying Internet hate mob.

Restoration of Wharton's kingdom had its costs. Not being able to get himself fired, Fink walked out of a party in honor of Fink's own promotion. A note left on Wharton's desk by Fink said simply that he had lit out for the West. Later, word leaked back to Piazza's sources that Fink had kept cutting a path westward and ended up in the Far East. The birth of Wharton's daughter, Krockett, did not bring about a thaw within K.K.—who had taken his risk-taking in Iraq personally, though she took to mothering more than his projections had anticipated (it did help that she had a lovely staff to assist her).

Oil was still down. Wharton had decided to test a nonbinding accord of engagement with his parents, now that a child had been added to his nuclear family. He began volunteering at the H.E.A.R.T. Program, which promoted structured independence and job training for people who are mentally handicapped. He referred to himself as an "urban pioneer," exploring on walks less wealthy neighborhoods, communities that he had never known existed in a city where he spent his whole time zipping around by car. And after Houston got wrecked by another annual five-hundred-year flood, Wharton got involved in politics for the first time in life to fight back against the unchecked developers terrorizing his hometown.

Six months after being promoted to CCG partner, Wharton rolled around like a dying crawfish for a challenge. Then one day a package arrived from Fink. Inside the package postmarked from China was a business plan proposal and a hardback copy of the Russian novel *Dead Souls*, a red feather tucked inside the worn front cover where Fink's unmistakable handwriting had inscribed:

"WHIRL IS KING" —ARISTOPHANES

Wharton wrote back that they should meet up when Fink next came into town. And so it was on a lazy late autumn afternoon, while K.K. was at her family's ranch for polo, that the chimes of the doorbell sounded. "*Gracias*, Inés," Wharton said, putting down the strange con man's tale of *Dead Souls* and getting up from the couch, "but I can get the door." Wharton ushered Fink into his house for the first time and brought him a cup of hot tea with sugar and declared, "Neither one of us knows the first thing about starting a company."

"With your talent officially joining forces with my talent for the first time as partners, we could be legends."

"Let's aim for being normal."

"Consulting wildcatters! Only downside is that it might take some time. Also, we might not make a ton of money the first year or two. And there's the risk that most first businesses fail. You're still married, right?" Wharton nodded, unsure how his precarious marriage could make the gamble more attractive. "We might need some of your wife's capital."

"We are going to have to change the name from CrossConsult."

"Why? It's perfect. Special Operations Forces are cross-trained and we apply the same unconventional leadership techniques to business. I see a real market opportunity for a couple of hucksters like us. You might even be in a position to steal away a few CCG people. Katie would come if you asked her."

"The name sounds like a fitness cult, for one. And isn't that what that fired general is selling?"

"The disgraced general busted because of the email affair? Or the self-promoting Special Operations admiral who leaked stuff to the movies while on active duty? They weren't fired, they just abruptly resigned. Kind of like what we need you to do to make this happen. You're lucky I'm around, as dramatic resignation letters are my forte. We're selling America."

He could almost believe in such an enchanted mission, if Fink had not cross-trained him in awareness. Still, it was easy to lapse into believing the wonder that could be sold in the new world. And the fear, the wars . . . Wharton thumped his chest. He knew they had time to figure it out. "Well, I guess if even the richest of men in this green land can rise from humbly privileged beginnings to become working-class populists . . ."

"Only in America can you muck about with such tall tales."

ACKNOWLEDGMENTS

I am grateful to Tom Bacon, Laura Bacon, Drew Bacon, Katy Madigan, Michael Skelly, and Anne Whitlock for their extremely generous support and ideas. Many thanks to Ed Djerejian, Francoise Djerejian, Sharie Fountain, Taylor Nichols, Mike Quinn, Michael Zilkha, Nina Zilkha, and my family. And especially to Andrew Stuart, Nate Roberson, Kirby Thornton, Elliott Walthall, and Ben Fountain for helping turn the manuscript into an actual book. Thanks as well to Alexis Washam, Julie Cepler, Rachel Rokicki, Lindsay Sagnette, Annsley Rosner, Molly Stern, Robert Siek, Elina Nudelman, Jessica Heim, Christopher Brand, Gwyneth Stansfield, Becca Putman, and the rest of the Crown team.

I would also like to thank the following for their generous help over the years in either reading a draft of the manuscript or for their support/ideas: Manny Acosta, Ben Ahn, Bennie Flores Ansell, Chad Atlas, Helen Atsma, Alice Bailey, Joe Bailey, Jimmy Battista, Sarah Schwaller Betancourt, Jim Blackburn, Jane Borochoff, Douglas Brinkley, Bill Caesar, Chetna Cates, Justin Clark, John Coleman, Brendan Collins, Matt Cook, Erik Cooper, Al Danto, Aly DeCamp, David DeFilippo, Rachel Deinhart, Chris Delao, Amber Dermont, John Dyke, Lynn Elsenhans, Nate Erdman, Todd Fertitta, Danny Fields, Jerry Finger, Kris Fitzmorris, Lance Fitzmorris, Adam Foote, Doug Foshee, Lee Fountain, David Frank, Bud Frazier, Russ Fusco, Stephanie

George, Luke Gilhooly, Bill Glick, Lynn Gosnell, Cybele Greenberg, Shane Gregrow, Bryan Gubba, Ed Han, Pat Hanlon, Michael Hardy, Eric Heaning, Peter Hotez, Nick Huber, Nick Hyunh, Brian Ivany, Sean Jump, Jonathan Kalaher, Toby Kamps, John Keenan, Kami Keoho, Pete Kingston, Bubba Koehler, Kyle Kras, Jennie Latson, Jerry Leehy, Sara Loewy, Jake Logue, Rick Lowe, Will Lyles, Weezie Mackey, Brian Maginn, Mat Melcher, Greg Merkl, Chris Mersinger, Angelbert Metoyer, Lauren Thompson Miller, Lucas Miller, Anton Mueller, Jackie Munn, Drew Nelson, Scott Newton, Steve Panagiotou, Danny Perez, Josh Prueher, Pete Quinn, Jonathan Reichek, Rachel Fleck Render, Adam Robinson, Dan Runzheimer, Justin Searor, Chris Seger, Judd Serenko, John Shaddix, Alex Sonnenberg, Justin Springer, Tim Stephenson, Dave Stevens, Mimi Swartz, Farbod Tahbaz, Chase Tanton, Ethan Taranta, Lily Thompson, Jeff Tompkins, Andrew Treleaven, Bart Truxillo, Emmett Walsh, Emily Walthall, Matt Weiland, Earl Wells, George Witte, Kyle Wittenbraker, and Michael Woodrum. Lastly, this book owes a debt of gratitude to the generations of writers who have reflected on returning home from war, especially many of our greatest living literary lions who both courageously served in the Vietnam War and then fought to write about their experiences in a way that reverberates fifty years on.

ABOUT THE AUTHOR

MIKE FREEDMAN was born and raised in Houston, where he received his MBA from Rice University. He volunteered for the infantry after 9/11, later serving three tours in Iraq and Afghanistan in the U.S. Army Special Forces. His first novel is *School Board*.